CW00496013

This story touches on domestic and sexual abuse.

Dedicated to Michael

Chapter 1.

Alone in a silent office, Jackson Maddox was startled by the knock on the door. He was perplexed. no one other than Montgomery Moon, his boss, was due to arrive at the house (and he would let himself in with the security code). He opened the door to find a gorgeous, curvaceous woman standing there, with long, thick, dark brown, hair which blew around her in the sudden gust of wind. She wore blue faded jeans and a lilac 'Montgomery Moon' hoodie.

"DARN!" The word escaped his lips in his thick Tennessean drawl before he could think or keep himself in check.

'Darn fine!' is what he thought to himself. His stomach gave a little flip and a feeling in his chest he hadn't felt for years, it was as if a tumble weed had blown in to his lonesome prairie from a wild frontier. Another die-hard fan, he thought to himself, ready to escort her off the premises and change the security code for the gates.

"Alright I'm Alva Moon!" she smiled brightly extending her hand to him, her East London accent ringing out.

He knew his boss was English, but he had elocution lessons to ensure he sounded Texan. Montgomery was an international country music sensation. Known as 'Moody' Moon, he dressed always in black other than a silver belt buckle and mirrored aviator sunglasses.

"Wait there!" Jackson barked at her in his southern drawl ignoring her outstretched hand, almost sneering at her. He was never caught off guard.

He spun around on his Cuban heels shutting the door and locking it. He didn't want her getting in if she was a stalking fan. He went to the office he used and quickly shut down the 'project' he was working on and hid the files in his bag.

He returned a few moments later.

"If you are who you say, why is that the code for the gate?"

"Mum and Dad's wedding anniversary! Mont told me ages ago!" she replied confidently.

He went back in to talk on the phone then came out with his mobile.

"You're on video!" he said and continued to talk to his boss.

"Jack, yes, that is Alva, pass the phone to her please…"

Jackson handed her the phone indicating to come inside.

"Why didn't you call to let me know you were coming, I'd have got Jack to meet you!" he could hear his boss telling her.

"I wanted to surprise you!" she giggled down the phone.

She slipped in the house beaming at Jackson, who thought her smile was charming, she was a ray of sunshine in the dark clouds of his being.

"OK. I will be home soon! Jack will take care of you until then, pass me back please."

She handed the phone back and Jackson turned the video off. He turned to her and smiled brightly. She can wait a few moments he thought. She stood there waiting in the hall whilst Jackson flitted about in the office and running up and down the stairs. He finished the call dumping the phone in his indigo-coloured jeans back pocket.

He was a good-looking chap with longish dirty blond hair and beautiful piercing blue eyes. Jackson was native to Nashville; he was a little shorter than Montgomery by an inch or two, but a few, inches taller than Alva. He had put her in mind of the country star 'Keith Urban'. Jackson was not a stereotypical Personal Assistant, he worked in his jeans and always wore a band t-shirt, (unless out with Montgomery, then he would wear Moon merchandise). Jackson worked and owned a musical instrument store and often served the elite. Jackson had met Montgomery when the latter first moved to Nashville and Montgomery was buying a keyboard and guitar, Jackson advised him well. They became chums, once famous, Montgomery walked into the store and offered him a job. Jackson had shown Montgomery around when he was settling in and showed him the best of the drinking establishments, especially on Broadway. Something had just clicked with the pair.

"Hello Miss Moon, I'm Jackson Maddox, Mr Moon's personal assistant. Welcome to 'California'. I am sorry for not believing you and welcoming you immediately when you arrived." He apologised, "I also apologise for almost swearing."

"That's quite alright Mr Maddox. I'm pleased to know that no crazy fan can get to Mont. Thank you so much for doing your job correctly and keeping my brother safe! Please call me Alva and I don't remember any swearing." She winked at him.

She was rather pretty, no more than 5ft 4ins and on the plump side, but nicely proportioned. He guessed she weighed about 200lb. She was a fine-looking girl and precisely twenty, Jackson knew this as about six months ago Montgomery had returned to the UK to celebrate her birthday, when he returned and was wild with the dislike he felt for her boyfriend, Drake Trent, there was something that didn't sit right with him. The one thing that made Jackson take instant notice of her was her lavender scent, it was a smell that took him back to a happy place and the magic of his childhood.

"Thank you for understanding, allow me to show you around the house and pick a bedroom, also please call me Jack!"

Jackson's mind wandered, is love at first sight real? Some people believe love must grow, like a plant, it needs the correct nurturing and care to flourish, like a lavender bush in Tennessee, it needs perfect cultivation, because it is not a native plant, it is native to say England, where the soils are different, but it is possible to grow. Others believe in the concept, whilst some do not. Is having a soul mate an actual thing? Is there really another half of you out there waiting for you and only you? Could this Alva be the other half I've had missing? Neither Jackson nor Alva subscribed to such hypothesises, nor did they ever think about them until today.

She had noted the grandeur of the house on her arrival, the outside was a rather country styled two storied weatherboard house, the planks reminding her of the US flag that adorned the flagpole near the gate. There was a stereotypical a veranda imposing the entrance, like some lyrics to country songs that mention the porch. A white stone chipped drive that sparkled like stars in the August high noon, like stars to the moon. Montgomery had bought the place just after he got back from England that February.

Jackson gave her a tour of the house; she dumped her sandals in the hall and sunk her toes into the the burgundy carpet that led up the middle of the house. There were several rooms, a living area, reception area for parties, a kitchen, dining room, music room with a piano, a bar room which also was a billiard room. The walls of which were lined with his music trophies, awards, and discs, a library and Jackson's study/office. Upstairs were several bedrooms all ensuite and tastefully decorated with equally plush furnishings. Jackson returned to the lobby and asked her to follow him. He hauled the heavy red suitcase up the stairs to one of the eight bedrooms.

"That one is Mont's, but he said other than that, please pick a room to stay in."

Alva walked up and down the hall settling on one at the far end.

"This will do, thanks" She turned and smiled to him.

He offered to make her a drink and they returned downstairs, to the well-lit bar room. He poured her a white wine and slid it over to her before he cracked open a sparkling water to keep her company.

Montgomery's bar and games room stretched across the back of the house, the walls were bare brick, except for one adjacent to the main house which had been painted white and adorned with his awards in cabinets and gold discs. One end was a purpose-built bar with bar stools and optics that sparkled with the coloured glass and liquids. The other end was a full-sized American pool table with green baize. There were a couple of beech tables and a mahogany wood laminate floor. The length of the room was bi-folding doors which led to his garden, down to the lake and the rest of the ranch.

"So how long have you been working for Mont?" Alva enquired perching herself on a bar stool.

"About a year and a half!" he answered.

"That is good! He speaks very highly of you!"

They sat and chatted for a couple of hours; he was very animated when she was asking him about his musical interests. She told him about her eclectic taste in music, of course she liked Moon and now had a like for Country but really liked a lot of retro bands and easy listening.

"I like your t-shirt!" she told him.

He wore merchandise of a group called 'The Fishers'. She told him she particularly liked that group. They were a siblings duo comprising of brother and sister Ethan and Scarlett Fisher respectively.

"I know them…" he laughed. "…they used to come in my shop years ago…"

"Really! I don't believe you!" she retorted.

With that he whipped out his mobile and video called someone.

"Hey guys! Would you mind saying hello to Alva, Mont's sister for us, please?"

"Sure!" came a recognisable voice.

He passed his phone to her and she smiled at meeting her idols. He planned for her to meet them in person later in the week at the shop he owned, but now had a cousin managing the place. He enjoyed talking to her. He thought to himself if she was older and he were younger he would really like to date her, but he felt that being the nine years her senior was a lot. Also, he didn't think Montgomery would be too thrilled. There had also been mentioned the boyfriend that was disliked. He felt a sense of relief he now knew he wasn't as completely broken as he once thought.

The evening cast long shadows over the lawn in the garden, Montgomery waltzed in and greeted them. He booked a table at 'Nelson's Country Club Restaurant' on the outskirts of Nashville. Alva popped off to get showered and changed. He asked Jackson if he wanted to join them, he agreed as he wanted to talk to Montgomery about business and it couldn't wait besides, he had enjoyed talking to Alva so much and was keen to find out which acts she liked he knew quite a few and thought he might have to show her around whilst Montgomery worked and figured he might as well use the opportunity to catch up with people.

He had been shocked earlier his genitals had a tingling after he had felt broken for about seven years. He had spent a fortune and a dime trying to get his virility back to no avail and believed that it was probably his type II diabetes that caused it, none of the treatments worked. He vowed that if he ever found a woman that could turn him on, he would marry her there and then and do whatever it took to keep her, yet Alva posed a massive problem, she was his boss's sister and he was sure she was out of bounds, forbidden fruit.

Stepping in the shower, he could not stop thinking about her and there his manhood was again, begging for attention. Standing with the water cascading over him he had no option, his mind whirring with fantasy with Alva as the main cast, tears streamed down his face. He had to quickly retrain his mind as he couldn't afford for any embarrassment at dinner.

Half an hour later the three of them were headed out. Jackson noticed how elegant Alva looked as she came downstairs. Montgomery wore his trademark look, he was always clothed in a black satin western shirt, jeans, belt, with a solid silver buckle and a pinched top, felt broad rimmed Stetson, that hid his brown short back and sides haircut, black leather cowboy boots completed his outfit. He sported the thick short darkest brown beard and mirrored aviator sunglasses. A must so no-one could see his eyes or recognise him. He had wanted to remain mysterious, almost anonymous.

"Watch yourself!" Jackson whispered to Alva. "The fans will think you are his date! He will be swamped in a matter of seconds so please grab on to my hand or arm, so you don't get parted from us."

Montgomery exited the sleek black car and was almost drowned in a sea of fans. Alva slipped out, behind him. Jackson grabbed her hand, it felt so small to him, she looked nervous as they arrived and saw the mass of people. Montgomery turned to Jackson nodded and with that they swept through the crowd. Montgomery said hello and apologised he wouldn't be able to meet everyone. He explained his dear sister was visiting and he wanted to spend time with her. He hoped to meet them all soon and thanked them for their support.

Alva was dressed in a pretty black sundress dotted with tiny yellow flowers dotted. Her make-up was perfect and she had 'scrubbed up well' Jackson thought. Alva tripped on a loose paving stone and Jackson caught her around her waist before she fell, he gave her a kind smile when she thanked him. It seemed in that moment there was a spark that ignited a flame, for Alva she had never had a man treat her like a lady. She felt like a rose that was just about to burst open, her insides awakening.

They sat down at a secluded table; the waitress went around the table flicking the napkin open and draping it across their laps. Montgomery ordered wine for Alva and him, Jackson ordered a sparkling water with slices lemon and lime, they sat, sipping their drinks.

"So, Alliwoo how long are you here for?" Montgomery asked. Alliwoo was his nickname for her, she had called him 'Kendo sauce' (as he always like kindo sauce from the Chinese takeaway), which then had gotten shortened to Kendo.

"About four weeks if that's OK Kendo? I have five from 'uni' so that gives me time to stay here."

"Jack, can you organise outings with Alva for the next two weeks as I am in the studio. I'll let you know when I have some gaps, one of the days you can come and bring Alva to see the studios and I'll give her a tour."

Their meals arrived, huge portions as always, Alva could eat hers and theirs too! Jackson and Montgomery chatted about business, occasionally stopping to explain things to Alva.

Jackson took out his notebook and pen in anticipation of jotting ideas down for their day trips.

"What are you studying?" Jackson asked.

"I'm a student nurse, just finished my second year." She smiled.

Jackson was impressed, he was thinking of her in a tight nurse's dress, quickly putting it out of his mind as he felt his penis start to throb.

"Do you enjoy it?"

"Yes, most of the time, the shift work interferes with my social life and Drake my boyfriend hates!"

Jackson's heart sunk, he knew her brother would be opposed to their match, he watched the siblings' interaction across the table.

"You're still seeing that prick?" Montgomery sighed.

Alva glared at him; it was a sore subject.

"Does he know you're here!"

Alva shook her head. Montgomery huffed.

"I hope he doesn't turn up too wanting a free holiday!"

"So, Alva, I know you like the 'Fishers' but who else?" Asked Jackson sensing tension between the siblings and attempting a change of subject.

"Well, until Mont started singing country, I didn't really listen to it. Since then, I realised I do like most of it." Alva replied.

"Which country acts are you into then?"

"I really love 'Common Ancestor'!"

Jackson and Montgomery looked at each other and Jackson fell about in hysterics, whilst Montgomery stifled his humour.

"What's funny?" She asked.

Common Ancestor were a group made up of Janey and Jason Day, Felicity Stapleford, Craig Johnson, Joanie, Jimmy, and Johnny McDonald, siblings and cousins who had formed a family group when they were all teenagers. Janey and Jason were of mixed heritage, the others were all dark haired and brown eyes, reflecting their Italian ancestry of their great grandmother Giovanna, known as Jane to her American comrades.

"They have a really good vibe and harmonise beautifully." She told the guys.

Jackson was almost in tears from laughter and Montgomery was trying to keep his moody image in check.

“What did I say that was so funny?!” Alva got annoyed.

“You will meet them, I’m sure!” Montgomery choked out. Montgomery struggled not to laugh. It wasn’t in his image to be seen laughing, but let a small titter escape momentarily. His chuckle made Jackson laugh even harder. Jackson hadn’t ever seen Montgomery laugh. But the paparazzi were beginning to reach for their cameras and ‘Moody Moon’ had to come back out.

“They are good friends of ours! They are Mont’s support act for the tour…They are doing a lot of rehearsals together! I knew Jason and Janey from High school and kept in touch. They were up and coming and when I got this job, I introduced them to Mont!” Jackson told her.

“It’s comical because you are thinking of them like they are superstars and we drink and jam with them so often, they are part of the furniture. Seen them all drunk and at their worst.” Montgomery explained.

Montgomery turned to Jackson

“I hope you can put up with her this length of time, because you are going to have to drive her everywhere as she never learnt! That prick stopped her.”

“So, who else do you like what do you want to do? Oh, and I would love to chauffer you around this holiday Ma’am.” Jackson said in his best Tennessean drawl.

Jackson knew these next four weeks would test his nerves; there was a strong possibility of him falling for her, like fallen both ways with nowhere to land. He knew he liked her and she was the only one (who he had got an erection over in years). He wondered what to do, his boss and friend was relying on him to look after her, but knew how protective of her he was and didn’t want to cross the line.

Chapter 2

Alva stood in the Country Music Hall of Fame inspecting the displays. She had been in Nashville less than twenty-four hours. She stopped to look at Elvis Presley's Cadillac.

"I never knew he was an inductee." Alva announced as Jackson caught up with her. "Elvis Presley, the King of Rock and Roll, a country musician?"

"His music appealed to a variety of people. I love his music!" Jackson said.

"Me too! He was so talented and such a short life. I'd love to go to Graceland one day. It's quite a way from here, perhaps I can get Mont to take me another holiday."

"It's one of those things on my 'bucket list' too." He announced. Hoping she would ask to go there; it was about three hours away.

Jackson enjoyed watching her walk around, she moved with a little cute wiggle, her hair long down her back over her blue denim jacket, sunglasses on top of her head and her gorgeous smile. He had visited the attraction many times showing people around, but today was something different, he had never paid much attention until today; Alva was shining whilst chatting about Elvis and was very knowledgeable about his music and his life. Jackson would adore those days, the time he would spend with Alva.

He enjoyed that week and took her to see the usual touristy things. They enjoyed the Grand Ole Opry and The Ryman Auditorium; Jackson managed to get tickets and took her to a few shows. He spent a couple of blissful evenings with her, Common Ancestor, and Montgomery drinking on Broadway. Jackson had been pleased Montgomery had kept his drinking in check, but knew it wouldn't be long before he would ramp it up a notch, and Alva would realise there was a problem. She told Jackson she liked museums and art galleries so he took her to several he knew.

During the first few days Jackson introduced her to his brother, Maxwell 'Mad Mosquito' Maddox, as 'Max', a retired wrestler. Max was big in his time, he explained she might see him some days, as he trains Montgomery. It was the first time Jackson had spoken of family.

Some days he took her to various recording studios and visited various musicians he knew including 'The Fishers.' She was so very excited at meeting them. She had loved their music from the first note, he took her to a vineyard and took her wine tasting.

Jackson carried his little note book with him always, he would often stop and write something down she said or a remark.

"Jack, do you mind if I ask what you write down?"

"Ideas for lyrics, or songs… sometimes you might say something such yesterday you mentioned you liked the artist Barcham Grice. I might want evidence about you later" he laughed.

She pushed his arm in reply. Barcham Grice was renowned for beautiful watercolours of animals in particular birds. Jackson, used to transfer notes to a book he had at home. He had lists of people in his life and he would note a like or an interest in there or anything that would help him if he needed to buy a gift. He enjoyed talking to Alva, she always seemed happy with whatever he would suggest for her to do. She never asked for him to do anything specific. Jackson got the impression she always felt supressed and felt she couldn't ask.

Jackson was a kindly soul, and would unbeknownst to those closest, volunteer at the homeless shelter once a week. After the Lainey disaster he left Chicago and with no work he had to somehow get home. He had no means to call home and ask for help, he wanted to, needed to work his way to Nashville, besides he didn't want people thinking he was a failure. He set out walking each day, slept rough for a bit but managed to get in a few night shelters for which he was grateful. After about eight weeks he ended up home much to the relief of his family who hadn't heard from him. He vowed he would give something back. He would arrive on a Thursday evening after work and stay until just after midnight and drive to his white weatherboarded house surrounded by colourful flowers and as cheerful as him.

He would merrily do all sorts of work, cooking, laundry, cleaning, administration work and would spend time with their guests, he was a valued member of the team, he never told anyone about this, his family were unaware he volunteered and why. The manager of the centre Bob approached him as he arrived, was a man who was in his fifties with a balding head and a goatee beard, his arms were sleeved with colourful tattoos.

"Ah Jack! I need you to do me a favour. I had a telephone call from a young lady yesterday she is coming to volunteer tonight, I wonder if you would mind showing her around and inducting her, please?"

"Sure!" Jackson replied brightly.

"Thanks Buddy! I'll come and find you when she arrives."

Jackson arrived just as rush hour had faded and chatted to the other volunteers, Liam, Austin, and Lila. He heard two familiar voices approach the room, one being Bill and the other Alva!

Jackson spun round, he was secretly pleased to see his friend, but this could mean some of his untold work might be exposed, better this than the other surreptitious work he was undertaking, he thought. She smiled when she saw Jackson.

"Hey Honey, long time, no see!" he joked, it had only been two hours since he had last laid eyes on her pretty face.

"Alright!" There it was, the Essex twang he loved.

"So you know each other? No need for introductions then! I'll leave you with Jack and let me know if you need anything!" Bill told them.

"Hey, I'm Alva!" she held out her hand to Liam, Austin, and Lila.

Jackson introduced them.

"Right how do you want me?" Alva asked showing enthusiasm.

Lila stifled giggles; she had noticed how Jackson's eyes lit up and the way he looked at her when she walked in the room.

"Excuse us guys I need to do an induction of the newbie!" he smiled, indicating to Alva.

Jackson told her all important information, fire exits, rules and showed her around.

"So… cards on the table… are you stalking me?" he asking in a serious tone.

Alva looked puzzled; she wouldn't do that!

"No! why would I?"

Jackson burst out laughing.

"So, what brings you here? No one knows about me and this place."

"Mum and Dad always encouraged us to do some kind of volunteering… I used to volunteer for the night shelter at home… so thought I would here. I guessed it might help me make a few friends whilst I'm here and if I come back again to visit, I'd know a few people."

"So why a night shelter?" Jackson was interested.

"There was a girl in my year at school, I only knew her to say hello. Well, she had 'problems' undiagnosed mental health stuff, her parents had pleaded for help from the authorities, she had symptoms for years, since she was tiny, I remember her from nursery. No one would help and when they did, it was because the secondary school noticed her odd behaviour. When she was fourteen, the waiting lists were long, years in fact. We found out when we went back in January, she had committed suicide! She had always been a kind kid and was often raising money for the homeless and domestic violence centres near us. It was almost an obsession for her. She had a box in the school reception for toiletries and food, kids took the mick out of her because she would rock up on a Friday with her pink shopping trolley to take the stuff to Blake House or the Women's refuge. People were horrible to her, yet she was so kind… I like to think of it as carrying on for her. I regret not being more friendly." She told him looking sad.

"That's awful! What happened?" Jackson asked cautiously, he felt sad.

"I don't know any details… just she had died, I guess the school wanted to protect us, her name was Alyssa, I always thought it was pretty."

"It is a pretty name, I'm sorry, she sounds like such a nice girl, some people wouldn't carry on with that type of work if they were being bullied. I know what being bullied is like."

Jackson tried not to show too much of a reaction other than empathy, although the thought of a young girl feeling so awful she would want to end her life abhorred him and he contemplated the reasons.

He introduced her to a few more people.

"What about you Jack? Why do you volunteer here?" she asked gently.

He looked at her suspiciously, his lips forming a thin line.

"I'll tell you later! I take it Mont knows you are here?" Jackson asked, changing the subject.

She shook her head.

"You come downtown on your own, one of the most dangerous parts of the city and Mont has no idea!? No one would know you were here? So how were you planning on getting home?" He sounded cross.

"Bus or taxi?" she smiled weakly realising it wasn't perhaps the best idea.

Jackson smacked his forehead with his palm.

"So where does Mont think you are?"

"I said I had made some friends?"

"Alva! It's a good job I'm your friend! I'll run you home tonight… and… any other night you volunteer on two conditions!"

"What are they?"

"One you only volunteer on a Thursday, when I do and two, you don't tell Mont or anyone about my volunteering!"

"Deal!" she held out her hand enthusiastically.

Jackson shook it, he liked her petite. He found himself craving her touch. His life had been like a sandy prairie in a western movie and he was a tumbleweed bouncing alone, like he had been when he blew home from Chicago after Lainey. It was strange having these sensations and urges in these years, Alva seemed to caused these feelings, he wasn't sure what to do, only that he felt like a man once again.

She wondered why he didn't want his boss to know. She text Montgomery that she would be getting a lift home and not to worry. They strived the rest of the evening, enjoying the ambiance of the place, people were made to feel welcome. Jackson found himself watching Alva showing her interest in the clients. She had chatted to a man who had an aroma of festering leg ulcers, she somehow managed to pursued him to let her redress to them.

"He could really do with seeing a medic." Alva had said whilst treating Bert.

Alva had remarked to Jackson about the healthcare system in the UK. She told him about how it was free at the point of delivery. This guy would have to go to the welfare homeless places Jackson noticed how genuine she was. She mentioned she was a student nurse, she seemed natural, she was clearly good at it and dedicated.

At the end of the evening Bill asked how well things went, Jackson had said to Bill she was a great help and she could come again!

The August night was warm as they walked to Jackson's car, a contrast from the air conditioning of the building, the heatwave was like an oven, his mum would cook meringues in the conservatory at home and it reminded him of that.

"So, Jack it is later now… did you want to tell why volunteering here is so important?" she tentatively asked as they climbed up in his silver SUV car.

"I will… but this is in the strictest confidence Alva…"

"My lips are sealed!"

He sat and told her some of his story. He told her the last part after he had split up from Lainey, deciding he might tell her one day if he ever felt able to tell her his secrets. He told her how he had worked in Chicago and needed to come home. He wasn't ready to tell her the first part of that story and how he was shattered from the relationship. He said he had left his work in a rush without pay and travelled by foot back to Tennessee, at that point he'd had a bit of a breakdown and didn't call home, because he couldn't face asking for help and he was ashamed of being homeless. He had a bad time. He had chanced on a night shelter and how people were non-judgmental. They helped him, but didn't force anything on him. Alva sat and listened carefully. She had compassion and for him but didn't feel sorry for him, she felt rather proud of him. There she was and only known him a short while and he was bearing his soul to her.

"Thanks for sharing that with me Jack. Have you ever told Mont about any of this?"

"No! I'm too ashamed!"

"But it's something that could happen to anyone! Please don't be embarrassed with me Jack, and Mont wouldn't think less of you, you know? But I won't say anything!"

"Alva, you said you used to volunteer at home… do you not anymore?" steering the attention away from himself.

"Na, Drake doesn't like me volunteering for the homeless… he says they're all drug addicts and prostitutes and doesn't want me being led astray. I tried to get him to understand it's a mixture of people. I keep asking him to join me to see what it is and most are just a product of their circumstances, but sometimes I can't argue with him and it's just easier to keep the peace!" She sighed.

Jackson thought her brother's assessment of the guy was probably spot on, he was indeed a prick.

They drove up the white gravel drive to the door, the chippings pinging on the undercarriage.

"Thanks for your help tonight, you were great, by the way you were excellent with Bert, he won't let anyone touch his legs let alone listen to anyone getting him medical help. He finally asked Bill to drop him to the homeless welfare medical place in the morning."

"That's good! I hope he gets them sorted! Thanks for bringing me home safely… I didn't think about getting home if I'm honest!"

"Anytime Honey, goodnight and I'll see you in the morning. You have my number call me if ever you need me… any time of the day or night."

"Thanks! Night, night Jack!" she said exiting the car.

He watched her bounce up the steps, turn and wave, then give him the smile that lit up the moon.

Jackson fidgeted all night with broken sleep. Why did she turn up like a beautiful category five storm? Raging in, messing him up, making him tell her things he told no one? She would be perfect if the age gap was better and she wasn't Mont's sister and she wasn't spoken for! I hope he treats her well, he's such a lucky man, he thought! Little did Jackson know how badly Alva needed him.

□

Chapter 3

The morning rose with its clear skies. Jackson could hear Montgomery's raised voice as he got out of his car at work. As he entered, the row coming from the kitchen was reaching a crescendo. He could see Moon's reflection in the black gloss of the cupboards and him pointing at Alva. Montgomery was towering over his sister, who was perched on a stool, trying to eat her breakfast.

"SO, WHO WAS THIS FRIEND THAT DROPPED YOU OFF AT BLOODY 1AM ALVA?!" Mont shouted, waving his arms furiously.

"A friend!" she replied in her small voice, looking at the floor and squirming in her seat.

"MALE OR FEMALE? I WANT A WORD, IT'S TOO LATE TO BE OUT!" Montgomery paced besides her.

"Mont, it's ok they wouldn't see any harm come to me!"

"Alva! You are in my care! I don't want Mom and Dad thinking I can't look after you if you end up in a gutter somewhere! TELL ME HIS NAME!" Montgomery demanded slamming a fist on the breakfast bar, making the spoon clang in the cereal bowl like a bell, causing her to tremble.

"I'm nineteen! I'm not telling you anything." She squeaked in a meek voice, looking away from her brother and studying the floor.

She was almost trembling, she hated arguing, but she had made a vow to Jackson.

"Getting you keeping secrets! Bloody like that fecking Drake Trent! I'd bet he would be furious if he knew you were out galivanting with another man… I'd better phone him." He snatched

Alva's phone from the counter top, it was never locked and started scrolling through.

"PLEASE DON'T TELL HIM!" Alva cried in an anguished tone.

Jackson now by the kitchen door couldn't withstand listening to Montgomery upsetting her, there was something in her tone, disclosing her fear.

"MONT!" Jackson commanded in a firm voice, appearing in view at the kitchen door.

Alva and Montgomery turned to look at him.

"Alva was with me last night. I saw her out and offered her a lift home. I'm sorry it was late and might have disturbed you."

"OK! Thanks Jack!" he turned to his sister "So what was the problem of you bumping into Jack then!?" He slammed her phone back down on the kitchen counter.

Alva flinched at the bang of the phone. It was clear to Jackson his boss had been on a bender that last night. The alcohol stinging his body like a demonic venom

"Thank you, Jack!" Alva blew a sigh of relief.

She was anxious about Drake; he was very possessive and if he thought she had been out enjoying herself she would have been 'punished' when she got home. She knew she would face consequences of having time away from him, she just needed her space and to be herself and have fun. Although he had never been physically violent, yet, he was psychologically and emotionally abusive Montgomery stormed from the kitchen, ready to face his battle that day with Della his manager who, like Trent, was full of coercive behaviour and control.

"Where do you want to go today?" Jackson smiled after the quiet settled around them.

"Promise you won't laugh, it's really nerdy!"

"I promise!"

"I'd really like to go and buy some binoculars and go birdwatching!"

Jackson smiled a big smile.

"You said you wouldn't laugh!"

"I'm not laughing! Did Mont tell you about my guilty secret pleasure?" he asked.

Alva cocked her head and looked at him inquisitively.

"Why? Mont hasn't said anything to me about bird watching… he usually takes the micky out of me! I asked him yesterday if he thought you would mind taking me and he almost died laughing."

"Mont laughed? Huh! You hear something new each day. He shouldn't laugh at that… I've never met a girl who's into ornithology too! I've got a few pairs of field glasses at home and some books on native birds, I know some places with hides. I'll tell you what we can get a picnic, drop past mine and get my kit and I'll show you the best places!" he offered.

"So, you really won't mind taking me!" she enthused.

"I'd love to take you, I'm so pleased to be asked, it's one of my favourite hobbies and you never normally ask for anything either."

She was so pleased.

They found a hide, shrouded amongst a copse of trees, there were no other twitchers around and they settled themselves down.

"You hardly mention that lucky boyfriend of yours!" Jackson enquired.

"He doesn't think he's fortunate!" she sighed. "Have you anyone special in your life?" she asked trying to deflect the attention around that relationship.

He shook his head and looked forlorn, looking out across the reserve, illuminated and warmed by the bright sun.

"Well, if you ever decided to ask me out, I wouldn't refuse you!" she smiled.

She regretted blurting that one out and blushed.

"I'm too old for you honey! You are off limits according to Mont, besides you have a man."

The silence was palpable. Alva thought she had embarrassed him.

"So, what about this Drake character?"

Could she tell him? Should she tell him she had begun to hate Drake? He was putting her through hell or would he then feel obliged to her if she told him? Then imagine Mont going off on one if he knew! Her head was a washing machine of what ifs.

"Not much to say really — Oh look is that a Nashville warbler?" she asked, changing the subject.

They whiled away the day watching various birds swoop and soar. Jackson was an expert and took delight in teaching her about the Native birds.

"Some days I wish I was a bird!" Alva remarked thoughtfully. "Then I could escape! I need to escape sometimes!" She looked wistful.

Jackson wondered about what she had said and felt his heartstrings pulling in her direction.

He noticed a tear roll down her cheek and she quickly wiped it away with her sleeve hoping he didn't see. Jackson was just about to ask her, when a few others joined them and the moment had gone, like she wanted to be.

Chapter 4

Another sunny warm day dawned and today the zoo awaited them, Alva had mentioned to Jackson she would like to go and she had read they had 'clouded leopards,' she also wanted to look around the aviaries. The zoo had different species to what she had seen in the zoos back home in England. Her love for birds was incredible and Jackson could see the enthusiasm and animation when she spoke of her passion. It was like all the timidness, anxiety and fear fell away from her in those moments. Alva would love the brightly coloured varieties and the squawking and twittering as they walked through the aviaries, some were indoors and felt humid, she worried about her hair frizzing up and looking a sight to Jackson. She would take her time reading the information boards. Jackson loved to watch her, his body craving her more and more with each day, like a plant needing water in a drought.

Jackson started to notice Alva was flagging, she seemed washed out and tired, as the day wore on, she looked pale and unwell. He offered they take refreshments in the cafe nearby. He kept asking her if she was alright and she kept telling him she was. She was so enjoying being with him in her fantasy, they were a couple dating. If only he would ask her out, she thought, she could then be 'rescued' from Drake. She felt a horrible searing pain in her abdomen, all day she had had cramps. As she stood up, she felt a gushing sensation and felt dizzy, Jackson caught her in his arms to stop her falling. They started out again as she walked away from him Jackson noticed she was bleeding; he could see blood seeping through the crotch of her jeans. With that he took his jumper off and tied it around her waist. Placing his hand in the small of her back.

"I think you might want to go to the emergency room… you're bleeding!"

He was worried she might be miscarrying. Alva was mortified. She had a condition that caused very heavy periods embarrassment washed over her in a wave.

“I just need to go home. Thank you for telling me. I’m sorry you have had to witness that!” she blushed as red as her own blood and felt hot with shame.

She spent the whole journey praying she would not leak through to the seat.

They arrived home and Alva ran upstairs and showered. She appeared half hour later in the laundry room, soaking the clothes in cold salted water, then washing her clothes and his jumper. She avoided him at all costs. He was worried as there seemed to be a lot of blood, more than he thought there should be for a period. He called Montgomery who appeared within the hour, then after a quick drink, a chat with Alva and a call to the medical plaza, Montgomery had Alva in the car on the way to see the gynaecologist.

“Thanks Mont! I’m relieved to get that sorted out, there was such a wait on the NHS to have it fitted. I’m SO EMBARRASED that it happened in front of Jack.” She told her brother.

They were in Montgomery’s truck on their way back, the windows rolled down and the radio up, his latest hit came on the radio, that song was going to be a hit, it was the umpteenth time she had heard it today on the radio or elsewhere.

“You know he thought you were having a miscarriage and was so worried about you that he rang.” He told her as the last bars faded out and the DJ spoke.

“Aw that’s really sweet of him! I guess I need to explain about my condition. How humiliating! And no, I’m not pregnant, the imaginary ‘penny’ mum put between my knees is still there!”

“I can always tell him, you know you shouldn’t worry about what you can’t control, it’s a medical condition. Oh, and you should keep yourself chaste, especially around that Drake Trent, he shouldn’t be allowed to breed!” Montgomery offered.

“Would you mind telling Jack? I can’t face him!” she buried her face in her hands.

As soon as they pulled up outside, she leapt out and ran as fast as she could upstairs and out of sight. Jackson met Montgomery at the door, the August heat contrasted with the house's air conditioning.

"Is Alva OK?" Jackson was keen to know.

"Let's grab a drink and I'll explain it to you."

They went to the bar room sitting with a drink each at the bar.

"She is really embarrassed… but she was really touched by your concern. Alva has a condition called polycystic ovarian syndrome, or PCOS. I'll let you internet search it if you are interested. One of the symptoms she has are really awful and heavy periods… She's been waiting for a procedure, to have a gynaecological device fitted in England for months… She has now had that procedure. I offered to explain it to you because we feel that you should have an idea about what occurred today."

"Will she be, ok?" Jackson enquired.

"There's no cure but she might need a bit of a rest from the procedure, see how she goes"

"Thanks for trusting me with this!" Jackson replied. He spent that evening researching the condition, he was concerned for Alva's suffering.

When Jackson arrived the next morning, he brought a bouquet of beautiful colourful flowers for Alva. They were picked from his garden and tied with ribbon. His mum was a noted florist in the area and Jackson and his brother had observed the way she would put together bouquets. Jackson's older brother was a famed wrestler, Maxwell 'Mad Mosquito' Maddox, and he and their mother had done the flowers for his wedding.

Alva as sitting in the kitchen drinking coffee at the breakfast bar. She was wearing a floral dress, when she looked up and saw Jackson in the doorway, she blushed and smiled.

"Good morning, Jack. Here's your jumper back…" Thrusting his jumper towards him. "Thanks for giving me a bit of dignity with it yesterday."

With this he presented her with the flowers.

She reached up and kissed his cheek. It felt like sparks were starting a fire in his heart and love filling his soul.

"I hope you are feeling better. No worries with the lend. I was hoping you'd want to go out today. Please promise me if you want to rest or come home let me know."

Alva blushed and thanked him putting those beautiful flowers in a vase and taking them up to her bedroom. They were a riot of roses, coneflowers, daisies, zinnias, dahlias, lilies and Black-Eyed Susan, they all were various colours. Jackson had wanted to give her a bouquet of only roses, but didn't want Montgomery becoming suspicious. Jackson had de-thorned the roses to ensure she didn't prick herself.

They sat and ate breakfast and planned their day.

Perhaps Jackson was the tonic she needed.

□

Chapter 5

During their long days they would have deep conversations. They were driving home from a day of bird watching. Jackson was always such a careful driver, Alva felt safe with him. For some reason she would place her life in his hands and know he would gently take care of it. She also found him frustrating, she just wanted him to kiss her, she would love him to push her up against a wall and kiss her. Not slam her against a wall but push her firmly. She wondered how he kissed, how he tasted, her heart was flipping.

"Why are you called Alva? It's an unusual name and I've never heard of it before I knew you." Jackson asked.

He broke her fantasy about him kissing her.

"Mum and Dad saw it once on a documentary about a Finnish midwife, who founded the Salvation Army in her country, they thought it was a pretty name. It's also happened, to be the first two letters of mum and dad's names. It apparently means 'elf' and is the female form of Alfred, my mum's dad." She answered.

"So… Why Jackson?"

"My parents are huge Johnny and June fans and it's a song they did, and A Boy Named Sue… you've heard us call Max Sue? Johnny Cash sang 'Dorraine of Ponchartrain' too."

"I've not heard the one about Dorraine."

Jackson told her to play them on his phone. He forgot to mention he had sister.

No, Max is named after our Mum's father, Max did toy with changing it to Memphis as a stage name at one point, but it never went further. Our Grandfather was Maxwell Barnes, you may have heard of him, he was an eminent oncologist! As for calling him Sue,

Dad always joked about it and it stuck as a nickname. After all he was the only one not from a Johnny Cash song."

"Maxwell Barnes was your Granddad?"

"He was!"

Alva was seriously impressed.

"I was sorry to hear he had died last year; he was quite well respected amongst those I worked with. I read his paper on prostate cancer and quoted it one of my essays."

Jackson smiled. Not many people had heard of him and he was proud of his grandfather, knowing she was a student nurse he did wonder if she had heard of him.

"Did you know he was not just a physician, but had a doctorate in Astronomy too." Jackson asked.

"Is there anything else you like other than ornithology?" Alva enquired.

"Yes! I do have another guilty pleasure… or 'nerd fest' as you call it." He answered.

"Go on…"

"I like astronomy, I have a telescope in my garden shed and have made it into a little observatory. It's good where I am as there are no street lights so no light pollution and you can see them. I'd love to show you one day."

Before Alva knew she was on the driveway at Montgomery's. He came in to chat with his boss, he would check in always after bringing Alva home and see if there was any work to be done. Tonight, Montgomery asked him to dinner. He had missed his friend and fancied a catch up over the Della situation, the narcissistic boss who fancied the pants off Montgomery.

The three of them arrived at the restaurant they had first frequented. It seemed as if was a favourite place of Montgomery's. They all ordered their usual meals and drinks. Alva sat scrolling through her phone. Montgomery always ordered Steak in a peppercorn sauce, chips and buttered carrots and broccoli. Jackson would have a plain medium rare steak with a jacket sweet potato and steamed veg and always asked them to omit the butter. Alva liked to sample the menu, today she would try the beef stroganoff.

"So where would you like to visit tomorrow?" Jackson asked Alva.

It was her last week. Her flight was booked in three days.

"Can we go to the planetarium please!" Alva requested.

Montgomery shot Jackson a look. He saw his friends' eyes light up.

"Only if you really want to, don't ask to go to please me."

"I'm not, it's just you mentioned about astronomy earlier and it's made me curious and I would like to educate myself a little." Alva told him.

Montgomery could sense there was something brewing. He would need to think of a way to discourage this.

"Would you like to look through the telescope tonight?" Jackson invited.

"I'll sort out an evening and bring her over with me, if she comes again!" Montgomery interjected.

Montgomery wanted to be clear she was not going out with him alone during the dark to that secluded den in Jackson's Garden. All he had to do was find out who those pesky friends were that she met up with on a Thursday and put them off and she was sorted. Only thing was he wouldn't be able to tomorrow as he had a business dinner with Della, much to his annoyance. It would be her last evening tomorrow so she would not be meeting up with them again anyway.

□

Chapter 6

It was Thursday and Alva had finished her last shift, at the night shelter. Jackson was driving her home. She was ready to go back to England the next morning. It was their last chance to have a chat on their own.

Jackson had said something in his small-town accent.

"Love your accent!" Alva giggled.

"I love your cockney!" Jackson replied mimicking her.

"You're only said to be a cockney if you are born within the sound of the 'Bow Bells.' But yeah, you can say we speak cockney or estuary English."

"What's 'Bow Bells'?"

"It refers to the bell at the church at St Mary-le-Bow in the east of city of London."

He spent the rest of the journey time trying to learn 'rhyming slang.' Alva taught him all those she knew including the doubles and triples.

"I love how you talk 'real' slow!" she mimicked him.

He really liked her accent it was a major turn on for him. He found the expressions she would pull when she said certain things, super cute. His face changed to a serious one like he was about to announce his undying love.

"I love your perfume. It reminds me of being a kid and staying with my aunt and uncle in England. You are a 'lavender moon'!" He told her.

“There’s no such thing!” she answered him.

“My aunt and uncle would use the term for an event that was so rare and beautifully exquisite. It happens less often than a blue moon, but the event is twice as precious. You’re like a lavender moon, you are rare and precious… I find you so very sexy, I find your accent so very sexy, it really turns me on.” He blurted out that last bit.

“We should stop Jack… you said you don’t want me in that way so don’t make me fall in love with you. You keep complimenting me and that and you really shouldn’t if you don’t mean it, because I will fall for you and if I do I will be obsessed by you… so stop please!”

“Alva, I do mean it! Any bloke would be lucky to have you… but…”

“I know you have said you are too old for me and I’m Mont’s little sister! Trouble is I like you and I could easily fall in love with you I would walk away from Drake if I really thought you wanted me. I don’t think Mont would be a problem if he found someone special and as for being too old it’s a number, I don’t know what your problem is Jack. I’m going to leave it there. I’m going home tomorrow, back to my reality. I’ve loved being with you. I’m happy to just be friends if that’s what you want, but if you want more I need to know, sooner rather than later.”

“We are friends…”

They pulled up outside the door; Alva quickly alighted the car.

“Thanks for the ride, Jack, I’ll see you tomorrow!” Alva said jumping out and running as fast as she could.

She raced off up the steps on to the white painted veranda and disappeared in doors.

He put the car in gear and drove off quickly in case Montgomery saw him, his mind wandered during his journey; she had told him she could fall in love with him. He wanted to tell her he was already deeply in love with her but terrified to admit it. It was a mess.

She had asked what was his problem? He took to pondering that question the rest of the night.

Jackson drove Montgomery and Alva to the airport early that morning, thew sky took on a ruby hue. Mont sat in the rear, and Alva was sat in the front seat with Montgomery in the back. Alva, she kept looking at Jackson and then out of the window. The car journey was tense. They arrived and parked in the grey foreboding multi-story.

Montgomery instructed Jackson to wait for him by the car as he would see Alva through. Jackson had wanted to tell her all his deep fears, anxieties, and explain. Montgomery sensed something, he didn't want them getting together and they seemed different towards each other.

"Well, I best say farewell here then." He opened his arms towards Alva.

She reached up for a hug and wrapped her arms around his neck.

"I've had the best holiday ever! Thank you so much!"

She squeezed him close. He held her tight. She fought the tears threatening to fall, like torrential rain.

"If you ever need me, you have my number just ring me anytime, day or night!"

"Come on!" Montgomery barked impatiently.

Jackson squeezed her and kissed her cheek.

"I hope I'll see you again someday soon." He honestly told her.

"So do I, I'll see you when I see you!" She replied.

She released the embrace and turned away quickly, and sped off.

She raced through to departures with her brother, needing to get away from the tears welling.

"You, OK?" Montgomery asked her.

She smiled. He could see she didn't want to go home. He felt bad not letting Jackson walk with them, she was always so animated around him. Montgomery wondered if Jackson would have softened the blow. She hugged her brother, as she walked through the gate she turned and waved. She waited until she was out of sight before she burst into tears and was swallowed by the rising tide of her emotions. She sat on the plane in seat 7A weeping softly, and reaching for some wine. She wanted Jackson and she knew what was in store for her when she saw Drake.

Jackson had sat in the car waiting patiently for his boss, he was fighting his urge to run after her and sweep her up into his arms and beg her not to go and stay there with him forever. All holiday he sensed things were not happy with her boyfriend but didn't want to pry. The country radio started playing Cole Swindell's Love You Too Late, it was too late now to tell her, he was sitting there certainly staring goodbye in the face and he couldn't take back what he hadn't told her. He saw Montgomery sauntering towards the car, Jackson hit the steering wheel in frustration.

"Hey what's up Jack?" Mont asked as he got in the car noticing the gestures as he was walking toward the car.

"Nothing Buddy, I just forgot to do something really important and I will have lost my opportunity now."

He put the car in drive and drove back in silence.

***

Alva alighted the plane and was relieved to see that only her parents were waiting for her, Drake was nowhere to be seen.

Vaughn drove the hour journey home, the motorway a long stretch of black tar returning her to her monotony. They chatted in the car and pulled up outside their house. Drake was waiting for her with a huge bunch of flowers. He rarely bought her anything, only to 'show off.' He once stole some flowers off a lamppost that had been left in memoriam after a recent car accident and fatality. Alva had been horrified, she thought it despicable. When she had let him have her opinion, he had told her what an 'ungrateful bitch' she was which was why she was touched when Jackson had given her a bunch, especially that he had picked them from his garden. Jackson had touched her heart that day.

She went to put the flowers in water and pricked herself on a couple of thorns. Tears filled her eyes as she stood in the kitchen. He laid on the schmooze thick, especially in front of her parents. He told Alva how he had missed her and was so gushing. He invited her to dinner and told Vaughn he would have her back no later than 11pm. He was excellent at charming her parents, it seemed as if it was only Montgomery that saw through it.

Alva willingly went with him. He was being nice. He had been lovely like this the first month they were together. He bought her dinner and they went back to his flat. He made a telephone call. He was pleasant.

"Did you miss me?"

"Of course, I did!" She smiled.

He grabbed her ponytail pulling viciously it was the first time he showed his physical side.

"Don't lie, fucking bitch! YOU MADE ME LOOK LIKE AN IDIOT! You went over there; didn't tell me I've had four weeks without you! You are going to start with making up for all the lost dinner dates." He screamed in her face.

She could smell alcohol and cigarettes on his breath.

He ordered a takeaway and forced Alva to eat it until she passed out for a couple of minutes, she awoke to him stubbing out cigarettes on her bare thigh.

"I'm sorry I had to punish you. You really shouldn't push me like that. I really missed you. Come and have a cuddle…"

He snuggled her on the settee next to him and wrapped his arms around her.

"You can eat the rest tomorrow." He said gently to her.

She liked him when he was sweet, when he wasn't he was a pig.

He took her home and arranged another date.

***

Across the town in his 1960's office and factory complex, Enrico Capozzi, a muscular grey-haired guy in his fifties, phone rang in his pocket, reached in and looked at the caller identity, he stood up from his desk and paced up and down his coffee scented office.

"Uncle, it's me… I've found someone I'm obsessed with… I wonder if you can keep tabs on her please?"

"Of course! Consider it done! Send me her name and details and I will follow her as best I can without her knowing, it will be at a distance though and I will not get involved directly you understand! I will call you later and discuss what you need."

"Yes, Uncle and thank you, love to Auntie Kim!"

Enrico Capozzi the feared Mafia Don returned his mobile back to the inside pocket of his jacket to await his nephew's instructions. He returned to his desk and continued the meeting in Italian.

***

For three awful months, sometimes he was sweet, sometimes he wasn't, mostly he wasn't the majority of the time, he was cruel and spiteful, he abused her every single way possible and always out of view and behind closed doors and always in places no one could see or were easily covered up, certainly never her face. Sometimes he would apologies but would always turn it to being her fault, when he did, she would crave those moments of kindness and validation. He was like a drug, she knew he was no good, yet in those junctures she would get 'high' then come crashing down to earth messed up. Enrico or one of his men would have stepped in and crushed Drake like the bug he was if they had known what he was doing to her, but couldn't see through walls, so would let the path of true love take its course.

The weeks continued and Drake tried to wear her down about moving in with him. He asked her to marry him, he tried everything to get her away from Vaughn and Alison, bit by bit he wanted to control her. He would stop her going to work some days, eventually she got into trouble and failed placements and ended up leaving. She told her parents she didn't want to nurse, but it was a blatant lie.

The only ray of sunshine in that time was the parcel she received one morning. The postman delivered a heavy package wrapped in brown paper with airmail stickers and pretty stamps, although the proof of postage was printed, an array of stamps with birds on had been found to decorate it. She opened it in secret away from her parents and certainly not in front of Drake. Jackson had sent her a book on birds that are native to the US and attached was a notelet. The card had a painted picture of a 'Nashville Warbler.' By the artist 'Barcham Grice' She read the letter he had written.

'My Dearest Alva,

I hope you are well,

Please accept this little gift from me, I saw it in the book store and hoped you would love it. It reminded me of our glorious times together. I hope you like the card; I remembered you like Barcham Grice's paintings and saw it and thought of you, Honey.

It has been very quiet here; Mont is keeping me busy.

Bert and Bill often ask after you and send their good wishes. The night shelter is not the same without you, we miss you! Hope you will visit soon.

I hope your boyfriend is treating you well, because Alva you deserve the best, because you are a 'Lavender Moon'.

Merry Christmas.

Yours always

Jack x'

She felt the tears flowing and she hid the card in the book and put them on the top of her parent's wardrobe so that Drake couldn't find it in her room and read it. That would cause a punishment. This past week he started to get more violent, and physically attacked her twice during that week, somehow making her feel it had been accidental or she had provoked him.

Time continued at home for Alva, Christmas had past painfully slow and without respite. All she could think about was her book, which she hadn't had chance to look at. Drake hadn't been thoughtful in his gifts to her, he'd bought her loads of sexy underwear which was four sizes too small then told her to slim into them, whilst shoving a huge box of chocolates under her nose. In front of her parents, he'd bought her an expensive watch to show off. She hadn't noticed the men who followed her, they noticed the sadness in her eyes and wished to help her.

Today was the first day of a new year, her last straw, she was forced to change. She kept think about the words Jack wrote telling her she deserved the best. Today he went for the kill, he was so frustrated that she would not move in with him. He had tried again to seduce her into his bed, she wasn't ready, he'd forced her into oral sex, she'd agreed on a couple of occasions to stop him from having sex with her. It had been enough to keep her virginity for now.

She kept thinking back to her book received from Jackson, his gift was thoughtful, he knew her interests and it was about her pleasure and enjoyment not his. She felt bad for not sending Jackson anything in return, but she didn't get an opportunity because Drake now wouldn't let her shop without him.

She snapped out of her reverie and back to the moment she was in. She was in his flat again! One moment he was doing what he wanted. Forcing her to do something she hated, then he beat her, kicks and punches were thrown and other injuries inflicted, cigarettes were used in the aftermath whilst she lay in a foetal sobbing heap on the floor by the end of his bed. She lay there shocked and dumbfounded. He left the room to make a phone call. Alva scrabbled the rest of her clothes on.

The next thing she knew he was back in the room, making her jump.

Next, she was headed for the door.

Next, he had his hand tightly gripped around her throat and up against the door.

"If I squeeze hard enough you will pass out and I will have you here on the floor without you knowing about it! Fucking cock tease!" he growled.

His face was so close she could feel his breath and smell the cigarettes. The tears started. What was worse? Losing her virginity to him or not knowing anything about it? Either way terrified her.

Drake jeered at her applying more pressure. He wanted her to see he was serious he was in charge.

She started seeing stars.

She wasn't going down again without a fight. She kicked and screamed and manged to use her weight to push him off, getting out and running as fast as she could.

She could hear him shouting after her.

"NINE FUCKING MONTHS I'VE BEEN WAITING FOR A SHAG! YOU'RE RIDICULOUS ALVA… NO OTHER BLOKE WOULD TOUCH YOU! FRIDGED BINT! I'VE BEEN GETTING IT ELSEWHERE!"

Somehow, she managed to get out of the block of flats. She knew he wouldn't be far behind. A black taxi was there waiting for her? It seemed odd it was like it had been placed for her, she directed the quiet driver to where she wanted to go, he hardly spoke just nodded.

She got home and asked the driver to wait for her, she asked him if he saw Drake's red car coming to call the police, whilst she got packed. Alva left a note for her parents, not telling them where she was bound but promised to ring as soon as she arrived. She grabbed her most treasured possessions from the top of her parent's wardrobe. She ran down the stone stairs to the street, with her luggage, slamming the street door in haste and straight back into the taxi. She thought she could see his distinctive red car in the distance which was at the end of the main road about 200 yards away, what she didn't know was Drake had been held up in his flat. She ducked down in the taxi and told him to drive to the airport as she clasped her passport, bird book and notelet in her hands. The driver looked familiar, like she had seen him in the newspapers, he reminded her of the feared mafia lord Enrico Capozzi.

Once down the road she bravely sat back in the seat and cried. The driver passed her a packet of tissues.

She read the notelet again. It had given her some courage; she knew who would help her.

"Where are you going?" he asked.

"I'm going to Jackson!"

"As in Jackson Mississippi?" he said almost laughing.

"No, this one is in Nashville Tennessee!"

She quickly looked on her phone for tickets there was a flight in two hours.

"How long until we get to the airport?" she asked.

"Forty-five minutes tops!" he told her in his East London accent.

"Thanks! There's a flight leaving soon and I can book it."

She tapped out and paid on her phone.

"So, what's the deal with him? Do you owe him money?"

“No, he’s just my ex and I want to get away from him as soon as I can!”

“He’s part of that Drake family?”

She nodded.

“How did a nice girl like you get involved with thugs like them?”

She shrugged in reply. She honestly didn’t know. She certainly didn’t know she was born involved, she started crying again

“Oh, Luna di lavanda!” he muttered, “You will be fine soon!”

Alva looked at her phone, she looked in the stored cloud at pictures of Jackson, she had deleted them from the phone because Drake liked to look at her phone, so she had put everything in a secret cloud account that only she knew login details for. She hovered over his number hesitating, she had saved it under Jackie, so Drake would assume it was a female friend. He, told me to call if I needed anything… but it is 4:30am for him… day or night he said… I’ll give it a bit longer, she thought to herself.

Jackson was lying awake, he glanced at his clock 3:39 something had jolted him awake. He had celebrated New Year with his parents and got home at 1am. He worried about Montgomery being drunk somewhere. He couldn’t get back to sleep. He felt ‘bothered’ by something and didn’t know what. He put on his radio. The song that came on next reminded him of Alva. It was one of Montgomery’s. He looked at his phone, no missed calls, no texts, nothing. No Happy New Year from her. Why was I expecting a call from her he wondered. He looked at the pictures on his phone of her. I miss her! I want her, and I need her, he finally admitted to himself! He lay there a few more minutes and decided sleep would not come. He was shattered from New Year celebrations, yet he couldn’t sleep. He didn’t have to go into work today as it was New Year’s Day. Montgomery was in the studio, because it was more convenient.

Jackson got up and showered, Alva was on his mind again, he couldn't shake her, for some reason today she was there. He decided he would go to work, he could tidy and clean the office worst case scenario, but he could do some more of that secret dossier he was working on, at work certain information was more available and would look less suspicious. She had been like a ghost in the house after she had left, he felt her presence, he would hear a noise and be convinced she was back.

Alva arrived at the airport and went to pay the taxi driver, but he insisted on no payment only on staying with her until she could board, he made a few calls out of her earshot but she was always in his line of sight, he kept his hand on the pistol in his jacket pocket. She kept looking around worrying Drake would work out her destination and arrive and who was this driver, he seemed to want to protect her for some reason? She kept looking at her old watch around her left wrist, she had dumped his at home, planning to return the expensive one as soon as it was safe to. She found a bar and the driver bought her a whiskey to steady her nerves. She kept checking the board and was on the flight as soon as she could board. She wouldn't be happy until she was in the air. She just prayed Drake hadn't thought of it too, and would appear on the same flight. She didn't know Drake was still at his flat being detained by some men, he was wondering when he would be beaten but they were to just wait until Alva's flight landed in Nashville. The driver walked her to the VIP gate and passed her through to a tough looking man, he spoke commandingly to in Italian,

"This man will see you on the plane piccola luna di lavanda. Oh and please give my regards to Jack… I see you have him in your phone as 'Jackie' presumably to fool that parasite, Trent?"

Alva nodded. Who was this man and how did he know about Jackson?

Next thing she knew she was in the sky saying goodbye to London. She read her card again, then looked through the book. The illustrations were incredible. It was a really thoughtful gift, now she was able to really appreciate it. She wondered if Jackson would welcome her.

□

Chapter 7

It had been just over three months since Jackson had taken Alva to the airport for her flight home. He had enjoyed the weeks she had been there. At the airport she kissed his cheek and told him she'd had a wonderful time and it was the best holiday she had ever had. His friend had stood to attention again that day, he hugged her and whispered in her ear.

"If you ever need me Honey, I'll be here for you!" or words to that effect.

He immersed himself in Montgomery's work. His and secret work. The manager, Della Fontaine, had, only seemed to be interested in making money, and was clearly after him sexually. He knew Montgomery was hopeful to find a lasting love but wasn't interested in his manager. She could be a pestilence. Jackson found himself doing more and more managerial duties and Montgomery seemed to delegate them to his trusted friend.

Today Montgomery was in the studio and Della was there. Jackson avoided the woman at all costs, she was rumoured to be behind many a disappearance of many stars who had fallen foul of her.

Jackson had decided to go to Montgomery's house to do some paperwork in the office and make some calls, perhaps clean, and organise his office. He didn't have to today as it was New Year's Day, he just had an urge to be there. All he had to do was collect Montgomery later and socialise, and that was a friendship arrangement.

He got up to make a herbal tea and was standing in the kitchen humming Montgomery's upcoming single to himself and recalling memories of Alva. He had written the song himself after Alva had gone home. It was called 'Lost Loves and Other Angels' Montgomery had accidentally heard him singing it one morning and insisted it go on the album. The lyrics had reminded Montgomery of

Georgette and it had spoken to him that way, little did he know he was singing a song to his ex about his little sister. That's the beauty of country music, you see, you can find a song that speaks in different ways to its listeners.

Suddenly, he was startled by a knock at the door, the sound ricocheting through the empty house taking him back to the first time he met Alva…

He abandoned making his tea to answer it. It could only be her he thought. He raced to the door and quickly opened it to the heart-breaking vision that stood before him — A sobbing and terrified Alva.

He lurched forward and caught her in his arms as she let out a howl, dropping to her knees. He held her as she let everything go. He kissed the top of her head. The lavender scent a reminder, in the depths of sorrow there is warmth. Seeing her heart breaking was like watching glass shatter over the floor, no way to restore it.

"Let it go! Let it all out, when you are ready you can tell me what has happened." He whispered, holding his strong arms around her, stroking her hair.

It seemed like forever that she had been kneeling on the hall carpet, like a terrified puppy, weeping and being held by Jackson. Eventually the cries subsided and he helped her to the bar room and poured her a drink and grabbed a box of tissues. He opened a bottle of fizzy water and sat opposite her waiting for her to open up. She was shaking. She stood up and slipped off her jacket, she had been in such a rush she hadn't put her cardigan on to hide her injuries when she left. Her cardigan was still at Drake's flat. She would always hide the injuries; he would always wound her in places she could cover up.

Jackson gasped when he noticed her bruised wrists. They were mottled greens, browns and purples, it was clear something untoward had been occurring and for some time. What had that

Drake Trent done to her, clenching his fists so hard his nails dug into his palms Jackson thought to himself?

"What happened?" he said breaking the silence.

"I… told him I didn't want to tolerate his behaviour anymore and he got really nasty!" she explained. He noted the fresh bruising to her neck.

"He's been unkind to you for a while, hasn't he?" Jackson remarked pointing to her wrists. "Oh Alva! I'm sorry! I wish I had picked up on it when you came last time!"

He tried to figure out why he had missed these cues before, perhaps he was too wrapped up in his 'other' work, or too busy trying not to fall in love again,

Alva burst in to tears again She couldn't tell him what had happened to her, what she told him was how she had refused to sleep with him and how he had told her he had gone to her friend because she was willing and that he was fed up waiting on her to put out. She then showed him the video he had sent her of him having sex with her best friend. It had been sent an hour after she left, and received it in the taxi from the airport. She let it all go. She had forgotten the taxi driver and his message to Jackson.

Jackson sat listening and not saying a word. Sitting silently in a world of shock, non-judgement of her and allowing her to speak her truth. He had understood from his sister Dorraine that these matters aren't as simple as getting up and walking away, the most dangerous time for a victim of abuse was this, the time of leaving your abuser, special help should be sought if possible and many charities will help make a plan to leave, plus a lot of numbers don't show up or need paying for. Dorraine was a specialist police officer who dealt with such situations.

"Firstly, I promise you that no one will hurt you while I am about! Do you want to go to the police? I know you'd probably would need to go back to the UK… but you need this documented if you want to pursue it later. I can speak to Dorraine she's a specialist police officer trained for such things." He offered.

"Who is Dorraine?" a pang of jealousy hit her.

"My sister" he replied.

"Oh! I didn't know you had a sister… Dorraine of the Ponchartrain! I remember now our conversation about why you are called Jackson."

"And a boy named Sue!" he said dead pan to her.

She started laughing.

"Alva! That's not nice! Laughing at my brother being called 'Sue'!" He chuckled.

For those moments of that conversation, she was transported on the tangent away from the horror.

"Wow! I just realised You have two famous relatives! Maxwell Barnes and 'Mosquito Maddox' Drake would be so jealous about me knowing your brother… he's a massive fan of his!" she sniffed wiping her nose with a tissue.

"Max wouldn't be a fan of his… we don't treat ladies like that!" he replied.

"I'm not worth it!" She bowed her head moving her legs underneath her on the bar stool and holding them on the bar at her ankles. He noticed her keep wincing with pain whenever she moved. Her demeanour had transited from devastated, to slightly cheerful, and then it plummeted back to despair at the merest mention of her being worthy of respect.

"Don't let Drake make you feel like that… that's how they work it, they make you feel like garbage and tell you are worthless, so you become dependent on them. They isolate you, little by little."

He grabbed her hand to reassure her. “I promise I won’t let anyone hurt you!”

Alva sobbed again at the thought of someone wanting to protect her, in those months she had been with Drake, he had zapped every ounce of her confidence and self-esteem. There was nothing left of her former self, she was like a discarded shell on a beach.

“You won’t tell Mont, will you? I don’t want to tell my parents I’m too ashamed and anyway, who would believe me?” She said looking pleadingly into his eyes.

“I believe you! I won’t tell anyone, but I would feel so much better if you had a chat with Dorraine, she will be discreet.”

“Do you have any painkillers please?”

Jackson went to the kitchen and got her some ibuprofen and paracetamol. The way she was holding herself he was guessing they might not be strong enough.

Alva eventually agreed to speaking to Dorraine, who was over within fifteen minutes. First task was to get Alva medically seen, so she drove her to an authorised doctor.

Alva was examined and x-rayed, and swabbed for DNA and STIs, it felt intrusive, but the doctor and Dorraine made it bearable. Dorraine took a statement and pictures of the injuries; plus, a number that Jackson wasn’t aware of. She explained that she couldn’t do much from her end, but gathering evidence with a qualified officer and an affidavit should be admissible in a court should she decide to proceed. It was also important for Alva to be believed and acknowledged, which Dorraine did.

Dorraine took Alva back to ‘California’ and went in for a cup of coffee, with her and her brother. Dorraine liked Alva and got the impression she was genuine and very impressionable. She thought she would really suit her brother, who at twenty-one and come home dishevelled from Chicago, he had not had a girlfriend, she didn’t even think he had dated. Something was unhappy about him the day he rolled in like a tornado, and this sadness never seemed to go until about August last year, it seemed to coincide with the girl she was looking after today. When she was gone Jackson was alone with Alva once again, Alva went and changed to hide her bruises and tidied herself up and put concealer around her neck. She returned to the bar room and had another drink.

His phone pinged:

Do you like your gift? I took great care sending her to you Jack.

The message could be easily misconstrued as a threat.

Thank you, Uncle, a very precious gift, like a lavender moon, I will take the best care from now on. Love to Auntie Kim and y'all.

Jackson put it in his pocket and went and found Alva in the bar after seeing Dorraine out.

"How are you doing? Would you like to come for lunch? I'm going to collect Mont in a few hours fancy killing some time with me? It's a new year, fancy a new start?"

"Sure! I'd like that. I'm just going to tell Mont, I broke up with him because, I caught Drake in bed with Ella, my best friend and leave it at that."

"Whatever you want Honey." He replied. "Do you need to let your Mom and Dad know you are here? You can ring from the office and I can wait."

She dialled the number with a +44 prefix the telephone was picked up, a relieved Alison was pleased to hear her voice. Drake had been pestering them to her whereabouts. They didn't like him. They had realised early on he was the son of Diana Drake, the half-sister of Vaughn and a cousin of Alva's and Vaughn's nephew. The boy had been influenced heavily by the Drake family. They had always given him the benefit of the doubt, because he was always so well-mannered and polite with them, during those last few days his mask slipped and they heard him say vile things to their daughter.

Alva had been there a week and spent most of the time reading, she couldn't do any birdwatching, she had trouble standing. The doctor had called her to tell that her tests were negative, which was a relief for her. She was in excruciating pain, the worst she had ever been in, even worse than the time she had fallen out of the window at school trying to get away from a bully and broken her arm and collar bone, the doctor had suggested it would be about six to eight weeks to heal her fractures, they were all in places that could not be cast.

Montgomery felt she needed to socialise and had spoken to his trainer to see if he was able to accommodate her watching wrestling. They had asked Jackson to suggest it to her. Although Jackson had just wanted to leave her to do her own thing

"My brother is at the wrestling today. Mont thought it would be nice for you, if you would like to come." Jackson asked.

"Yeah! That will annoy Drake!" she laughed "He's mad on wrestling. I can do a load of selfies and put them on social media. I'm guessing his mates will show him…"

She liked that idea, Alva wasn't a vindictive person, but for Drake Trent she might make an exception.

"…Thanks Jack, let me know what time you want to leave."

The Nashville grey sky had set the backdrop to his for Jackson's journey that morning, the to work, his windscreen wipers swished intermittently, like a metronome to a song about her he would write. Alva appeared at the kitchen door ready in her jeans and a black 'Montgomery Moon' hoodie, she liked to advertise her brother, plus he gifted her any merchandise she wanted.

They set off to the arena and met Maxwell, the wipers scraping the window. During his reinvention Montgomery had hired Maxwell 'Mad Mosquito' Maddox, or Max as he was known as was a retired professional wrestler and now a personal trainer. He showed Montgomery how to build muscle. Montgomery hadn't realised until their first meeting that 'Mad Mosquito' and Jackson were brothers as there was a ten-year gap, Jackson being the younger. Dorraine was smack in between the brothers. When they arrived together that first morning Montgomery realised, they had to be related and asked. Max would work him hard and encourage him so that Montgomery would become the best version of himself.

The morning was spent watching practice matches and rehearsals. Alva hid the pain well that morning. Maxwell introduced them to many of the main bill athletes and lots of pictures were taken. A group of the lady wrestlers collared Jackson and were chatting and flirting with him, much to her jealousy. They all knew he worked for Montgomery and had hoped that was a way of meeting Montgomery Moon, the country star. Jackson was used to this and paid no attention. A couple of the male wrestlers took a shine to Alva, or appeared to, one of them arranging a 'date' for the next evening.

Ashley 'The Incinerator' Ashdown, had organised to meet her in a restaurant and hired a private room. Ashley, was very tall and bulky, he was tanned and muscular, he was very popular with his lady fans. Jack begrudgingly gave her a ride to her date, there was something that set him on edge with Ashdown. Jackson decided he would sit in the bar and wait for her, talk about dating on the rebound, Jackson had thought. It was Thursday, and he didn't want to miss his turn at the night shelter, Alva had already rung to say she couldn't help, that had annoyed Jackson, yet he found himself dialling Bill and saying he couldn't be of service. He wondered if it was jealousy on his part made him want to wait for her, or was it something else?

The private dining room was upstairs, Jackson sat in the bar with a fruit infused soda. His stomach churned, as he felt a sense of foreboding.

Alva sat at the table chatting to Ashley, the first half an hour was sweet whilst they looked at the menu. Alva was dressed in a pretty dress. Ashdown had now downed half a bottle of Jack and was plying her with the liquor. She was now feeling uncomfortable with his comments, for some reason she felt unsafe. Her eyes started frantically searching the room planning an escape, she felt uncomfortable his demeanour had changed from sweet and kind into menacing, she wanted Jackson, she glanced at her phone wondering if she should text him to come back.

After sitting for fifteen minutes nursing his drink, Maxwell came running in, with a worried look on his face.

"Jack, where is she? We need to get her out now!" Maxwell puffed.

Jackson leapt from his seat, almost knocking his drink over.

"Why what's up? She's upstairs in a private dining room." Jackson said, hurrying towards the stairs.

"The other guys told me what he was wanting to do to her. They were worried about her." Maxwell explained.

Jackson was bounding up the stairs two at a time, frantically opening every door to see which room they were in, apologising for disturbing people as they went.

"He's got a reputation Jack, I only just out found that he was meeting her."

Jackson could hear crying and begging him from the corridor he burst in through the door, the ferocity imprinting his sole of his boot into the wood.

"Please stop! You are really hurting me!" she pleaded.

“What the hell do you think you are doing!” Jackson shouted, launching himself at the wrestler.

“FUCK OFF!” Ashley shouted at Jackson, pushing him off.

He had Alva pinned down on the floor, his whole muscular body suppressing her. His hand groping at her breast ferociously. Jackson and Maxwell pulled him off her. Maxwell then dragged him out of the room, down the stairs and out of the restaurant. Alva was shaking, her dress was torn at the top exposing her bra, he had broken the strap. Jackson helped her to her seat and helped her take a drink of water. He took off his hoodie and wrapped it around her shoulders, then he sat with his arm around her, trembling like an earthquake.

“How did you know I needed help?” her voice quivering.

“Max showed up and said he heard you were on a date with him and he has a reputation. We can report him… I’m sorry I didn’t get to you sooner! I let you down badly. I won’t ever be able to apologise enough!”

“Jack, you didn’t know what he was like… I’m grateful you came when you did! I feel a fool this happening again. You must think I’m a tart. This has happened twice in two weeks!”

“I don’t think anything more than you have really bad taste in men and you are just really unlucky!”

As they made their way out of the restaurant, they noticed the police had arrived and Ashley was cuffed in the car. Maxwell had made a citizen’s arrest and had called Dorraine for advice; she was on duty and headed over with her partner. Dorraine escorted her to the police station to make a statement, Jackson and Maxwell followed and made theirs. Alva’s injuries were again photographed and her dress and underwear taken for evidence.

Jackson snuck back to the house and slipped like a ninja in and upstairs to grab Alva a change of clothes. He was used to being stealthy around Montgomery, his undercover work required it, he wondered what Montgomery would make of it all when it came to light. He stood in her bedroom and opened her underwear drawers to pick something. He felt horrible looking at her lingerie, they were all pretty sets, he supressed his carnal urges knowing what had just occurred. He grabbed a matching set, found a pair of jeans, top and wrapped them all in her lilac Moon hoodie.

She didn't want Montgomery finding out. He had been sitting in the lounge drinking whiskey and hadn't noticed, Jackson creeping in and out.

Eventually the police had all they needed. Jackson wanted to scoop her up in his arms. He had never seen anyone so broken in his life. He felt guilty he had not insisted on chaperoning her, but then she was twenty and entitled to her choice in men, however awful they were.

They were sitting in Jackson's silver chevvy SUV in the car park of the police station.

"Let's get a meal!" he started.

She smiled and nodded. Food always made her feel better, or so she thought.

"Thanks, Jack, for today. Will Max say anything to Mont?" she asked in a shaky voice.

"No, he won't. He is just glad you are safe now." He reassured her.

Jackson reached over and squeezed her hand.

"You know you are not to blame?" he said, shifting the car into drive.

"I think I am… I thought he would be nice, being famous you know? You missed volunteering tonight! Sorry Jack!"

"Men can be bastards whatever walk of life they are from. There are also decent guys from all areas of life. We don't come with labels! Plus, I would drop anything for you!" he smiled reassuringly.

They drove to the edge of the city and found a steakhouse. Parking up they disembarked and Jackson offered her a hug.

She liked his scent, he smelled of safety, he smelled manly. It was like an animal urge, sniffing their mate. Jackson loved the scent of lavender even more now. He wanted her so much. The more time he spent with her the more he felt like a jigsaw that wasn't complete, yet each time he was with her he got another piece and the picture was now emerging. He had to keep denying himself. He was nine years older; he didn't want anyone thinking he was taking advantage of her, especially her, after what those thugs had done. If they did date and split it could be awkward with his boss and best mate.

He felt like a knight in shining armour who had just rescued the princess from the dragon. He drew an analogy in his mind that if this was the Jackson and Alva show it was going to have to carry on with the cliff hangers for now. Jackson vowed in that moment he would have to make sure she was treated well and like the lady she is.

Jackson was sitting in the study the next morning, Montgomery had gone to the studio and the coffee he had made Alva had gone cold on the kitchen counter. He thought she was late getting up and wondered if he should go and check she was well. He heard her coming down the stairs. She walked slowly and he went out of the room, he saw her wincing as she descended the stairs.

"Good morning, Alva." Jackson called cheerfully.

"Hi" she managed weakly.

Jackson went to the kitchen and poured her a fresh coffee. She followed him to the kitchen. She went around looking for food to binge on. Flinging open cupboards, and checking everywhere. There was very little and Montgomery had asked her to get some groceries and cook dinner today. Jackson offered to make her toast and she agreed, but she needed something to blot out her pain.

He could recognise the want in her to binge.

The next thing Jackson knew was clinking sounds coming from the bar room. Alva was stood looking at the bottles of spirits wondering which would drink them off her mind.

"Alva… are you alright?"

The tears started again.

"Which one will make me pass out do you think?"

"What!? Why do you want to pass out?"

"Because I need to blank out all the pain! Yesterday and Drake!"

"There is no alcohol strong enough! You know a binge of any kind is not the answer?"

Jackson reached her hand and took the bottle of rum she was grasping. He put it on the bar and wrapped her in his arms. She sobbed into his chest, her tears soaking his Luke Combs t-shirt.

"Can I suggest? I can see you are in agony and don't want to be walking too much, that we make a grocery order online, then you let me order a takeaway lunch and collect shopping later? Then you can rest on the sofa today… I will cook dinner for you both and he can heat his up when he comes home."

Alva nodded. She felt embarrassed by everything and Jackson was so sweet to her. Today she would trust her heart and allow Jackson to take care of things at least for a while.

Chapter 8

The annual Country Awards for Music and Other Entertainment or CAMOE's was held each year. Montgomery was up for awards in several categories: best song, best album, best collaboration, best music video and best artist. He had been ordered to go with Della Fontaine, yet he wanted to take Alva. Jackson also happened to be nominated for awards with Montgomery. Jackson had written 'I've missed you so much it's stopped hurting' and 'Death on Love Row' with Montgomery both songs were up for song of the year. Montgomery had performed the former at last year's event. He also had written many songs on Montgomery's album 'Lost Loves and Other Angels.' Jackson was also going to keep Montgomery company and there was 'safety in numbers.' As Della was insisting Montgomery to escort her, Jackson thought that Alva might like to go as his guest. Alva liked the idea. Of course, Alva liked the idea she was smitten, she felt he was her knight in shining armour.

Montgomery organised a day of shopping for his sister to buy a dress. She had visited a few shops and boutiques and was either ignored or laughed at because of her frame, she got back in the car on the verge of tears. Jackson turned to her,

"No luck Honey?"

"No! they ignore me or say there is nothing in my size."

Jackson pursed his lips.

"They have no idea that you could be showcasing their designs at the CAMOEs next to the latest country music sensation?" he pondered rubbing his chin. He burst out laughing. Alva looked dejected.

"It's like that scene in the film 'Pretty Woman' when she returns and tells them what a huge mistake they made." he dialled a number on his phone.

"Eduardo! Yeah, it's Jack Maddox… you know you said if you could ever do me a favour just ask? Well, I need one, but it could well work in your advantage. My guest for the CAMOE's needs a dress designed and made for her by Saturday. Can you help? Yeah… Yeah in half an hour? Yes… her name is Alva, Alva Moon… she is related… she's his lovely sister." Jackson winked at her. "Thanks! See you soon Eduardo!"

"Jack who was that?" she asked.

"Eduardo Cavalieri!" Jackson put the car in drive and drove off.

"THE Eduardo Cavalieri! The designer!?"

"Yes!"

Alva sat dumbfounded.

Eduardo Cavalieri was one of the most sought-after designers. He was well known for making dresses for the more Rubenesque lady and to have him make you a dress, meant you had 'arrived'.

"How on earth do you know him?"

"We've been friends since high school, he knows Janey and Jason too." Jackson grinned

Jackson drove a few miles across town and parked up. Alva felt like she was in a dream. They trotted into a very modern glass fronted boutique, which sparkled in the high noon like a diamond in a desert.

"Jack you old rogue!" Eduardo greeted him "Who is this fine creature I see before me!" he smiled at Alva.

She held out her hand, he took it and kissed it.

"Eduardo this is one of my best friends, Alva. Some of the local designers have been rather rude to this beauty because of her stature. They clearly don't realise she could be exposing their designs to such a wide audience!" Eduardo walked around her looking at her from all directions.

Jack, said I was one of his best friends she thought to herself, turning a slight pink with a blush, wondering what being his 'best friend' might actually mean?

Jackson sneaked off leaving Alva to enjoy the experience. She needed to be treated well, she'd had so long being bullied, scorned and ignored, Jackson wanted her to feel amazing.

"Champagne for Miss Moon please!" Eduardo clicked his fingers and a young girl walked over with a glass of ice-cold fizz, condensation forming on the bowl.

"Thank you, Dania! Will you please get my fabric swatches silk and watermark taffeta I think!" He smiled at his assistant.

His assistant scuttled off and collected what was required. He drew a few sketches, made measurements and took some photographs, whilst chatting to her and getting some style ideas.

"Miss Moon would you kindly call-in person tomorrow at 10 am and I would like to show you, my designs. Then if you would like to go ahead, we can organise fittings etc!"

"Thank you so much Mr Cavalieri! But please call me Alva!" She went to shake his hand.

"NO! NO! NO!" He wagged his finger at her. "It's Eduardo to Jack's friends, Alva. I wouldn't be here if it weren't for him helping me out with some troublesome bullies! He gave me back my confidence and I am eternally grateful to him!" he said with a bow, then he hugged her and offered her his arm to escort her to Jackson's awaiting car, opening the passenger door for her.

She sat with Jackson a huge smile plastered over her face.

Alva enjoyed all the fittings each day for the week. She appreciated all the work Eduardo was putting into her outfit. She also enjoyed these because Jackson would drive her and wait in the car and then they would go and do something together afterwards, often lunch then bird watching.

The day of the CAMOE's came. They would meet Della there, but Jackson would drive Montgomery and Alva. Jackson had brought his tuxedo to change into, but went out after lunch time, Alva had been whisked off upstairs with the makeup artist and hairdresser Montgomery organised.

Jackson had a new haircut, short back and sides but still lengthy on top and he had decided to wear a black pinch top cowboy hat too. Montgomery paced in the hall waiting for his sister with his trademark gloomy look. Eduardo and Dania then made their way downstairs. He gave Jackson a knowing wink and left.

Alva stood at the top of the stairs. Her makeup enhanced her features, her eyes looked amazing with a smoky eyeshadow.

She walked with grace and poise down the stairs. She looked radiant, her beaming smile lit up the hall.

"DARN!" Jackson exclaimed.

"You look nice!" Montgomery said.

"She looks amazing! Smouldering." Jackson blurted out in correction of his boss, lavishing the praise. Then Jackson realised he had thought aloud. He stared at her, she was stunning, he really noticed her beauty.

"Well, I'd probably think the same if she wasn't my sister!" Montgomery laughed.

It surprised Jackson to hear his boss laugh a second time recently, he never usually smiled. He obviously made these things an exception when it came to his sister.

Jackson tipped his hat to her before removing it and leant forward to kiss her cheek, and to apologise for the 'cuss' word. He offered his arm to escort her to the car. Once at his silver SUV he opened the door to the back seat and she climbed in, gathering her skirts. She thanked and smiled at Jackson,

"Your hair looks nice! I like it! The cowboy hat looks cute on you too!" she smiled.

"Thank you, Ma'am! You look stunning and gorgeous!" he told her.

Alva blushed. No man had ever complimented her like that and she had heard him thinking out loud to her brother.

Montgomery sat in the front seat and took a nip of neat whiskey from a hip flask to calm his nerves. He was aware his friend and sister were in a 'moment' he would shut that down, later. No man would ever be good enough for her and no girl would take his best mate away from him.

As he drove Jackson, kept looking in the rear view and realised just how beautiful Alva was. It was hard not to keep looking at her, he kept having to remind himself to concentrate on the road, he could easily get lost in a fantasy of her, especially when her eyes would meet his and she would smile, he needed to get everyone to the event safely, so had to focus.

Della was standing waiting for them outside the auditorium, her arms crossed, tapping her foot, denoting her impatience, yet they had time to spare. Della's bright scarlet off-the-shoulder evening gown reminded Jackson of the danger she posed, although she was sultry looking as always. She greeted them big smiles and gushing. They didn't like her insincerity. She grabbed hold of Montgomery's arm and barged her way through, almost dragging him. Alva took Jackson's arm and floated in with him. They found their large round table and sat down. Della poured out the champagne, Jackson moved it to his side; he did not drink alcohol. He ordered his usual sparkling water from the waiter. That was one thing Alva had noticed, Jackson was so respectful of everyone. Della demanded of the waiting staff, yet Jackson was really polite and always spoke to them kindly, like they were doing him a massive favour by getting him fizzy water, Alva admired this quality.

Della was quick to aim an insult and started jibing him about not drinking alcohol. Jackson kept his cool.

“I forgot you are driving us! Thank you, Jack, for thinking of our safety.” Alva said making a point and shutting down Della.

Montgomery leant over and grabbed Jackson’s flute downing the drink in one.

“Slow down Mont!” Alva whispered to her brother sitting next to her.

Jackson was sitting next to Alva on the other side. There were a couple of other executives from the record company on their table and they had all been introduced. Jackson used this opportunity to listen to furtive conversations from these executives. Common Ancestor were on the next table. Alva remarked to Jackson how much better it would have been if they were sitting with them. Jackson was happy where he was, he gained quite useful information that night, no one would suspect him, the quiet, innocent PA of Montgomery Moon.

Montgomery performed his set, then returned and continued listening to the other acts. The awards were read out, Montgomery won each of his nomination and therefore so did Jackson. Alva filmed for her parents as the show wouldn’t be shown in the UK for over a month. Alva was proud of Jackson. Once all the awards were done Montgomery continued to drink. Della tried to drape herself over him like a mink fur.

“I thought she was married?” Alva remarked to Jackson.

“She is! Her and Bryan have an arranged marriage and an ‘understanding’.” Jackson told her.

Alva was shocked.

"EWW! I don't think I'd want to share anyone, if I had someone, that was done to me and it stings!"

"She's after your brother big time. I think we should get him home, don't you?"

"Yeah! One either side?" She suggested.

They pulled up outside 'California.' Jackson got out and opened the door for her, then the front passenger door. Montgomery stood up and vomited. He covered Alva and her dress. She let out a huge sigh! His vomit seeped down her neckline and her dress had been plastered in the foul-smelling emetic. Alva was so upset, although tried not to burst into tears. She had gone through a lot and she loved that dress. It was the only time she had ever felt sexy and her brother had ruined it in a moment. Jackson noticed the shattered look on her face that sang a thousand songs.

"Mont! You are proper rat-arsed!" she scorned him.

They got him to his bedroom and sat him on his bed.

"Alva, you go and shower and then you can come back and help me." Jack suggested.

"OK, Thanks but can you just unzip me please." She asked.

"Sure" he undid the zip.

He caught sight of her purple lace corset, which stirred him.

She flew out of the room and into the shower and put on her pyjamas.

On her return she heard Montgomery's raised voice, but couldn't hear what he was saying. When she arrived back Jackson was trying to get him to drink water. Montgomery was crying and getting upset over Georgette.

"What set him off?" Alva asked.

"He saw me unzip you and convinced something is going on between us! I told him he barfed on you and now he is going on about Georgette."

"Do you think she will watch it, Alva?" Montgomery asked.

"Of course she will and will be so pleased you won. Now you need to go to bed and sleep this off! What if you ever meet her again, will she want a drunk man?" Alva spoke firmly.

"I'm sorry I puked on you and your pretty dress!"

"It's OK it can be dry-cleaned" she reassured him.

She wished she had told him it wasn't OK she wasn't happy with him, but it just wasn't in her nature, she would always spare feelings.

Montgomery was wasted. Jackson offered to stay the night. Alva accepted feeling happier if she had back up. They sat on the bed with him until he fell asleep. Alva went down and made her and Jackson a hot drink. He came out of the office and had changed into a pair of joggers and a t-shirt. Jackson joined her in the kitchen. She was puzzled. Why would he have another change of clothes? Unless this was a regular occurrence and Montgomery got paralytic so often that Jack would stay with him.

"Jack how often does this happen?"

"Once a month or any occasion we go out like this. It's worse if Della's there!"

"Do you think he's alcoholic?"

Jackson went quiet.

"He has to admit he has a problem; he has to hit rock bottom before we can help him. We can't force him; he has to want it. I'm not enabling him, I don't buy the drink, what I do is stay when he's like this to keep him safe. I will check every hour to check his breathing etc."

"Tonight, we check between us! You are not doing this on your own. I'm going to get him to go to Alcoholics Anonymous tomorrow."

Jackson went to the study and showed her a copy of 'the big book' of Alcoholics Anonymous and pointed out a couple of chapters that would change her tack about how to approach him.

"You might want to read these chapters before you start insisting on anything… I'm in a twelve-step fellowship!" He told her, reeling off a few examples in the navy-blue linen bound book.

Chapter 9

It was the end of January, it bowled in with two days of snow last week and lengthening days. Montgomery was going to start his US leg of his tour next week, he would then go back with Alva and continue his UK tour concluding with a night at 'The City Empire' on the first day of May. The flights were booked for the second week of February.

Jackson was in the office at 'California' working; it wasn't unusual for Jackson to arrive and start before Montgomery was up, especially as he was gathering information. The scent of toast and coffee and toast wafted upstairs, hitting Montgomery as he descended the stairs. Montgomery's room was directly above the office, so as soon as Jackson could hear movement, he would make the breakfast. Alva followed shortly after and she would be down 7am on the dot. Jackson had a coffee waiting for her. She would change what she would eat daily rather than her brother, keeping to his two slices of toast with peanut butter.

The din of cutlery and the frothing of the coffee machine came together like a symphony asof a second cup set a cheerful tone, Jackson appeared in the kitchen doorway.

"Are you and Alva coming Friday Mont?" He asked.

Alva looked up from the coffee machine at her brother puzzled.

"It's Jack's birthday Friday and he has asked us over! I'm coming but forgot to mention it to Alva."

Alva smiled; she was touched he wanted to ask her.

"I'd love to Jack!"

Jackson returned to his work pleased she was coming. Alva slid a coffee across to her brother.

"Mont, what do you think he would like for his birthday?"

"A good shag and you're not going to give it to him either!" Montgomery laughed salaciously. He'd been on a bender that night so had a harsh tongue, this black double espresso should straighten him out.

Alva glared at him.

"Don't be so crude! Jackson is nothing but chivalrous! Anyway, if a girl wanted to give herself to him, she would be very lucky! Anyway, you don't have control over me, you're my brother, I'm over the legal age of consent, in England and here in Tennessee! You'd have no say over my sex life!" She chastised him.

"So, you would sleep with him!? I knew there was something going on between you two from the other night, he undid your dress and spent the entire evening gawping at you! I'll fucking kill him! No one touches you! He's nine years older than you!" Montgomery yelled at her.

"Nothing has happened between us and even if it did, it's none of your business! You were drunk out of your skull! That's why he stayed to help me. You are bloody lucky to have a mate like him! He clears up your mess stays with you to make sure you don't die choking on your own vomit or get alcoholic poisoning!" She retorted.

"I pay him!"

"Not enough in my opinion! He goes above and beyond what an employee and a friend would You are so lucky to have a pal like him. I just think you could acknowledge him better, he's a nice man!"

They sat silently for a few moments.

"Alva, I know what you are thinking and please don't bake, him a cake, he won't and he can't eat it!"

Montgomery knew his sister would want to make him something, normally some kind of food item.

"We'll go out this afternoon and look." he reassured her. "And yes, I am aware he does a lot for me. I know less scrupulous people in the industry would have fed me to the lions by now!"

Alva couldn't decide what to wear, she subconsciously wanted to look heavenly for him, she wanted to attract him, but didn't want to look over the top. She settled on a pair of smart black jeans, black cowboy boots as he'd once remarked how nice her legs looked in them and finally a black, long sleeved chiffon blouse with a pussy cat neck bow. Alva felt rather elegant. She straightened her long hair and applied her party make-up and her large, hooped earrings. She took the gift bag from the bed with his card in and joined Montgomery.

The long winding dirt roads were contrasted by the bright highways that led to Jackson's home, which was situated down a lane and Montgomery parked in front of the white picket fence. Alva noted what a sweet house it was. white painted weatherboarding, much like her brothers, but smaller. It was dark so she was unable to see its true beauty in the moonlight.

"What did you buy in the end?" Montgomery broke the silence of the car as they parked.

"I bought him matching leather-bound notebook and music manuscript books, and a nice fountain pen for writing his music, I hope it suits him."

"Alva he'll love it!" He reassured her.

Alva enjoyed the evening and the food was most enjoyable. To a compulsive eater like Alva, the buffet was the best part, because you could eat and eat and there were often leftovers to eat too. The urge is so cunning, baffling and powerful, and she had no control over her disease. Alva chatted to various people and hadn't noticed Montgomery having a binge of his own. She found him only an hour into the party drunk in the armchair in the lounge, she had trouble rousing him. She went and found Jackson in the kitchen.

"Sorry, Jack have you got a number for a taxi please. Mont's rat-arsed again!" She asked trying to be discreet.

Jack put his arm around her shoulders.

"He can stay here. We'll strategically take him up to my box room and he can sleep it off." Jack smiled at her.

"I will still need a number; Mont drove and I can't get home otherwise."

"Honey, I was going to suggest you stay too." He whispered, his lips almost kissing her ear., his lips almost kissing her ear.

"I don't want to impose on you, and I haven't got a nightie or a toothbrush."

Jackson chuckled.

"I can find you a t-shirt and I have a few new toothbrushes; you can have one of those! It's no imposition at all. I'd love you to stay."

He still had his arm around her and squeezed her. Her warm smile and nod showed her agreement. He ended up buying a multiple pack as the shop one day because the shop had run out of single ones, he decided that he could work his way through them. He had at that point given up with looking for love, so hadn't held on to one 'just in case'.

He and Alva got Montgomery to the small bedroom, stripped to his underpants and put him in bed, with a glass and jug of water next to him and a bucket next to the bed in case he should vomit.

"Thanks Jack!"

"No worries, the night is young yet, we've time for a dance." He told her, with a wink.

Alva went back downstairs, Jackson rummaged in the back of his wardrobe. He found the oversized XXXXL 'Fishers' t-shirt he used to wear, she liked 'The Fishers.' He found the pack of toothbrushes, picked a pink one for her and put them in the other spare room on the bed. This one was more luxurious than the room he had put Montgomery in, he quickly checked it was tidy and clean, before he returned to his guests satisfied. He noticed Alva was chatting to Dorraine in the kitchen. He went and found his friends from 'Common Ancestor' they were all sitting around in the living room, Craig the youngest and most immature of the family group was quite harmless, yet the quickest to blurt out the most insensitive waffle.

"Aww! That Alva is SO pretty. I'd love to have her. Those boobs, so big bouncy and fresh! I'd put my dick in her cleavage and rub them all over it and cum all over her!" He smirked.

"Yeah! She looks like she could do with a good seeing to… I bet she's a proper slut when she's horny!" Johnny laughed.

"Guys! Have some respect! That's Mont's little sister!" Jackson spoke.

"I bet I can shag her before the week is out" Craig betted with Johnny.

"Na! bet she'd fuck me first! I'd make her orgasm over me!" Johnny licked his lips.

The girls were tutting and telling them they were idiots, crude and disgusting. Jackson was getting annoyed, he rarely got involved, he didn't like the sleazy talk, they were being disrespectful to Alva and he was mad. The urge to protect her was overwhelming.

"You know nothing about her! She's an absolute lady! I don't like you speaking about my friend in this disdainful manner! I didn't invite you so you could be lewd about her!"

They were shocked. He rarely spoke up for himself. The girls patted his back in approval, they would be even more shocked if they knew what he was doing in front of them all but covertly.

Craig and Johnny got up and found Alva, trying to chat her up, much to Jackson's chagrin.

"If you like her like that tell her!" Felicity whispered in Jackson's ear.

"How do you know? I haven't told a soul!" he whispered back.

"You've never looked at anyone like that!" she told him.

"You won't tell anyone? I don't want to upset Mont. He's protective of her, and quite rightly so, I get the impression she's been through a lot. Plus, I'm nine years older than her and don't want anyone thinking I'm taking advantage. She's in the UK and I'm here and don't know how it will work, but Flick I love her so much!"

He was also terrified if his secret work came to light it would make her a target.

"Jack you wouldn't exploit anyone! You are such an honourable man. If it's meant to be it will work out, you need to mark your territory before they do… if you say you are interested the pair will back off!" She pointed to Craig and Johnny trying to shower Alva with compliments.

Alva stood there looking bemused, she was uncomfortable with the attention, especially with everything that had happened to her over the last six-months. She looked like she was going to burst into tears. Jackson stood up and walked over to her and put his hand in the small of her back guided her away in the pretence of her meeting another family member. She felt sparks from Jackson's touch.

"Are you OK? Were they being too much?" Jackson asked.

"Yeah! They are nice, but not my bag." She smiled.

"They mean no harm. They just see a really beautiful girl and like most men they try and get her. They are cousins and very competitive, especially when it comes to dating pretty women!"

"Do they really think I'm pretty!" she asked.

"Very pretty!" he smiled at her.

She blushed as red as the pearl snap shirt Jackson wore.

"They will do anything to try and talk you out of your clothes so just be wary!" He winked at her. He wanted her so badly yet was so frightened she would reject him, his heart leaped in his chest.

One by one the party dwindled in numbers until just Alva and Jackson remained. After a drink and a chat, it was half past midnight and Jackson said he would show her to her room and show her where the bathroom was. They checked on Montgomery who was snoring. Alva nipped in and opened his airway a little and he stopped snoring.

"Thanks for everything Jack! Goodnight." she threw her arms around his neck and hugged him. He wrapped his arms in the small of her back and squeezed her. Her legs felt weak.

"Goodnight, Honey."

She lay there in his t-shirt, her loins growling for him. She hardly slept thinking of him in the next room.

Jackson lay there knowing her head was right next to his just through the wall and if there wasn't one, he could reach out and stroke her. Every time he closed his eyes there she was. He got up in the night to check on Montgomery and saw her sleeping through the open door. He saw her plump pink velvet lips, how he wanted to kiss her, he berated himself for his carnal thoughts.

The morning came and Alva rose early, she found a scrunchie in her purse and scrapped her hair up into a messy bun. She nipped downstairs and found a bin bag and set about collecting the waste, glasses clinked as she carried them to the kitchen and placed them on the counter. Jackson had been so kind to her she wanted to return the favours. The house was almost done and Alva was standing at the sink washing up. She had loaded the dishwasher but thought she would save time by handwashing the next lot. Jackson stood watching her from the door, she looked like she belonged there he thought to himself. He had put on his black horn-rimmed glasses; he would have put in his contact lenses if he'd remembered Alva was there, his vanity always took first place when it came to her. Today he forgot, then figured if she would love him, she would accept he wore spectacles.

She looked up surprised. She hadn't seen him in glasses. She would never have worn hers around him. She had woken up with dry sore eyes this morning. She had forgotten to remove her lenses last night; her pride didn't want Jackson seeing her in her 'dowdiness.'

"Thank you! The house looks spotless, you didn't need to clear up." Jackson chirped.

"Jack it's my pleasure, you have been so kind to me." She replied.

He wished he could wrap her in his arms, she was so sweet. She genuinely was so grateful for his kindness.

"Leave that!" he indicated the washing up.

The suds on her hands making the tea towel damp. The sound of the coffee percolator broke the otherwise silence of the house and, then he made his peppermint tea.

"Should I wake Mont up and get out of your hair?"

"No; unless you are desperate to get away from me!" he jested.

She shook her head; she would happily stay all day with him if he asked.

"Good. We can have breakfast together and I can open my presents with you! I can make some porridge or toast, but I only have wholemeal bread." He offered.

"I'll happily have what you are eating!"

Jackson made some porridge with fruit and nuts. He put a jar of honey on the table as she had a sweet tooth. After making another drink and checking on Montgomery they settled in the lounge to open his presents. Montgomery had bought him a very expensive watch and a bottle of whiskey. Alva had been puzzled over the aged liquor and mentioned that Jackson did not drink.

"Why booze, when he knows you are T-total?" Alva enquired.

"Because he knows he would have drunk the one I bought for the party and has replaced it, that way he knows I will always have alcohol in the house."

He saved Alva's gift until last.

"Alva! They are awesome! Thank you so much!" He leant across hugged her and pecked her cheek.

He was so touched by the thought; he had seen them in a store not so long ago and loved the quality of them. He liked the smell and the tactile olive-green leather. He felt she knew him better than he knew himself.

They sat chatting for a couple of hours.

"Jack, shall I strip our beds and take home the washing and bring it back later for you?"

Jackson laughed.

"Honey, you are my guests! Leave everything now and sit and chat."

Montgomery woke, he looked around the room, this wasn't the one at Jackson's he would normally wake up in. This room was like a storage room. There was a bed, but it housed boxes and stuff.

Shit! Alva! He thought. She is going to be pissed! I did it again! He yawned.

He went to the bathroom and splashed water on his face and went to pull on his black out glory and went downstairs. Jackson would see him without the hat and aviators but would never comment or take photos. He knew it was part of the act and without the 'act' there would be no work.

He arrived downstairs and was greeted by a look of distain from Alva. Jackson went and made him breakfast. Alva was surprised her brother didn't have a hangover. He seemed to tolerate this bit well other than his wicked tongue.

"Mont! You got drunk and passed out again!" she chastised him in a hushed tone.

"Yeah and I bet you stuffed your face with food!" he retorted.

They both felt bad by pointing out the other's addiction.

"Did you stay here too?" Montgomery asked.

"Yes, because you didn't give a frig about me and got off your face! Jackson took pity on me and invited us to stay!"

"I bet you had a good time sucking him off last night! Bet you loved him in your knickers!"

"HOW DARE YOU! I told you before, he has been nothing but a gentleman! I stayed in a spare room and he kindly lent me a t-shirt and had a spare toothbrush!"

"He has a packet of spare toothbrushes for when his whores stay here!"

"Shut up Mont! You are being a pig."

"Bet you were a pig with the buffet!" he retorted, with a snorting sound.

Alva sat ignoring him sipping her fresh coffee. His words ringing in her ears about Jackson having a lot of women and she felt rather green with jealousy.

There was a knock at the door which hailed the arrival of the gang, Common Ancestor arrived with food to make lunch.

Craig and Johnny continued to take an interest in Alva, they sat either side of her on the settee, vying for her attention. Montgomery sat watching; disgusted with his friends, he knew very well what they were like.

Felicity sat next to Montgomery, noticing the thunder roll across his eyes, she knew what he was thinking.

"Don't react… just listen to me and hear me out!" she told him quietly.

Montgomery nodded.

"Look at them… they were saying their usual things last night… you know the stuff they say when they fancy a girl, but they go on stupid teenager mode…"

She could see him rising up.

"…Sit! LISTEN to me… Jack wasn't having any of it and shut them down! He NEVER does that!"

"NO one can have her! She is too precious for me to allow any of them to go out with her!"

"Not even Jack? Sweet Jack? The guy who hasn't ever had a girlfriend since we've known him?"

"NO! she's too good for any of them!"

"You'd better look at these…"

She showed him some pictures and film she had taken last night. They all showed Alva looking at Jackson and vice versa and he had never seen two people look so in love.

"They are denying themselves because of you! Now, you know what Jimmy and Craig are like, they will wear her down until she gives into one of them and it will go tit's up! You know that, they've done it before, with Marie your fiddle player! If Jack claims her, they will back off, you know that…"

Montgomery pondered. Felicity continued,

"…Would it be so bad if Jack was to be with her. You know he won't do anything to harm her! Would it matter if he chose her and she him? Don't deny either of them happiness Mont! Please!"

He took those words around with him the rest of the day. Alva and Montgomery drove home.

“I’m sorry Alva! I shouldn’t have said those horrible things to you and not about Jack… he’s a decent guy. I shouldn’t have remarked about the toothbrushes… I’ve never known him to have a girlfriend in the few years I’ve known him… the one date I know he went on wasn’t suitable.”

“I’m sorry too Mont! I think you have a problem with alcohol and I worry about you. People could take advantage of you. Jack is a gentleman!”

Jackson didn’t wash the t-shirt, he lay with it on his pillow, drinking in her lavender scent and aroused at the thought of it touching her bare skin.

Chapter 10

"Stop checking my sister out!" Montgomery jested.

He stood up from the desk in the office, paced to the door which gave the view of Alva sitting at the breakfast bar, with one hand on a mug and the other holding a novel she was engrossed in, and clicked it shut.

"I wasn't!" Jackson protested.

"Bro! You can't take your eyes off her!"

"I was thinking about the song we're writing and she happens to be in my line of sight that's all!" Jackson sounded flustered.

Montgomery stifled a laugh. Of course, Jackson was checking her out.

"Put your tongue back in your mouth, it's hanging out drooling like a dog!" Montgomery joked, trying to lighten the mood.

Jackson let out a false laugh, he was worried that he would be caught looking at Alva. It was strange, she wasn't what he was attracted to normally. He usually went for skinny, blonde 'birds' as Montgomery called a lady. It was the only time he ever used an Estuary English vernacular.

They both continued with their hot drinks.

"Jack whilst I'm on tour I'm going to need you to stay here and look after Alva please. I get she's not a baby and old enough to be here on her own, but she doesn't know anyone and it will be her birthday the day after I leave and I don't like the thought of her being alone. I also worry in case her ex turns up, he's been pestering Mom and Dad about her whereabouts, I never liked him and I wouldn't put it past him to do something nasty."

Jackson's stomach churned at the thought a tight knot making him feel nauseous. He only knew a little of what had happened to her, what would Montgomery do if he found out the full extent?

"Sure Mont. Would you like me to arrange something special for her birthday?"

"Yes please! Do up the dining room with some balloons or something whatever you think, you know what she likes, you like her and she likes you and you seem to like the same stuff, you've gotten to know her quite well… I TRUST you! I'll leave my present here and you can give it to her."

Montgomery emphasised the word 'trust' he wanted to let Jackson know he gave his blessing but didn't want to say it nor did he want to embarrass him. Jackson then set about thinking of ideas, he had expected to go on tour, but was happier to stay with Alva it also meant he could carry on with his 'extra work' he could find excuses to go to the studios with Alva.

It was the morning of her twentieth birthday. She woke up at the crack of dawn and she could hear the birds almost singing happy birthday

She felt lonely, as alone as if she was in the wilderness.

Montgomery hadn't told her Jackson was staying behind and was going to sleep in the house. A day or so before Alison had telephoned Montgomery to say Drake Trent had pestered them in search of Alva and said he was going to go and meet her in Nashville and bring her home. They knew he was trouble; they knew he could be violent; they didn't know of the abuse Alva had suffered. They also knew Alva had categorically stated she would never get back together with him, however, they were aware that he may lay it on thick enough to con her. She was always sweet enough to give him or anyone the benefit of the doubt, she always liked to see the best in people. His mask had slipped a few times in front of Alison and Vaughn that last week they were together. They were consumed with anxiety that she could potentially be in danger. Drake had told them he knew where Montgomery lived, he told them the address. He said if they got her to come home on her own, they would be safe. Vaughn and Alison were not intimidated by him and told him so, yet Alva could be vulnerable.

It was early, Alva lay in bed, wondering what she should do with herself and her loneliness; along soak in the bath, binge eat and read her books/ She planned what she would buy and have delivered to stuff on, and no one could stop her. She rolled over, '6am'.

There was a tap on her door, she shot up on her feet; no one was meant to be here?

"Alva? It is Jack may I come in?"

'He is early, why wasn't he was on tour with Mont?' she thought to herself.

"One sec!" She replied quickly putting on a robe, brushing her hair and dabbing a little make-up on.

Jackson waited patiently.

"Good morning, Jack! How are you?" She greeted him opening the door.

"Hey, Happy Birthday!" He greeted her with a peck on the cheek.

"Aw! Cheers babe!" She giggled; blushing.

"We are going on a trip to 'Graceland' it's quite a drive so we need to leave as soon as possible. Breakfast is ready to take with us and eat in the car."

"That would be lovely! Are you sure you don't have anything better to do?"

"I'm looking forward to taking you!" he told her.

He had wanted to take her there since the first time she mentioned she liked the music of Elvis Presley and she wanted to go.

Today he wanted to tell her he had feelings for her, he was always happy in her company. The thing he would most like to do in the world was make love to her. But as it was her birthday, he decided to leave it for another day, just in case she didn't feel the same especially after her suffering. He had heeded what Felicity said to him about making sure she knew he wanted her.

"I'll just shower and be down, I'll be so quick, I promise!" she smiled.

He had to try and shake the thought of her in her shower and had to fight himself offering to help her scrub her back.

Alva appeared downstairs in the kitchen ten minutes later dressed in jeans and a t-shirt and noticed the balloons and decorations.

"Oh Jack, the dining room looks gorgeous! Thank you!" She gave him a hug.

He had always stated friendship and she was happy with that, she would have liked something more, but after the experiences with Ashley Ashdown and Drake Trent she was well and truly off men for the moment. She carefully unwrapped the gifts, an Elvis hoodie and an Elvis double CD which he insisted playing on their journey to get in the mood. She spent a lot of time laughing at Jackson's Elvis impression and how he would lip-sync to the music. He loved hearing her laugh. He hadn't heard it yet this visit, she had been so morose over Drake and worrying about Montgomery's drinking. There it was, he thought. He loved her chuckle and her smile, she truly brightened his day with those. He could quite easily get lost in her.

Jackson made her a breakfast wrap to eat in the car. He'd borrowed a couple of thermal mugs from the kitchen and filled them with hot drinks. They chatted the whole drive. When she first met him, he was very quiet. She had been used to Drake and his cousins, who were all loud and obnoxious and had been nervous around them. They all had 'wandering hands'; she shivered at the thought. Jackson showed her his Elvis moves which had her crying with laughter.

Alva and Jackson strolled around the mansion and grounds taking photos, learning about Elvis and getting a sense about the man himself. They both knew the pitfalls of stardom as they were witnessing it with Montgomery and could see the potential lifestyle traps. Alva was fantasising again like she had at the zoo that day, they were a couple, kissing his lips would be the best gift ever! Jackson was a complete contrast to Drake Trent, Jackson was a gentleman, he was attentive, opening doors, polite, complimentary, kind, supportive, all she could ever want or need a partner to be.

They stopped at a restaurant outside Nashville for dinner. The waitress showed them to a little booth with brown vinyl seats. Alva perused the menu, her eyes settling on a picture of bacon mac 'n' cheese, Jackson choosing a steak. They sat waiting for their meals chatting there wasn't much going on in this diner, other than another couple seated at the other end and an elderly looking man sitting at the counter, his cowboy hat placed on the seat next to him, nursing a burger and chips, he looked like he knew the terrain well.

She slid a little wrapped gift to him across the table.

"Thank you for a lovely day. I'm so sorry I didn't get you anything for Christmas… I was never allowed out by myself let alone buy something for another man. It's just a really small token." She smiled at him.

He unwrapped the TCB logoed keyring.

He took out his keys and added the fob and smiled at her, then he leant over to kiss her cheek.

"Alva that's so sweet of you… I get it must have been so hard for you at that time, I will treasure it forever! I loved the notebook and song writing things for my birthday too…"

"TCB… Taking Care of Business… you take care, such good care of Mont's business and I really appreciate that too!" She explained.

"You know I'm keeping you company at the house the next few weeks" Jackson smiled at her.

"Oh okay!" she looked at him puzzled.

"I'm sleeping at the other end of the corridor! Mont and your parents would feel happier if you had a chaperone." he explained.

Alva burst out laughing,

"Oh my gosh, that's so 1950's like I will be having blokes around after Trent and Ashdown!" she sighed. "I'm off men! Present company excluded! Jack, you have always been a gentleman and any girl would be lucky to know you! But honestly if you have somewhere better to be don't feel you need to 'babysit' me!"

"I'm happy to be there, besides you are far more fun than that Della, Mont has to tolerate, if she was a man, I'd have straightened her out by now!"

Alva laughed.

"Yeah! Mont has told me what a P.I.T.A she is!"

"What's a P.I.T.A?" Jackson asked

"Pain in the…" Alva laughed. "She's a right nutjob!"

"She must have problems I think, let's say if they were giving out awards for it, she would be winning them all! I tolerate her for business, and she's very astute in the music industry and good at that."

"I met her the other week… at first, she thought I was a bird of Mont's, almost nasty to me she was. She told me she would get rid of me and how much trouble I would cause if people saw him hooking up with me. I was like 'Yuck! Urgh!' and she asked if I didn't fancy him why I was hanging around and I told her I was his sister... suddenly changes her tune and all friendly. I'm going to warn him. If he does get a girl, I'd hate for her to put them off! He's capable of doing that himself." Alva laughed.

They set off on the last fifteen-minute journey. The fishers came on the radio and Alva lip synced the song. It was her favourite.

"You always lip-sync don't ya honey?" Jackson stated.

"Yeah! No one wants to hear my wailing." She jested.

The grinding creak of the wrought iron gates announced they were at 'California', Drake Trent suddenly appeared from behind a dense thick bush with a bunch of flowers.

"Happy Birthday Alva!" he shouted following the truck through the gate.

Jackson could see fear and panic well in her face, she was shaking. He hastened to the top of the drive.

"Do you want to talk to him, or shall I get rid of him?"

"I don't want to see him; but he won't go until I have! Stay with me Jack, don't let him take me away!" she burst into tears.

"He won't take you anywhere! Go inside and lock the door and I will get rid of him. I promise you he won't harm you anymore!" Jackson said calmly.

Alva did as she was asked and peered out of the office window. She watched Drake assume Jackson was Montgomery and was extremely polite. Although he had seen pictures and film of Montgomery, he wore his look so it was easy to confuse the two men.

"This is private property sir; I must ask you to leave immediately. If you persist, I will call the law."

"I'm Alva's boyfriend I'd like to wish her a happy birthday!"

"You are an intruder on private property leave now or I call the County Sherriff!" Jackson took out his phone.

"ALVA! TELL 'IM! TELL HIM YOU LOVE ME! ALVA GET OUT HERE AND SORT THIS YOU SILLY COW!" Drake shouted at the house.

"Don't you dare speak to her like that! Police… please." Jackson was riled, but kept calm, he didn't want her upset anymore.

With that Drake legged it down the drive and left. Jackson checked the gates and went back to the house. As he entered, he could hear Alva vomiting. He tapped on the toilet door.

"Are you alright? Do you need a doctor?"

She cautiously opened the door ajar, half expecting Drake to have charmed his way in.

"He's gone!" Jackson reassured her. "You can come out."

What had the guy done to her to make her physically sick? he wondered.

"Alva what did he do to you to react so badly?"

"I can't tell you; you will hate me!"

"I could never ever hate you Honey… but I understand if you are not ready yet." He smiled reassuringly.

They sat in the lounge watching telly. Alva was suspiciously silent. Her laughter and smiles were replaced by fear and sadness. The atmosphere between them changed. Every little noise, she would jump. Each time Jackson moved she would flinch.

“Jack, will you come around with me and check all the doors and windows tonight please?”

“If you want but he can’t get in.”

“Is that why you stayed because you knew?”

“Mont thought he might, but I stayed because I wanted to hang with my friend! We have such a good time together.” He reassured her.

She felt bad for him, he was missing out touring with his friends for her. He sat in silence with her. After a while she said her goodnights and went to bed. Jackson made a quick patrol around. She was clearly terrified of this man. He nipped into the office and took the pistol, a colt 45 and holster from the locked drawer. He had bought a hand pistol to keep in case of a stalker or a crazed fan. He strapped the belt around his chest he covered it with his hoodie so that Alva wouldn’t be aware he had one. Alva had been scared to find one in the glove compartment of his truck last week, when he had asked her to pass him a tissue. He explained whilst the UK had stringent gun laws and would be rare for her to see one, in the US it was on the second amendment and it was his right to bear arms.

Unbeknownst to him she had found one in Drake’s flat once and it was a worry to her because of the laws in Britain.

As he walked up the stairs, he decided to check on Alva, he knocked on her door. No answer, he knocked again, still no answer, he carefully opened the door to find her sobbing into her pillow trying to stifle the sound. Jackson’s natural reaction was to go and comfort her. He placed his hand on her shoulder and she panicked. It broke his heart, he was such a gentle chap. She looked up realising it was Jackson. She tried frantically to stop crying. Why did he always see me crying, she chastised herself. She sat up, he sat on the bed next to her and put his arms around her and held her tight. He suggested they lay and watch telly in her room to take her mind off things and asked if she felt safer if he stayed in the room with her.

She fell asleep safe in the arms of love, wondering what Drake had done to her to cause such an extreme reaction. Montgomery had once said she could be emotional because of her medical condition, but he was sure there was more to it.

***

Alva woke in Jackson's arms he hadn't moved as she got up, he murmured.

"My Lavender Moon!"

She crept to the toilet. She stood looking at him from the door. What a nice man. He stayed all night fully clothed in my room and didn't try anything. She made her way downstairs to make him one of his teas. Montgomery had him so wrong all those nights, the accusations of him always trying to seduce her.

"JACK! JACK! HELP ME PLEASE!"

Jackson woke suddenly to hear her terrified screams. He leapt up and dashed to find her in the lobby near the door and Drake banging on the door. He was getting more and more frantic and was kicking it now.

Jackson hurried to her side.

"I'm going to have to talk to him." She cried in an anguished tone.

"I'll get rid of him! Stay here and go in the office and ring Dorraine and Max and ask them to come over, then lock yourself in the shower in there." Jackson calmly asked her; he had once told her the shower room in the office was also a panic room and she knew how to use it.

He opened the door, Drake tried forcing his way in. Jackson stopping him and hauling him out the door.

"No buddy! I TOLD YOU YESTERDAY! YOU ARE TRESPASSING ON PRIVATE PROPERTY!" He told him pushing him out of the door and locking Alva in.

"TELL YOUR SISTER I'M NOT LEAVING UNTIL I SEE HER!"

"I'm not Montgomery Moon!" He let out a manic laugh. They now stood sizing each other up on the drive.

"WHO THE HELL ARE YOU THEN?" Trent seethed. They squared up to each other.

"I'm her boyfriend! SHE'S MINE! I OWN HER NOW! HEAR THIS, COME NEAR HER OR HERE AGAIN AND I WILL RIP YOUR HEAD OFF!" Jackson finally exploded.

Trent tried throwing a few punches and as Jackson had been trained by his brother, he dodged them. Drake kept trying to land a punch and was getting more frustrated as Jackson swerved each and every one, Jackson was quite amused. He carried on eluding any contact allowing Drake to wear himself out. Jackson was someone who avoided violence at all costs.

Dorraine and Maxwell came racing up the white stone chipped drive, the car screeching and sending up dust.

Drake was suddenly star struck as meeting his idol 'Mad Mosquito' he faltered and held out his hand to shake his.

Maxwell and Jackson started frog marching him down the drive. Dorraine walked behind filming him. She had filmed the damaged caused to the door.

"Sir, I now have you on film. You were politely requested to leave the property by persons residing here and you continued to harass them. We are now using reasonable force to escort you off the premises. I will be making a report, if you come back, you WILL BE ARRESTED!"

Maxwell marched Trent to the gate and tossed him into the street. He stood up and Jackson took out the pistol. He was a crack shot and fired, the boom echoing around the private lane, the bullet grazing Drakes earlobe.

"IF you come near here or her again, I won't deliberately miss!" Jackson firmly told him.

A car was waiting and the occupants picked his luggage off the pavement and pushed him in. The car screeched off and out of sight. The gates were locked and the code changed. Dorraine and Maxwell returned to the house with Jackson to have breakfast and get Alva out of the room.

After an hour a phone rang, Dorraine nipped out and came back in.

"All my sources say he's on the plane home. He'd not booked a hotel. I think he thought he would stay here. The nerve of that guy!"

A couple of Dorraine's 'friends' had driven him to the airport and very strongly 'suggested' he get on the next plane home. They saw him through to the gate and escorted him onto the plane. He was gone.

"I'm so sorry for causing all this trouble!" Alva mumbled.

"Not your fault!" the three siblings said in unison.

She worried what they would think if they knew what had happened would they think she was dirty?

□

Chapter 11

There was no sign of Jackson that morning. It had been three days after her birthday and two after Drake had been ejected from her world, albeit temporarily. Alva was concerned, he was an early riser like her and both normally and naturally up by 7am. She carried on making breakfast and tea. Still no sign. She walked up the burgundy carpeted stairs. She tapped on his door.

"Jack, it's Alva, are you alright?" she called.

She heard mumbling within, she opened the door, Jackson looked unwell, he was clearly burning up and was trying to get up.

"I'll be down in a minute, I'm sorry I overslept!" he whispered weakly, coughing until he was struggling to breathe.

"Jack, You are not going anywhere; you are not doing anything!" She ordered him.

She felt his head he was so hot, although he insisted, he was cold. Alva opened a window and sponged him down with tepid water.

"I'm cold!" he protested.

"You've a fever and to stop feeling cold I have to cool you down!"

She ran downstairs. She had been a student nurse and trained for almost two years before she was forced to give up but had enough training to know what to do. She grabbed some paracetamol and a thermometer and ran back up to him. She took his temperature and gave him the tablets, he continued coughing. He didn't look well yesterday and had a cough but insisted they go out birdwatching. They had got caught in the rain and the gentleman he was he had given his coat to Alva. The car was parked two miles away, she felt a pang of guilt. Insisting he stay in bed; she padded downstairs and went to the office and found the list of numbers Montgomery had left in case of emergency. She picked up the telephone and heard the tone, her fingers trembled at dialling the numbers, she knew he was poorly.

"Good morning! I hope you are able to send a doctor on a house call please. My friend has a persistent productive cough. A pyrexia of 102 and rigors!"

"One moment Ma'am please…" came the voice at the other end.

She was put on hold. A minute later she was giving Montgomery's address and was told a doctor would be there shortly.

Half an hour later a gentleman arrived and knocked on the door. Alva opened the security gates in anticipation.

"Good morning, Ma'am, I'm Dr Ola" a kind looking man of Nigerian descent greeted her, with a huge smile, as she opened the door. He was about forty and wore a smart shirt, a red tie and smelled of peppermint.

"Thanks for coming so quick! My friend is Jackson Maddox, you may call him Jack. He has a persistent productive cough with green sputum. A pyrexia of 102 and rigors. I've given him 1g paracetamol or Acetaminophen as I believe you call it here, about 45 minutes ago and he still hasn't affected his temperature! I don't know anything about his medical history." she was telling him as he followed her upstairs. She saw him into Jackson's bedroom.

"Jack, Dr Ola is here to see you love. Do you want me to step out of the room whilst you chat to him?"

"You can stay Alva." He whispered weakly.

She watched the doctor listen to his chest and take some notes. He told the doctor he was type II diabetic. Perhaps that's Was that why he is so careful with his food she thought to herself. After a while the doctor diagnosed a chest infection and gave him an injection. Jackson didn't like needles but was too weak to protest, it nipped his skin, making his eyes water. Dr Ola suggested Jackson have injections for the first two days and he would come back that afternoon to administer some more.

"Doctor, I used to be a student nurse and have given a few intramuscular injections, if you would watch me administer this afternoon and leave me the equipment, I am happy to continue for the next few times."

They arranged the care Jackson needed and Alva was willing to look after him. The doctor gave her his work mobile and said should he deteriorate; she should call 911.

Alva spent most of her time nursing Jackson. She watched his breathing and counted them, occasionally checking his pulse. She cooked him soup, he was so weak she fed him.

Her phone started to ring for a facetime. Jackson stirred. Alva looked at the caller ID, it was Montgomery.

"Hi Mont! How's the tour?"

"It's great thanks! Is everything OK? I wanted to talk to Jack, but he's not answering… and Alva… why are you in Jack's bedroom?"

She blushed and confessed the innocence of the situation in a flustered tone.

"Jack's gotten sick because of me… he was coughing yesterday and we went out and got wet, now he has a chest infection."

"Has he seen a doctor?"

"Doctor Ola came."

“Good! Ask him to send me the bill Alva please! Are you OK or do you need help?”

“Na I’m OK.”

Jackson woke and sat up dazed.

“Can I talk to Mont?”

Alva handed him the phone; Jackson had a coughing fit and took some water.

“Sorry, buddy! I had planned to do those things you wanted doing today.”

“Jack, rest up! Do you want anything sending or are you alright with Alva?”

“She’s doing a great job; I feel better already!” he smiled towards Alva.

“OK, just get better, then get things done when you can.”

They said their goodbyes. Montgomery felt concerned Jackson was never ill.

Alva continued nursing Jackson over the next few days; when he felt better, she would sit and watch telly on his bed with him. They liked watching comedies, but inevitably would end with a coughing fit from laughing.

It was really hard for Jackson to allow anyone to look after him. He was always overly responsible. His father, Dirk had been a gambler and a workaholic, rather like Alva and Montgomery’s father. He had loved Alva looking after him, she was a good friend. Eventually he was able to resume his duties and Alva did her best to give him space and time to finish up what he needed to do for Montgomery. She was happy to read those few hours he would be finishing working.

***

Jackson was disappointed at Alva's reaction to the red rose and card he had put on her bed on Valentine's Day, two days after he'd got out of his sickness. He'd been wanting to ask her for a date. Time was like the sand in an hourglass, it was slipping away from him. She was leaving in three days. He didn't want what had happened last time, she had said she would have walked away from Trent if he had declared his love for her. He kept thinking over all their conversations and wondered how many times she had hinted yet he didn't pick up on them.

Although she had realised Jackson had put them there, but because Montgomery was still on tour, she genuinely believe it was her brother being sweet and thanked Jackson for helping Montgomery.

Jackson had gotten up at the break of dawn to drive to his home, picked the best rose he could find in his garden, he stood and pulled off the thorns as he didn't like her being hurt by a thorn, he likened Drake Trent to a thorn. He wanted to open his heart to her, but was scared, the women he thought he had fallen for in the past had badly hurt him and he didn't want pain like that again. He knew deep down that if he ever was a couple with her and they split there could be too much grief to bear. Yet he was now willing to take a risk with her. Something at the back of his mind pulled him in her direction, after all she had been the only woman to get his loins stirring even without touching her. He sighed and left her thinking it was from someone else.

***

Two days before she was due to go home, she had just finished her lunch with Jackson and was just tidying up the kitchen, a British telephone number flashed up requesting a facetime. She didn't recognise the number so she answered.

"Don't hang up Babe!" a voice came. "Please let me explain… I love you... I'm obsessed with you!"

Alva stood there shocked at the sight of Drake Trent pleading with her. She went into the empty office and sat at the desk not sure what to do. He had gotten another phone to ring her on. She sat in silence, her gut instinct telling her no, her head saying not to listen to his lies, her heart was guarded yet part of her was desperately seeking attention and validation from another man. He kept telling her how beautiful she was, how sorry he felt at the way he had treated her in the past. Spewing lie after lie. He hadn't even mentioned Valentine's Day.

Jackson overheard everything from the door willing her not to listen to it. He was so annoyed, he stood listening boiling with anger!

"Your mates say you are back soon, can we meet up? Sort this out? I promise to never hurt you again!" He recalled the men in his flat the day she left and how the expected beating never came, just a lecture in treating women nicely.

"I don't know, I'm not ready to talk to you." She answered.

She realised that he would try and control her again and she knew going back to him would be worse this time.

"I've gotta go…" she hung up and sighed. She slipped her phone into her pocket after blocking the number. She sat and thought, had Drake really changed?

Jackson felt pangs of jealousy and guilt, then an absolute rage at Drake. The nerve of that guy, he thought. After that altercation why was he trying to get back in her favour. He didn't want her going back to him, Jackson needed her and wanted to protect her and from the US there was little he could do.

He denied he felt something for her, it wasn't like anything he had felt for anyone. He'd cried for her some nights. The only woman that could get him hard and he felt she was out of bounds.

He wondered what to do, he knew from their days together she would end up back with him if the alternative was being single, or she could end up with Johnny or Craig and although they were reasonably decent, most of the time, no one could love her like he could, she had also told him she liked him and he would make a great boyfriend. He had always used his age or his employment as an excuse. He knew he had commitment issues after the previous women. He was scared to fall in love with her, yet he was so attracted to her, there was only one thing for it, he would have to tell her how he really felt. He waited until the evening; she was in the office printing off her tickets. Montgomery was touring the US and due back tomorrow late night ready to go on the UK and planned to go back with Alva.

"Alva…"

"Jack!" she smiled.

That smile would undo him, he would give the world just to see her smile.

"I was hoping you would let me take you out for dinner tomorrow evening…"

She was only half listening; her mind was still whirring about Drake. She hurried off, embarrassed, not sure if it was genuine, of if she had heard him correctly, she wasn't wanting to ask him to repeat himself. In her haste she accidentally left her unlocked phone on the desk. Drake had always demanded access to her phone, yet kept his secret, she never locked it. As much as Jackson realised it was wrong to invade her privacy when another UK number rang, he found himself answering to Drake, he didn't say hello, as soon as he accepted the call, all he could hear was Drake waffling about how she would 'get it' when she came back for blocking him on everything, one threat after another, the insults he threw disgusted Jackson, who listened quietly. He was getting the measure of the man.

Finally, Jackson spoke,

"I told you on no uncertain times she is MINE! If you ever call or speak to her again there will be trouble. She tells me everything so quit while you are ahead! I've got my gun loaded and I won't have any problem smuggling it into your country."

He hung up and left the phone on the desk. He had no idea how to smuggle in a gun nor did he have an ounce of disrespect for any country's law, although, saying that he was sure if he wanted a gun his uncle or cousins could get one, he just wanted to get him away from Alva at all costs.

Jackson was going to sleep at home that night, his parents were visiting him for dinner. Jackson went home feeling dejected. He sat in his lounge remembering Alva being there on his birthday and thought about asking her, he spoke to Michael his sponsor from his twelve-step fellowship and talked it out. She'd had a terrible time with blokes. He thought he would try again, once, and only once more, if he texted her, he would know his message been read. If it was in God's plan it would happen. He picked up his phone.

'Alva, I would love to take you out for dinner tomorrow night… PLEASE!'

Alva was in the house alone, with her own thoughts. Her phone bleeped at his message. She replied almost immediately,

'Like a date?'

A few moments later.

'I would love it to be a date if you do (winking emoji)'

Her heart flipped at the thought. The two blue ticks appeared; he knew she had seen it.

An hour came and went and he thought she wasn't interested; he had left the outcome to God. Her phone had died and it took a while to charge whilst spending the whole time swearing at the phone.

'I'd like that very much. (Blushing cheeks emoji, kissing emoji) Thank You.'

PS My battery died (Sad face emoji)

"Yes!" he shouted punching the air excitedly.

His mum remarked how happy he seemed that evening.

***

He went and found her first thing the next morning.

"You haven't forgotten our date?" he reminded her.

She blushed. She had fancied him the moment her eyes met his that first day she turned up in Nashville.

"No, I haven't. You really would like to date me?"

"Yeah! I'll pick you up outside the gate at 7pm? Perhaps we shouldn't tell anyone just yet I want to know if this is an option for us." He told her.

She was annoyed he wanted to be secretive but when she thought about the implications she could understand.

At seven o'clock on the dot she appeared at the gate. Looking ravishing in a blue floral print dress and black leather biker jacket. She got in next to him.

"You look pretty!" he smiled at her, pecking her cheek.

She blushed and smiled not used to compliments.

They awkwardly hugged and kissed. He drove to his favourite restaurant. He smelled divine again and looked smart but casual, smart, dark blue jeans, pale blue shirt, and navy v neck jumper and leather jacket. He looked rather co-ordinated with her. Again, he could drown in her scent.

He kept putting his hand in the small of her back, and the electricity between them was magic. She yearned for each and every touch. The waitress showed them to the same little booth and they ate the same meal, reminiscing about her birthday and trying to blot out Trent. A honkytonk bar was situated next door, they waltzed in and had a dance. It was playing all her favourite songs she swayed to the music with him as he held her tight, her arms wrapped around his neck, cheek to cheek. He held his arms in the small of her back, like he was holding his whole world. He liked feeling her close, she smelled of lavender and leather, it reminded him of the lavender bushes his uncle and aunt had in England, where he would stay as a child and had such happy memories of his cousins and the Palladian mansion that looked like the president's official home.

The more he was with her the more he had tried to fight these glorious feelings, now he could let go. As he lent in for a kiss a bar room brawl broke out ruining the atmosphere, a glass was thrown and shattered at Alva's feet. A shard of glass cut her calf. Jackson swung her away from the glass and decided to go home. People were starting to film with cameras. The guys that were fighting were well known NFL stars and they couldn't chance being caught on camera.

He sat her in his car and took the first aid box out of the glove compartment, he ripped her tights to gain access to the incision and gently cleaning and dressing her wound as he kneeled on the ground. He put a plaster over the wound and bent down and planted a kiss on top of the plaster.

They drove home in silence. Jackson drove up the drive this time they sat for a moment. He couldn't spit out what he wanted to say.

"Thanks for a lovely evening, Jack."

She turned kissed him on the cheek and got out running up the porch steps and into the house not looking back.

She always felt safe with Jackson. He had always been very chivalrous toward her. Tonight, she would love him to show her if he really liked her, tomorrow could be too late; it also may never come.

I should have kissed her! He berated himself. He hit the steering wheel in frustration, his palms stinging with the impact. His heart was beating so fast. He had just seen her home to 'California' and said goodnight. She was returning home to England tomorrow she had been there five glorious weeks and he had been paid to look after her and entertain her all the time, whilst Montgomery was in the studio recording and around the country touring. Although he decided that after the first few days, he would not take any money from his boss other than his basic wage.

How can I tell her how I feel he wondered? I made a point of telling her I am far too old for her, yet she is all I think about! Each and every time they were together, his feelings got stronger, every time he looked at her, he would linger longer, wondering what was she thinking and how pretty she was. But on the other hand, the turmoil was Alva was his bosses' little sister, Montgomery was protective of her especially since she had been there this time. He knew it would have been worse if Montgomery had known what Drake had actually done and if he'd known about the incident with 'The Incinerator' he would have been so much more protective. He loved his job and considered himself a good friend of Montgomery and didn't want to jeopardise that. What should he do? Then there was his covert operation if that got out, she might feel betrayed he didn't want to put her in danger, these people were nasty. He knew he was head over heels or cowboy hat over boots (in his case) in love with her. He lingered, looking back at the house from his car. He went to drive home… he turned the radio on, Cole Swindell was playing again… Saying I Love You Too Late, reminding him of last time she went home and then what happened. His heart burned at the memory, flashes of Alva in that awful state she turned up in on New Year's Day coursed through his mind. What was so wrong with him that he could possibly risk allowing that to happen again to the most precious thing, he thumped the steering wheel again this time with the side of his clenched fists.

From the window Alva watched him sitting in his car and fighting with the steering wheel of the car. I wonder what I did? Why is he so angry? Why doesn't he find me attractive? I guess I'm not what he wants, she sighed to herself. She had been praying all week he would kiss her or tell her he liked her. She had been willing him to over and over in her mind. This visit had seemed different, he never mentioned the age gap. Alva wondered if that was now out of his mind. When he asked her to go out tonight, she really thought that this was it. She knew he was wary of Montgomery and he didn't want to upset her brother as much as she didn't and if there was that spark surely, they could wait and work it until they both knew for certain they were going to last? She moved back towards the door and switched off the porch light and turned on her heel to retire to bed.

As Jackson bounded up the path, the porch light went out and his heart jumped.

He tapped gently on the frosted glass window, loud enough for Alva to but as not to wake her brother, who would have been back. He fiddled for his door key in his jacket in case she didn't answer.

A crack appeared in the door and Alva cautiously looked out. He smiled at her; she opened the door wider.

"Jack, are you OK?" she enquired, wondering why he was back.

"I'm sorry to disturb you…" he placed his hands on her hips and drew her close to him. "I want to claim you as mine!"

With that he put his hand behind her head and angled her and kissed her long and slow. His other arm snaked around her waist. She wrapped her arms around him.

Unbeknownst to them Montgomery walked past the door and saw. He hadn't initially liked the thought of his friend and employee falling for his little sister. He was worried if there would be complications. In the end he thought it was sweet and he was pleased for them. If only he could find the love of his life. A wave of sadness washed over him, as he remembered Georgette, he was in love with her at twenty-two and had messed things up. He knew he had broken an angel's wings and that was how he had become Montgomery Moon. He had reinvented himself from being Kenny Deighton to the international sensation he was just to be close to her. She had loved Country and the only way to be close to her was through the music. Moon's heart ached for his lost love. Montgomery, crept away like a moonlit shadow, leaving the two unaware.

After a time, the two stood holding each other breathless, neither one wanting break the embrace, he stood drinking in her lavender scent, she smelled how he remembered England.

"I hope you didn't mind me kissing you… I know I said I thought you were too young for me… but… what's nine years to a very mature lady like you and someone as immature as me?" he smiled tucking her hair behind her ear.

"WOW! That was the best kiss ever!" She panted, surprised at his gentleness. "I'd given up hope… if I'm honest… after them, I'd given up on men. I thought you didn't like me like that anyway!"

"Oh Alva! You have no idea! I have wanted to kiss you from the moment I first laid eyes on you."

"I felt the same! Anyway, you told me I was far too young for you!"

"Yeah! I did and you said it was just a number! Also, Elvis and Priscilla's age gap was ten years. We are going to have to be careful though… I dunno how Mont will react… I'm guessing that's why I've been cautious… we need to make sure we're gonna last. I worry about upsetting him… I've heard him mention someone called 'Georgette'…"

"She was apparently the love of his life; she is a memory he won't mess with. I never met her. Apparently, she was obsessed by country music and that was why he came here. I have often wondered if I could reunite them, he deserves to be happy… He told me yesterday she had got married… he had seen her wedding in the local paper Mum and Dad sends weekly. The guy is a decorated war hero and that sent him feeling low." Alva explained, remembering her brother's face and how he seemed to want to fight this man for no reason.

Jackson kissed her again.

"So how are we going to work this, Honey? Me here and you there? Do you think it can work?"

"With technology we can have daily calls and virtual dates?"

"Let's try that then!"

He left her with the promise of tomorrow.

The morning dawned, breakfast was made and eaten. Suitcases were by the door. It was time for them to head to the airport. Alva wanted to stay and be with Jackson a while longer and see if they could work.

The airport was a bustle of people, Montgomery insisted sitting in the back and pretended to sleep, but noticed Jackson reach across several times with loving touches and Alva smiling back. They parked up and suitcases were taken out of Jackson's trunk. Montgomery decided they should have space.

"I'm gonna look at the duty free I'll meet you in the departure lounge." He told Alva, wanting some alcohol to blot his misery out.

He turned to his friend and shook his hand.

"Thanks, Jack, for your hard work I shall see you in a few weeks."

He sped off trying to allow them a farewell and not wanting to feel like a third wheel and seeking a nip of whiskey to take the lonely off. If only I could find the love of my life, Montgomery sighed to himself, thinking his heart might break again. He looked at the photograph in his wallet of Georgette at seventeen, together with the paper cutting of her in her wedding dress with 'him'! His eyes misting over, only stopping when he was interrupted by fans and obliging for photographs.

As soon as Montgomery was out of sight Jackson grabbed Alva's hand and strolled along with her to check in. They grabbed lunch together trying to make the most of every moment left.

They stood at the gate until the last few minutes snatching long, slow, and tender kisses. She found him a pleasure to kiss, he was so gentle with her, they were not aggressive like the ones she's had in the past, these were like the ones in the flicks, when the guy gets the girl, or the cowboy rides away with his love together on the horse. She now understood the term that Montgomery had used about being loved like a country song, now here she was singing the chorus to her own song.

"I'll see you again soon Honey!" he reassured her.

"I... lo..." he pressed his finger to her lips to stop her speaking.

"Me too! But don't drop any 'L' bombs yet, not until I drop the first one!" he told her. "Promise me you won't go near that Drake without a proper chaperone." He continued.

"I promise. I spoke to Mont we are going to see him together when I get back and tell him never again! I will return the watch too. I shall also tell him I am spoken for!"

"Good girl, you are mine now, remember that!" He pressed his forehead against hers. "I did tell him I owned you when we chucked him out the other week!" he carried on laughing at the memory.

"Really?" she asked surprised he would say that.

"Yeah! I also told him I would rip his head off if he ever went near you again." He laughed, "not very Christian of me I know, but I am human."

Jackson decided he should omit the part about the firearm for now. Alva was surprised, but the thought that Jackson would do that to protect her, made her heart beat with butterflies. He was normally so reserved that he would have to be wild to react like that.

"I'd better go." She announced.

"Facetime me when you get home!"

With one last delicate snog, she went through the gate. He waved and blew her a kiss. She was soon out of sight. His heart yearned for her again and he started a lonely drive home.

Montgomery would be gone a couple of months. There was still plenty that would keep him busy and employed until he could see her face again, but tonight he planned to sit a look at all the pictures on his phone tonight, then he would sleep in the bed she had stayed in with her t-shirt, he missed her already. The first job he did was make another call.

"Thank you, Uncle Rico, can you please keep care of her whilst I am not able to be there."

"Consider La Luna di Lavanda protected." Enrico confirmed.

"I have an idea of what might have been done to her, but she hasn't told me yet, I don't want to pressure her." Jackson stated.

"When you find out just say and I can deal with them… I'm looking forward to an excuse to destroy the Drake Brothers and their family! ALL OF THEM!"

Jackson didn't know that could potentially mean his boss and Alva too!

□

Chapter 12

A few weeks of regular telephone calls and facetimes, minimum of daily often twice daily and sometimes thrice ensued.

"'Ello Darlin'" Alva's voice came as she answered the +1 prefixed number.

"Hey Honey! How are ya doin'?" Jackson enquired.

"Really good… Has Mont told you yet?" Alva asked.

"About Georgette?" Jackson said.

"Good, I'm so glad he's found her! He deserves to be happy" Alva stated.

"Apparently, he bashed, his truck in to hers. She was at her husband's funeral?" Jackson queried.

"That's what he told me too… he done her taillight and didn't contact him so he turned up at her house with a mechanic to fix it. She thought it was a wind up… sorry Jack a joke… I forget you don't always know our slang… she didn't recognise him at all and didn't know he was Moon until he sang to her." Alva confirmed.

Jackson continued with the part Alva hadn't heard,

"He's kept it quite until now, he gave her concert tickets and he took her out a few days. He has been seeing her two weeks, before he came home but has daily calls. He's not asked her to be his girlfriend yet. She is coming day after tomorrow for a 'holiday'. He's been busy doing up that large south facing bedroom, overlooking the garden. He's painting it himself, had oak panelling put in and bought a four-poster bed and had drapes, curtains, and matching bed things commissioned. He has not told her who he is yet. How's this… I'm taking him to mine tomorrow so he can pick her some roses and teach him to arrange them in a basket? He is going to write a note saying 'A basket of roses for my English rose.' How sweet is that?"

"Aww! So cute. I've warned him about Della! He can muck it up without her help… seriously I hope it works out for him. It will be good for us if it does." Alva stated.

"He's going to facetime her tonight! I'm praying for him. He's not been drinking so much which is good! But he could still need twelve steps!"

They chatted about their day and work.

"I'm going to look for another job… I hate it!" Alva announced.

She had got a job in a care home and her manager was quick to treat her unfairly.

"Come and live in Nashville! I'll look after you, you would never need to work with me!" Jackson asked.

"I can't leave Mum and Dad!"

"You can fly the nest, if you and Mont are both here, they'll have to come and live too!"

Jackson's thought made sense. But Alva would need to work on her parents. Every day Alva and Jackson chatted. They would often sit and have virtual dates. Alva stated that the technology was a wonderful thing allowing them to see each other daily.

Today Georgette had arrived in Nashville. As Jackson was chatting to Alva, a message popped up on his phone from Montgomery.

'She's here! Jumped into my arms and kissed me! Asked her to be my girlfriend! SO HAPPY!'

They continued to chat and his phone pinged again.

'First date picture… please publish on all social media!'

Jackson showed Alva, her phone chimed with same picture. He was really surprised to see a picture with him smiling, it was strange, no one outside the family had ever seen him smile, other than Jackson on those two occasions.

"She looks sweet!" Alva remarked "Jack, keep an eye on him, I hope he behaves himself!"

Each day Jackson relayed a bit more of the news from his end and Alva recounted things she had heard. Things seemed as if they were going so well for them and Alva and Jackson were delighted.

□

Chapter 13

Today the Moons were on their way to meet Georgette. Georgette was the love of Montgomery's life. He had gone out with her as a twenty-two-year-old, seven years ago and was besotted. An argument had occurred after a couple of months and she had left. She blocked him every way and there had been no way he could apologise or make amends. It was then he decided to reinvent himself from Kenny Deighton into Montgomery Moon. Georgette had been a huge country music fan and for Alva's brother this was the only way to get close to her again. He had hidden his true identity from the world, and hid behind a disguise of mirrored aviators, a thick black beard, and his hat. Montgomery had cosmetic surgery for his broken nose and teeth that he had got from protecting an innocent person. Although he was far removed from his original identity as Kenny, he'd kept the best parts and allowed them to shine. It meant the family would change their surname by deed poll. It would be a good thing in future as they were all related to the notorious family of the east end, The Drake Brothers, and Drake Trent, they were all cousins, unbeknownst to Alva, although Montgomery and his parents knew they hadn't realised Alva was unaware.

On the morning of her husband's funeral, Montgomery had accidently bumped trucks with Georgette in the car park of the crematorium. Today they were going to meet her. Alva was pleased for her brother, but more pleased to be seeing Jackson. She was disappointed that Jackson wasn't at the airport.

"This is my Mom Alison, my Dad Vaughn, and my little sister Alva..." he introduced them in the lounge at the airport.

"This is Georgette, my girl!" he told them proudly, wrapping his arm about her shoulders.

She was really pretty with shoulder length golden brown hair and dark eyes. They looked well suited. She could see they were shining and in love. Alva said her hellos and was hoping to see Jackson. Alva watched Georgette's face as things were clearly falling into place, she went pale like she was going to faint then just clung on tightly to Montgomery. Alva suspected that Georgette was expecting Texans, but got then got the 'extras from Eastenders', and had clearly thrown her. Montgomery drove them to a restaurant for a meal. He noticed his sister's disappointed look that Jackson wasn't meeting them or coming with them. Alva looked lost.

They arrived back at Montgomery's and Alison and Georgette made tea in the kitchen, whilst Vaughn and Montgomery took the cases upstairs. Alva nipped to the office. Jackson was standing in the office with his back toward the door. She ran to him and threw her arms around him. He turned and looked out of the door before he shut the office door and kissed her, he had missed her touch and her kiss.

"I'll come and say goodnight to everyone when I am ready and you can make an excuse to go to bed, jetlag or something and I'll meet you outside and we can have a date?" He smiled.

"OK. I'll let Mum know I am out so she can cover." She beamed.

Alva joined the others in the lounge and drank coffee and ate a couple of pieces of cake Georgette had made. Georgette was a great baker she thought. They sat and chatted a while. She watched Georgette snuggling with Montgomery on the sofa. He hadn't revealed himself to her yet. Fool Alva thought! Georgette clearly was in love and she had overheard her say to mother she would love him with a crooked nose and wonky teeth, with that and her reactions at the airport, Alva was convinced she knew, but it wasn't her place to say so.

"I best be off, see y'all tomorrow" Jackson said poking his head in the room smiling. Everyone said their goodnights to Jackson, who promptly left.

"I thought he'd gone ages ago!" Montgomery remarked.

Georgette noticed glances exchanged between Alison, Vaughn, and Alva. Alva got up and stretched.

"Goodnight! I'm off to bed!" Alva announced and disappeared, Georgette thought it was early yet, but Montgomery paid no heed.

They drove to a bar and sat and chatted all evening. It was nice to be in his company again. They planned to snatch as much time as they could, odd days birdwatching and the few shifts at the night shelter, as well as the time she had to spend with her family.

Again, time would slip through their hands and before they knew where the days evaporated far too quickly for anyone's liking. Alva held her tears in until she was in the Nashville grey skies, they were the colour of her heart at leaving her Jackson. One day we will be together! she kept telling herself.

This time there would only be a matter of weeks until they could meet again.

What seemed strange to her, when she was in England, was she would often see the 'taxi driver' about, he would wave and smile, he looked now as if he was a smart business man and seemed to have people, like body guards around him.

Chapter 14

Alva had nervous knots in her tummy as they flew to Nashville on the private plane. She was so excited to see Jackson again, she hadn't seen him for the month since her and her parents had left after meeting Georgette. She chatted with Georgette's grandmother Vera and her aunt Monica. They seemed nice, but she was very wary that if she mentioned her and Jackson being an item, they might inadvertently tell Montgomery or Georgette and it could be game over and she certainly didn't want anything to spoil Georgette and Montgomery's wedding, her brother had waited a long time for this.

Jackson was waiting for them at the private airport, he beamed as they approached him.

"Hello Jack!" Alison said as she greeted him with a kiss.

"Hey Alison!" he reciprocated and greeted Vaughn and Alva.

"This is Vera and Monica, and this is Jack" Alison introduced them all.

He shook their hands warmly and guided them to the awaiting cars Montgomery had laid on.

"Jack! Would you mind if Vaughn and I took Monica and Vera to the hotel with us? Then Alva can stay with you and perhaps you can do some shopping trips for the wedding please? It will be better if she is with someone more her age." She smiled and winked at him.

Alva's parents knew about the situation, as Alison had caught them facetiming each other, when they were first together. Alva had returned at the end of February, they were trying to allow the couple precious time without disclosing anything to the other ladies, so would make out Jackson was helping organise things as best man.

Over the next days they spent secretly together dating away from Nashville. Jackson would drop her to the hotel or to 'California' each night, depending on where they needed to be. The afternoon before the wedding Vera and Monica were staying in the hotel whilst the others had a pre wedding lunch, it was a surprise for Georgette, her relatives initially couldn't come, medical reasons had bumped the insurance costs through the roof and some airlines refusing to take them, but Montgomery chartered a private plane ensuring they would be there. The idea that evening Jackson would drop her at 'California' so she could partake with the ladies for a bridal soiree, again, Alva needed Jackson to 'help' her that afternoon and would join later. Georgette would be so wrapped up in her own enjoyment she wouldn't notice that Alva would be missing. She had thought she had decided to stay at the hotel.

Alva and Jackson spent a blissful afternoon at Rock Castle. Afterwards they drove back to Jackson's house. It was a three bedroomed house with a white picket fence surrounding a massive beautiful cottage garden. She commented on the flowers, they were like the ones Jackson had given to her the times she had seen him before.

She noticed the lavender bushes that led up the path to the door. The highly scented luscious purple spikes danced in the breeze. Lavender was hard to grow in Tennessee, yet it thrived in his garden. As you made your way along the path you would brush against it and the aroma would fill the air. He told her he took pride in cultivating the lavender.

"A lavender bush is common in England, yet in Tennessee it is tricky to grow, it needs care and attention. Like a special relationship, it needs tender care. I love lavender and I will take the time to look after them, just how I intend to be with our love." Jackson told her.

He explained that he had a gardener who grew the majority of flowers for picking, but was not to touch his lavender. His mother being a florist and owning a flower shop would often pop by and help herself as she needed, that was the sole purpose of this garden was for his mother's business, she thought how sweet it was. The grounds spread over a few acres, but also had a large expanse of lawn, from the back of the house and this was surrounded by several acres of flower gardens.

He showed her the rose garden and she happened to mention she liked a particular colour rose. He took a penknife from his pocket and cut one down for her. She watched as he flicked the largest thorns off with his thumb and forefinger, then running the knife detaching any small thorns.

She looked around the garden and suddenly realised. He always pulled off the thorns. Montgomery would never have thought to do that!

"Jack? You remember Valentine's Day?"

"Yes Honey!"

"That rose and card was from you and not Mont, wasn't it?" she asked.

Jackson smiled and put his arm around her shoulders.

"Why didn't you say?" She continued.

"Well, it's supposed to be from a 'secret' admirer. Anyway, I wasn't sure if you liked me anymore then." He smiled

"I would have snogged your face off if I had known!" she laughed.

"What made you guess now?"

"You always flick off the rose thorns!"

"I don't like the thought of anything hurting you! I had to get here at 4am that morning to find you the perfect one, before Mom came and picked them all for the shop." he told her.

He smiled that she noticed about the thorns.

Jackson had planned an evening picnic in his garden, the day was still long, the sun cast elongated shadows across his terrain. Alva had originally intended to join the bridesmaids' celebrations but she was enjoying being alone with Jackson. time with him was precious. Alva was feeling chilly as the sunset amongst the trees in the distance, the warmth and light of the house beckoned them.

They had sat watching TV, a documentary series about birds Jackson had streamed, on the sofa locked in an embrace eventually falling asleep in each other's arms it was 6:30 before an alarm on a mobile woke them. Montgomery and Georgette's wedding day was dawning that sunny mid-July day.

After a mad dash to her brother's residence to meet the bride and her entourage and swearing them to secrecy that she was not with them overnight, they were ready and set for the wedding of the year. The house had been a bustle of singing and floral scents, the sounds of cowboy boots walking across the marble floor, which quelled the summer heat. Alva was relieved to have arrived and ready prior to Montgomery's surprises, which Alva had been in charge of knowing, who were the surprise guests and gift that was arriving with them. Alva had felt proud her brother had entrusted these moments to her.

Alva saw Montgomery standing with Jackson, who was his best man and the other groomsmen, from Common Ancestor. Montgomery was dressed in his signature aviators, a smart black tuxedo a bolo tie and silver collar tips on his white shirt. Alva glanced over to Jackson, who was standing right beside him and was dressed similarly and looked rather dapper, he smiled and winked at her. Jackson thought she looked perfect. It was chanced that Montgomery had organised each bridesmaid to have a gentleman to escort them that day. He had made out this was important and sneakily put the pair together and hoped they would publicly acknowledge their union, but they wouldn't.

Alva choked back her own emotion; she was so pleased Montgomery finally was marrying his soulmate. She had also fantasised about being Mrs Maddox the whole wedding.

Jackson and Alva danced together much of the evening reception, but tried not to arouse suspicion. The chemistry between the pair of them was like electricity.

"I love you, Alva Violet Moon!" Jackson whispered in her ear.

"You Jackson Wesley Maddox have dropped the 'L' bomb! I Alva Violet Moon, reach down and pick up your gauntlet and accept! I love you too!"

"Honey let's sneak off and have a kiss." he winked at her.

"Let's hope we won't get caught!" she tittered, "Although, I don't suppose Mont would be too worried now!"

Montgomery caught Jackson on his own at the end of the evening.

"Jack, that girlfriend of yours… I'm guessing you have one… there's a new smile on your lips — Look I don't need any details about who she is, I'm guessing you want your privacy… but I was going to suggest that whilst we are on honeymoon and Mum and Dad are looking after Monica and Vera, you'd be very welcome to use our pool if you like. There's charcoal in the garage and you know where the barbeque things are. You, also know the security system so you can switch off cameras and have privacy. I don't even mind if you stay… but when we get back, they will all be coming to stay."

He didn't mention Alva, he knew and guessed they were still together. Now he had found Georgette and was married to her he had to concentrate on her and keeping his own secrets. Jack thought it was a lovely idea, he went and found Alva and told her.

***

The pool was glistening like a sea of stars in the sun at its peak in the sky, Jackson had been over that morning making sure it was pure and checking the chemicals and testing the levels. He had been grocery shopping for the day. Alva bid her parents goodbye and hauled her suitcase with her to wait in the car park for Jackson, as soon as Montgomery's truck had disappeared from sight, she figured might as well sleep at the house. Arriving back, she took her case up to the room she had claimed at 'California.'

Jackson hadn't expected she would stay so decided he would too. She changed into her bathing suit. A flattering black one-piece with white polka dots. She sat on the sun lounger, on the edge of the pool. watching Jackson and his red swimming shorts jumping in, trying to splash her. She noticed it was the first time she had seen his chest, he looked perfect to her. There was some muscle definition, but he wasn't toned or bulky he had chest hair and was turning her on. He kept calling her to get her to join him in the pool. She kept shaking her head. She was reclined on a sun lounger, pretending to read her book, Jackson splashed her and she continued trying to ignore him, smiling slyly to herself.

"Come in the water's fine!" He called.

"Nah! I'm alright here!" she flicked the page.

With that he leaped out of the pool and raced to the sun lounger.

He grabbed her book and put it on the floor, he bent down and kissed her. She reciprocated; she always loved his kisses; he was dripping water all over her, it was cold and it made her jump.

"You've got me all wet now!" she giggled pushing his shoulder.

"Good! I want you all wet!" He kissed her again. "Right! he tipped her off the sun lounger and into the pool and jumped in after her.

She kept swimming and he was chasing her. Eventually she allowed him to catch her. They stood there at the side of the pool kissing. She had her arms around his neck, he gently folded his arms in the small of her back. She started massaging his shoulders he moved his hands lower and started fondling her buttocks. She reciprocated by rubbing his chest. Jackson deepened his kiss and moved his hands to her hips. He started to kiss her neck and slipped the tips of his fingers just inside the legs and started following the line of the leg gently caressing her skin with the backs of his fingers, he worked slowly towards the gusset. That feels so good she thought to herself! Forgetting herself for a moment she allowed him to start petting her. She could feel a pressure start between her legs. He pushed her against the wall of the pool and she could feel his erection. She suddenly stopped and was shaking. Jackson stopped. He looked into her eyes. Alva looked absolutely terrified. Jackson didn't like that, he stepped back to give her some space. He thought she was enjoying it and was disappointed. Alva got out of the pool grabbed a towel and ran to her bedroom.

Jack decided not to run after her, although he wanted an explanation, he didn't want to freak her out any more than she clearly was. After a couple of minutes, he jumped out and went and showered, he replayed the moments before in his mind, like a VHS tape and wondered what was bothering her. He cried not out of disappointment but the look of panic and fear in her eyes, he would never want her to be scared.

Alva stood in her shower sobbing she so wanted Jackson, she wanted him to be her first and her only! It was going to take a while. She didn't want to break up with him. Her mind swirled with things from her past her heart wanting to forget. She was frightened he would go once she had given herself to him and what was a man like him doing with her in the first place she wondered? She'd suffered a lot of different abuse at the hands of Drake Trent and was almost raped by Ashley Ashdown too, although she knew in her heart he would never be unkind to her in anyway. She didn't like her body, there were things done to her that had scarred her not only physically, but mentally and emotionally too. She absolutely trusted him yet she freaked out. She had to speak to him.

Jackson stood crying in the shower adjoining his office. He kept replaying the moments before in his mind over and over, as if they were on a loop. He knew something really bad must have happened to her for that reaction. He hated that fear in her eyes, did she really think he'd be cruel to her?

She found him in the kitchen, preparing dinner

"Jack!" she spoke gently. "I'm sorry! I do love you, truly I do."

He dried his eyes on the tea towel, blaming the onions, he turned around to her and opened his arms he needed her to hold him more than ever. She could she he had been crying, her eyes were puffy and bloodshot. The raw emotion in that room was palpable.

"Oh Jack! I never meant to hurt you! I love you!"

She held him and he buried his head in her neck feeling instantly soothed by the lavender.

"Please don't leave me I'm sorry if I hurt you!" he said muffled by her.

"Baby you didn't hurt me. I want to one day, I'm just not ready yet. I've had an awful time with men before you. I know you wouldn't mistreat me."

"You looked so scared! I never want to see you look at me like that! Talk to me… you can tell me anything." He pleaded.

They held each other, the silence hanging in the air. Jackson finally broke it.

"Alva, promise me you will let me know when you are ready, I will wait as long as you need. There is no pressure at all. There is nothing for you to be frightened of I only want your happiness." He put forehead on hers.

She looked into his eyes.

"Jack, it will only be you, you are the only man I could love! You're the only one I can ever want to make love with!"

"Tell, me what happened, something awful must have happened to you to react like that."

"I will tell you soon, but I can't face it today! It was horrible!"

Tears started falling from her eyes again. He held her tight; she didn't want to relive it in that moment. Jackson wrapped his arms around her as she cried.

"I trust you will tell me when you are ready, I will be patient and there is nothing you can't tell me. I will always love you and there is nothing you can say that will change that." He reassured her.

He kissed the top of her head. She stood feeling safe and protected in his arms.

They decided not to use the Barbeque but cook in the house.

Jackson put the radio on, an advert played, then Morgan Wade's 'Run' started playing. Jackson danced with her in the kitchen.

"Always find a girl that will dance with you in the kitchen!" he told her.

"This could be about us if you listen to the lyrics," she laid her cheek on his chest. "I was looking for a way out and you saved me in the nick of time!"

They made a movie marathon of Elvis films. Jackson enjoyed lip-syncing.

"Why won't you sing? You only ever lip-sync?" she asked.

"Same reason as you, I think I sound awful and don't want to inflict it on anyone... I'm not a performer I like to be behind the scenes... tell me what you want me to do these next few days, do you want to sleep here or go back to the hotel?" He asked.

"Stay here! I want you to stay here too, I trust you Jack, more than anyone in the world!"

"Good! I want to spend time with you on our own! You are the only one for me and I will do whatever you need me to." he reassured her.

That night they continued watching the movies in Alva's room, they both lay on her bed and fell asleep watching 'Flaming Star.'

"You're my flaming star!" Alva whispered to Jackson, as slumber was embracing her.

"And you are my lavender moon!" he replied, as sleep carried him away to walk with her in his dreams.

The next day, the sun flooded Alva's bedroom, the drapes and window had been left open because of the summer heat and a gentle breeze wafted through. Jackson lay looking at Alva, she shivered with the cold so he pulled the blanket up around her and rose to shut the window and use the bathroom. The TV had timed itself off. Alva looked so peaceful, he decided to go and make her breakfast in bed. He crept downstairs and made a tray up with breakfast for them both, it was 8:30am and had both slept longer than they would normally. When he got back to the room, Alva was just about to get up.

"I thought you would like to have breakfast in bed with me?" Jackson smiled.

Alva felt her heart leap in her chest.,

"Jack! That's so lovely of you! Yes, I would like that very much! I was worried when I woke up, you'd done a bunk after yesterday."

Alva climbed back into bed as Jackson placed the tray down and slipped in the sheets next to her.

"Honey! I could never leave you!" he reassured her.

"I worry you know, with everything… I'm so worried Jack, that once you know everything you won't want me or once you see me naked, you'll go off me and regret everything!"

"I know you do…there is nothing you can't tell me that will stop me from loving you. You are stuck with me if you want. As for seeing you naked… there is nothing that will put me off you… I'm worried you will leave me, once you know me better, other women have!"

"Oh! Jack that could never happen! I need to work on my confidence and my body before I let you see me."

"Alva! How many times do I need to tell you, I already know I will love your body… I love your soul! Look, I get we both have stuff we need to get together and work out, I'll tell you what, let's go shopping I have an idea."

He stood outside a jeweller with her, looking through the window at the array of gems.

"Now, I'm not ready to commit to marriage just yet, and if I do it will be with you so I won't buy you and engagement ring… but here in the states some people, usually soppy teens, wear 'promise' rings to each other, you can wear it on which ever finger you like… I know we're not teenagers, but I'm showing you how serious I am about you! I hope you are dedicated to me!" he kissed her forehead.

"I've still got all this 'junk' to work out, Jack you are the only guy who I want. So, if that will work for you, I'll happily buy you a promise ring Jack. I will be pleased to accept one from you, but will wear it on a chain around my neck when I am around Mont!"

Alva chose a simple signet ring in silver for him. Jackson chose a plain silver band with a princess cut blue topaz. They weren't expensive in monetary terms but priceless to their hearts. Jackson also bought a silver chain to put her ring on and kissed it as he put it around her neck. He took his and put it on his wedding ring finger.

"I'm off limits now!" he said in a joking manner, but was absolutely serious.

After the honeymoon Jackson hardly recognised his boss, the beard was gone and he had started wearing brightly plaid shirts over t-shirts. Jackson arrived at the house later that evening after the couple's return. The men were looking through the wedding and honeymoon photos deciding which to release on the social media platforms, Montgomery noticed the ring. Jackson kept looking at it.

"Did you pop the question then?" Montgomery asked.

Alva had never said anything, Montgomery thought to himself, it piqued his curiosity.

"It's a 'promise ring'"

"Aren't those for high school kids not guys nearly thirty?" he jested with a laugh.

"We both have stuff to work out… the only things we can both commit to are our 'issues' I'm committed to working mine out in a 'solution', you know Mont with my steps in program."

Montgomery felt shocked, he thought and hoped things were going well, now he wasn't so sure.

The last few days the family spent together at 'Carolina' Jack would snatch time all the moments he could with Alva.

The next afternoon Montgomery drove Vera and Monica to the airfield, where the private jet was waiting to take them home. Jackson drove Alva and her parents to the airfield, Alva sensed a foreboding, the journey was quick, cars flashed past like they were being sucked into another world. Alva noticed Montgomery's truck empty and parked on the black tar which matched their current mood. Vaughn and Alison said their cheerio to Jackson and left the couple alone for a few minutes and joined the others in the waiting part.

"How long until I see you again? I can't bear this bit!" She asked longingly.

Tears welled in her eyes.

"It's getting harder to say goodbye each time." He remarked.

"We need to tell him so we can make a life." She told him.

"Now he has Georgette perhaps we'll try and see how the land lies?" Jackson promised.

"I'll try and get over and see you soon… once things are settled here a bit… Don't tell anyone but, Montgomery, Jason and myself are setting up a record company so we can branch out without Della and do our own stuff. Once that is sorted, I'll visit and we can tell him together! I'm trying to rid ourselves of her but she is tricky, look… I don't want to put anyone in danger, but please trust me."

Alva agreed and a long gentle kiss ensued. She had to 'hold it together' until she was alone with her parents at the other end.

□

Chapter 15

Four months passed with facetimes and calls. Alva started writing letters to him and he her. They were sweet and they both liked receiving them. Alva would send him small gifts that were small enough for the envelope. She continued to see the 'taxi driver' pretty much every day, he would often say hello to her, Vaughn and Alison always seemed worried that he was taking an interest in their daughter, they would smile and be polite, but steer Alva quickly away, they knew Enrico Capozzi was the local mafia boss. Vaughn was unnerved and was curious as to how and why Alva knew him, she just said he was a 'black cab driver' who had given her a lift which confused them even more.

One Friday evening Alva's phone rang and she found Jackson in a fluster on the other end.

"I need you to know something, Mont and Georgette had a misunderstanding earlier and I was involved, but I need you to know I would never cheat on you…"

Jackson went onto explain how Della had been upsetting Georgette all day at the recording studio, which had eventually accumulated in Georgette crying in the car park and him offering her a few seconds brotherly hug, which Della had filmed and made into a gif which she had looped for a minute making it look like a long romantic embrace and how this had been sent to her brother to cause trouble. Jackson continued to explain how Della was causing trouble and how the woman remained obsessed. Jackson continued with his secret work, every time he had an excuse to be at the record company he was, he was stealthy and would look quite innocent and could get into rooms when people were busy. He was more determined now to get his secret work complete. Weeks later Montgomery had insisted he and Georgette return to England to get away from Della.

Jackson was excited to be invited to stay with Montgomery and Georgette for Christmas, that meant he would spend Christmas day with Alva. Montgomery had mentioned eight weeks and the potential of touring the British Isles. His boss suggesting that he hoped that Alva might enjoy the company and return the kindness that she had been shown in Nashville. Of course, it was part of Montgomery's plan to allow them time together.

Jackson arrived with a suitcase within a suitcase and a rucksack. He marched through arrivals and found Montgomery waiting for him. They shook hands and hugged. On their way back Montgomery updated his friend on the goings on. What trouble Della had caused. How things were with Georgette and they were putting on a show. How excited he was about being a dad. He then shared with Jackson about his addiction to alcohol. Jackson reassured him of his unconditional support and asked questions to understand his friend better. Jackson reminded him that he too was in a fellowship, based on Alcoholics Anonymous' twelve steps. Montgomery and Jackson were one of a kind but had different addictions.

That evening Georgette handed around her scan pictures and the family increased as the baby bought love with it.

Alva and Jackson snatched as many secret moments as they could, it was as if they playing a game, but Montgomery didn't know he was playing, yet he did. The evening passed and they all retired to their rooms. Jackson wondered which room Alva was in so he could creep in and steal a kiss in the quiet of night. At four in the morning, he heard gentle tapping at his bedroom door, it woke up his wanting of Alva. The door creaked open; he rolled over to see her tip-toeing in. She was carrying a couple of gift bags and two mugs of hot drinks.

"Merry Christmas Darling!" she whispered.

"Morning Honey and happy Christmas to you too." he murmured back.

She sat next to him on the bed.

"As I can't give you your presents in front of Mont… do you want them now?" she said.

"Yeah! I'd like that!" he said reaching to put the bedside lamp on.

The semi darkness made her look desirable. He rolled over to the other side of his bed and scrabbled around in his rucksack and produced his presents.

"I've got one for you for when we are all together, but you can have your others now." He smiled placing five small presents wrapped in gold paper on the bed, next to him.

He was touched with the very carefully considered gifts of guitar picks, journalling notebooks, a book about Barcham Grice and a silver chain with a St Christopher pendant on it. She was moved that he had chosen such beautiful things for her. She loved the pair of diamond stud earrings; they were not showy, but you could feel the quality. Next, she opened the matching necklace and a solid silver bangle with their names engraved around the inside. The next present was a block shape. She opened the wooden box with intricate carvings symbolising her favourite things. Jackson had learned to woodwork from his carpenter father and made this; she appreciated the uniqueness of the gift, the thought, and the love in it. She swallowed her emotion down when he was explaining all the hieroglyphics to her. They lay in bed holding each other, by 7am alarms were buzzing throughout the house, as soon as this happened Alva nipped back to her room to shower and dress.

Within half an hour they had all congregated in the large living room and were all relaxing with their hot drinks on the grey chenille sofas. Georgette had made everyone a western shirt, with love in every stitch. Alva thought hers was really pretty and special. It reminded her of the dress she'd had made for the CAMOEs and the work that must have gone into both.

The news channel was on constantly that Christmas morning, Montgomery and Vaughn had been concerned as two days before Christmas, Brantley Clayton, Vaughn's nephew had been shot. His attempted assassination had been said to had been ordered by the Drake Brothers. There was a fear they could be in danger too. Montgomery had upped the security on his home and family, Alva remained oblivious to the connection with the Drakes. The pair had tried to get information as to his condition but as neither of them were down as his next of kin they were not allowed to know or even visit him and security was tight. They were to rely on news broadcasts. Georgette had mentioned the Nurse who had saved Brantley's life whilst walking past, was Maggie who had looked after Georgette, when she had been attacked in November and had been knocked unconscious when being hijacked.

"Ooh Alva! I keep meaning to talk to you, I was wondering if you would do me a massive favour next week… will you take Jack up to London and show him around, please? I'll pay for everything… use my card to book hotels, restaurants whatever you think he would like to see. I know when he showed you around you got on and I thought you'd like to return the favour. He will be here a few weeks so if you want to travel around the UK that might be good too. Obviously, you need to sort out work…" A mischievous smile played on his lips.

"Sure! I'd love to! Come then hand over your card!" She laughed, gesturing to Montgomery.

"Come on Jack! Let's get online and book some stuff!"

Jackson jumped up out of his chair, grabbed his flavoured fizzy water and followed her to Montgomery's study upstairs, relishing the thought of being alone with her.

Montgomery went to the kitchen to baste the turkey, the heat as he opened the oven door reminded him of the summer heat in Nashville on their wedding day, snickering to himself. Georgette followed him. She stood behind him with her hands on her hips and her lips pursed.

"No! they don't know that I know!" Montgomery told Georgette swishing the juices in the turkey he was cooking and returning it to swap with the potatoes and shuffling them around. "That's why I have given her the card so she can book and they can have time together without me."

"So, when are you going to tell them?" She asked.

"I wasn't!"

"Well, I think you should, because I can see they are desperate to be together! They clearly are worried about how you will react! Please Mont put them out of their misery! You know what secrets do to a couple!"

"Alright then, I will! Watch this Mrs Moon!"

He walked to the bottom of the stairs and called them down,

"Come on! I need to talk to you both! NOW!"

Montgomery walked into the large reception room where Vaughn and Alison were waiting almost knocking over the real Christmas tree. Montgomery deliberately paced up and down like he was a lion stalking his prey. Vaughn and Alison were worried, their son had never acted like this before.

Alva's heart was pounding as she walked down the stairs.

"Jack, does he know? Do you think he knows?" she wondered.

"Alva, if he knows, we'll figure it out, I love you and I won't let him stand in our way! I will be yours for all time and never want to let you go!" Jackson told her.

Montgomery heard the comment.

"Good! I should hope not! I'm glad to see you appreciate what you have in her! So, now you know I know. I've known for a while but been having you on! Georgette has quite rightly pulled me up over it… I can't say I'm pleased about it!" He continued. "I'm delighted!"

He turned to Jackson and shook his hand and hugged them both.

"So, can we please, get on with Christmas and you two can stop hiding! Go and have your holiday on me and enjoy yourselves!" Jackson grabbed Alva, pulled her under the mistletoe, then kissed her in front of everyone.

Alva was pleased and she felt the tension disappear from the room and the couple freely held hands and looked very well suited and comfortable with each other. Then a knock at the door hailed the arrival of Monica and Vera, the two families enjoyed dinner. Montgomery was animated recalling all the times they clearly were in love but obviously hiding it. Jackson explained that they wanted to make sure they would work before telling him.

Jackson and Alva prayed they would last, but would memories of their past be intent on destroying them?

Chapter 16

Christmas dinner was a success. Montgomery cooking was a revelation, his past attempts had been disastrous. Plates were cleared and tidied by everyone lending a hand.

"Jack… come to the music room and tell me what you think of these songs." Montgomery asked.

"Sure!" Jackson followed him fizzy water in his hand.

Jackson listened to the songs and they were great as usual. They tried adding different instruments to see what might work. The pair of them spent time working on the music. Alva appeared at the door holding a violin case. She took out the fiddle and started to play along with what they had started. Jackson stared, he hadn't known she could play and how well, her ideas to add in worked beautifully with all the songs. Jackson sat himself at the pedal steel guitar and played a few ideas. They enjoyed jamming, the room was a buzz of ideas and thoughts, notes and lyrics flowed and Montgomery would make sure his sister would get credit and royalties from the songs.

"I've started writing this duet, I wonder what can be added…" Jackson broached.

He produced a couple of sheets of lyrics and started singing. Alva was surprised he had a lovely voice as good as Montgomery's yet he was happy to do what he was doing. Montgomery told him Alva could sing and she blushed. He tried to get her to sing but after much protest she relented and joined in singing the female parts with Jackson singing the male fragments. Montgomery was impressed they harmonised beautifully.

Alva added some suggestions and wrote some lyrics, from her point of view. They could now be open with their chemistry and you could see it in the song. The song Jackson had written was called 'DARN, the first time I saw you!' it was about her and she kept smiling and blushing because she knew it was.

DARN, the first time I saw you!

DARN, the first time I saw you!
Darn is what I said,
you looked so pretty with your lips so cherry red.
Your big brown eyes were full of blue.
I just wanted to take the sadness from you.

You were broken and bruised
and I know your heart had been used.
Your heart was a shattered mess,
I just wanted to bless you.

Darn the first time I saw you,
I blurted out in haste,
but it was your lips I needed to taste.
You're so precious to me,
I had to set you free.

Darn the first time I saw you,
I wouldn't be the same,
one day I'll give you my last name.

The trouble you caused but,
DARN, the first time I saw you!
Darn, girl I thought I was dead, that day you said yes to a date.

Perhaps Montgomery could encourage a single with them both, they could both sing and the chemistry was out of the world.

"You know Alva, I'll give you a job if you want… you can fiddle play and be a backing singer in the band. I've been trying to find someone for ages. We keep having to hire people." Montgomery told his sister.

Jackson pulled her onto his lap and squeezed her. Kissing her neck, that lavender scent!

"That way we can be together… in Nashville." Jackson smiled at her.

"I'll think about it! I'm too fat!" she said.

"No, you're not and I'm only interested in talent!" Montgomery told her.

She could quit the job she hated and be with the love of her life, was life now going to be that easy?

Montgomery had given him eight weeks holiday to spend in Great Britain, he was grateful for Jackson's hard work, he always went above and beyond. Montgomery had noticed how his sister was around him. They clearly brought out the best in each other, she smiled more, she was bouncing with confidence and looked in love. Montgomery wished them luck even though life had been tricky with Georgette recently, they were getting on well and Montgomery had hoped she would be back with him as quick as a kiss. Della had caused trouble and had made out she was having an affair with Montgomery, which was absolute nonsense as he was devoted to Georgette and had been since he was twenty-two.

When Alva had realised Jackson was coming over, she took all her leave in one go and arranged to take unpaid leave. She missed him when they were apart and she also hated her job. She had always said that she wanted to find a job in Nashville, but had only stayed for her parents. She had mentioned this several times to her brother and he had said he would be willing to give her work as the fiddler in his band and was seriously considering the proposition as it could mean being with Jackson. Jackson had wanted to visit his uncle and aunt, but hadn't found the opportunity to yet.

Jackson and Alva had taken the train to stay in London for three days, before they would travel to York then Edinburgh. They were the three cities Jackson had always wanted to see. When he ever came to England as a young man or child, he would with his mother's sister Kim and her husband in a big house, stay near where Montgomery lived, the garden was full of lavender bushes, he liked the memories of those days, but growing up he visited less often, he would take Alva to meet them, he wanted her to know them.

The nights were long. They stayed in a hotel overlooking the river Thames. Alva had booked single bedrooms. She didn't want her brother knowing they potentially were being intimate, and she was still fearful of being carnal. I love him and I am so desperate for his touch, but I can't let him… I don't like my body, I was 'branded' by Drake and he will see my scars, I want to tell him, she would think to herself.

Jackson continued with his patience. He would have never told anyone about being with her, yearning for her yet waiting. I'd love to go a bit further than kissing and cuddling, but she is clearly terrified of sex… I wonder why? I wonder if she will ever tell me or let me? If she does, she will be worth the wait, she is so perfect and I could never look at another woman. She is the only one who can get him working, he thought to himself.

Tonight, was New Year's Eve, they sat in her room looking out of the window watching party boats pass along the Thames. Jackson reflected that this time last year he was in Nashville.

"Last year, I was at Dorraine's house seeing in the new year. She had a party… at one point it was full of cops… those on duty would come by for a coffee or a quick drink break. As I don't drink it was my job ferrying Max, his family and Mom and Dad around. I got home at 1am. What about you?"

"Thinking of you! I remember needing you like I've never needed anyone!" Tears escaped her eyes and rolled down her cheeks.

If I told him everything, how would he react, she wondered?

Jackson slipped his arm around her shoulder.

"I'm here now!" he told her.

"I insisted he saw the new year in with my parents, I didn't want to be alone with him that night. He was nasty that evening and said a couple of vile things to me in front of my parents. Dad told him off! He got annoyed and left about 10 o'clock. 7am the next morning he lured me over to his flat… well… he touched me for the last time. I sat in the taxi on the way to the airport, looking at our photos from my holiday and my finger hovering over your number wanting to call you, I looked at my watch, but it would have been 4:30am for you so didn't. What was really strange was the taxi was parked outside and seemed to be waiting for me."

Jackson smiled to himself.

"What's even more weird is the fact the driver waited with me, gave me a bodyguard until the plane and said… 'give my regards to Jack!'" Alva suddenly recollected. "Who was he Jack?"

"Perhaps I'll introduce you properly one day. I woke up thinking about you at 3:39 and I couldn't get back to sleep. I think I might be in tune with you, even if I was asleep, it wouldn't have mattered, I would have come and got you from the airport. I would have even come to London if you wanted!" he whispered.

Alva grabbed his hand, knowing his every word was true.

They saw the new year in with their fizzy drinks and toasted their future. They spent the next grey and drizzly days visiting the tourist places seeing the best of London making memories of them. London was mostly grey with the odd bus, pillar box and telephone booth splashing crimson on the palate.

***

The train journey from Kings Cross was uneventful. They had sat opposite each other a small table dividing them comparing their phones and planning where to go and stay from there. It was a few hours and towns flashed past, yet the countryside rolled. They had started the journey at dawn, now the sun was climbing up the sky. A beautiful blue sky with wispy high clouds was becoming a dirty grey with a yellow hue the further north they got.

They alighted the train and a blast of icy air hit them as they exited the train station. The road was busy and they stopped and looked at the map to locate their hotel. The walk was refreshing, the sun that had been shining was hiding in the jaundiced sky. The temperature seemed to suddenly drop. Alva hurried to keep up with Jackson's broad gait.

"Slow down! I have little legs!" she protested with a giggle.

"Sorry! I'm super excited!" he laughed.

He slowed down for her and she linked her arm in his.

"What shall we do next after dropping our bags off?" she asked.

"I think lunch, then a wander around. I'd like to take a bus tour like we did in London, that was cool." Jackson suggested.

"Yes, I was thinking of a bus tour."

They arrived at their hotel, a medieval looking wattle and daub building in the city centre and was told a mistake had been made and they would have to share a double room. Jackson noticed she looked nervous.

“Let’s have a look and I can sleep in a chair or on the floor if you want… or… I can share a bed with you and just sleep. I have done that before remember.” He reassured her.

After a hearty pub lunch, they walked to the city tours bus stop and bought tickets from the official and waited patiently for the bus. When it arrived, they made their way upstairs and sat in the middle section.

“York Minster coming up ahead was completed in 1472...” The tour guide was telling them. It was quite cold sitting on top of that open decker; however, the view was spectacular. “…you will notice the East window, which holds the largest amount of medieval glass in this country. You may see that one is heart shaped… legend has it that if a ‘loved up’ couple kiss under it… they will stay together forever.”

Jackson’s ears pricked up to these words. What if he kissed Alva beneath it? Would that reassure her that he would never leave her? Would it ease his own fears? He sat half listening to the rest of the tour, his mind wandering for the other half. Eventually they completed their circuit of the city and got off the bus. It was mid-afternoon and Alva was keen to look in some shops.

“I’m just going to go to the record shop along the way.” he lied to her.

“OK. See you in a bit” she smiled.

He got out of the shop and looked up and down the cobbled street, gathering his bearings he was looking for a particular shop, she was in a book shop so he knew she would take an age, she loved looking for books, he knew what he wanted to look at and buy, but he also had to make it quick enough so she wouldn’t see what he had bought and the get back to the record shop to meet her.

Standing in the shop he was mesmerised, by the light and sparkling array of stock and within a few minutes he chosen what he felt was perfect, paid for it and slipped it in the inside pocket of his grey woollen coat. He nervously telephoned Vaughn and ask him the second most important question of his life, so he could ask Alva the most important question. He was relieved by the response. He went back to the record shop and had just been there a few minutes when he heard the old-fashioned doorbell jangle hailing Alva's arrival.

"I think I'd like to go in the minster next!" he told her.

Why did she want to go in every shop on the way, he thought to himself? Eventually they arrived and paid the admission fee. They walked the length and the breadth of the church. The stained-glass windows reminding him of the shop he had not long patronised.

"Wait here I want to ask that guy something" Jackson indicated towards a worker.

He yomped off then returned.

"What did you ask him?" Alva enquired.

"I asked him if the legend is true, if you kiss under that window, you stay together forever?" He told her. Pointing towards the Heart of Yorkshire window.

"What did he say?"

"He, said we have to see for ourselves. Come on!" He grabbed her hand and led her along the side where it was roped off and had been given permission to be directly underneath the window. He knelt down on both knees in front of her, like in the LoCash song, and he would put a ring on every finger if she let him.

"Earlier… when we were on the bus, the man told us the legend. It got me thinking — You said you don't want to be parted from me and I don't want to ever part from you. We both have this anxiety about it. So, I figured if the legend is true and we kiss then that will make us both happy because we will be cemented together. I've worked on me and I have come to the conclusion I want more and I settled that if I ask you to marry me then that will be doubly sure… Alva Moon will you take my name and the rest of my life?" he took out the white gold and amethyst ring and offered it to her.

Alva stood there rooted momentarily not believing her ears. Did Jack say he wanted to marry me? A broad grin spread across her face.

"Yes please!" She cooed.

He slipped the ring on her finger and stood up snatching her up into his arms and twirling her around and then he went in for a long and slow snog. There was cheers and applause from the public in agreement. Jackson was so relieved he was worried she would say no. He thanked the guide for his help as they headed towards the gift shop.

Outside they telephoned their families to share their good news. Naturally Vaughn had told Alison that things were imminent and she picked up on the second ring, he had given his blessing as soon as Jack had asked. Jackson's parents were thrilled, they really liked Alva. Montgomery was pleased and Georgette was ecstatic.

They decided to take one of the horse-drawn carriages around the city, the minster bells were peeling in a full circle, as if for a wedding, the couple took this as a happy sign. However, back in the far corners of Alva's mind she was worried about having to speak her truth about what had happened to her. Jackson knew he would have to give up his secrets soon and hoped Alva wouldn't mind any of them.

Chapter 17

The snow was falling like confetti on their walk back to the hotel, it was bitterly cold. As they walked, Jackson had his arm around her shoulders and Alva with her arm around his waist. They were content and happy. It had been a long and lovely day. They were frozen cold by the time they arrived. Jackson kissed her in the hotel lobby.

"Thank you so much for agreeing to be my wife, I hope I make you happy, my love!" he told her.

"You have no idea how happy you've made me!" she replied.

They climbed the rickety stairs of the bed and breakfast to their room in the Georgian town house.

"I think a shower might warm me up! I think a shower and a cuddle in bed to celebrate!" she told him. He noticed her blushing. A naughty smile crept across her lips.

"You mean, you might want to try some loving?" He asked eagerly.

She nodded. His heart started to race, now she would know his secret, was he ready to show her? He had been so used to waiting and being patient, he doubted it might happen.

"Are you sure you want to?" he asked her.

"That is why I love the York Minster legend! I guess you are stuck with me now!" she smiled.

They showered separately, she first and climbed naked into bed, laying there in anticipation of her first time. Nervously Jackson appeared and bounded over and laid next to her on the bed, his towel was still wrapped tightly around his waist.

"Now… you are going to see a secret… NO ONE has ever seen this, no doctor no girlfriend. Absolutely no one. I am trusting you not to tell anyone. It's a secret!"

Alva nodded in surprise and wonder. He stood up and dropped his towel his erection sprang to attention with its shiny proud piercing through his tip. Alva raised her eyebrows.

"Doesn't it hurt?"

"Not now, but I need to take care not to pull it hard enough to rip it"

"So, how come I am the only one to see it? Didn't the person who pierced it see it and why have it done, I'm curious?"

"I was trained to pierce and tattoo when I lived in Chicago. The girl I was with at the time kept going on about getting a piercing down there. I done it myself as a surprise for her as I thought I was in love with her. She never saw it though because of what happened…" He saw the look of disappointment on her face. "…of course, I didn't love her… I only thought I did, until I saw you! I denied myself that I love you as I never wanted to hurt like that. So, when they said about the legend, I thought it was perfect!"

He slid between the sheets next to her naked warm body. He kissed her gently. He could feel her shaking.

"If you want to stop at any time we can." He reassured her with a smile and a kiss on her forehead.

She nodded.

He gently ran his hands across her breast and kissed her neck. She reached for his manhood with her soft hand and held it gently in her palm and wrapped her fingers around. She held on without any movement. His hands were wandering all over. He whipped off the cover and to look at her body. She went to cover herself up. He noticed several scars that looked like cuts across her tummy and so many what looked like had been cigarette burns. He didn't remark on them, he knew she would tell him in time. He was patient.

"You are so flipping beautiful!" he told her running his hand over her. "Open your legs!" He willed her.

She obliged. He gently ran his hand over her pubic area, repeatedly. Eventually touching her. She let out a gasp.

"Is that nice?" he whispered as he continued touching her until ecstasy hit her several times. He then started kissing her tummy working his mouth down her body slowly, he wanted her to have a third orgasm for him.

For some reason she started crying and freaking out.

She couldn't breathe as panic set in. What had triggered her so badly Jackson thought to himself. Was it to do with that night with Ashley? Or Drake? Or both? He, immediately stopped. She curled up into a foetal position on the bed crying and shaking. Jackson knew something terrible must have happed to her and grabbed a pair of underpants and slipped them on. When he turned around, she was in front of him kneeling on the floor begging him not to leave her.

"Alva! I'm not going anywhere! I promised you earlier, I am not ever going to leave you! Tell me what did I do wrong? We've been here before and survived it!"

He helped her up from the floor and sat her on the bed.

"What makes you think I am leaving? Hey?" he brushed her errant strands of hair from her face.

"You didn't do anything wrong, and you put your pants on so I thought you were leaving me!" She started weeping again.

"I put my boxers on, to show you I have respect for you. The way you reacted I'm guessing you are needing to disclose something that's triggered you. I'm going to sit here and listen as long as needed. You wouldn't tell me a while back… and it's happening again! Please talk to me! You can tell me anything and everything. I promise it won't change how I feel about you." He smiled reassuringly, handing her his t-shirt, which she slipped on.

She told him about she was worried about having to give him oral sex. Drake had forced her to give him oral pleasure on a few occasions and she hadn't liked him deep in her throat it was like he had deliberately tried to choke her. He had taken the micky out of her innocence. How he had threatened to rape her, with his hand around her neck that last time.

"So, you see Jack, between Drake and Ashley the only men I have dated they have ended up with me in danger and now I'm hypervigilant over everything! I also have a very strong gag reflex, and gag at most things, it's not me being disgusted by something it just is. My dentist has to keep stopping when I go even a check-up is tricky." She explained.

She then told him about all the cuts and burn marks being from him punishing her over her weight. In those last few weeks, he would weigh her and if she hadn't lost enough, or too much he would cut or burn her. She told Jackson how she could never win. She was on a roll; it was time to bare her soul to him. Finally, she told Jackson how he had been on at her to get cosmetic treatment for the little bit of Hirsutism or facial hair. Jackson reassured her she was still beautiful and he didn't care in the slightest.

They lay in bed talking away the afternoon wrapped in each other's arms. When the afternoon's light started to fade Jackon went out and got sandwiches for their tea, so they could sit together, allowing her time to tell him all the darkest truths she could face at that moment.

"Who else knows about this? Other than him?" Jackson asked calmly as they were eating.

"I told Dorraine, she had a way of getting me to tell her, she saw the cuts, the burns, and the bite marks too!" She disclosed.

"He bit you too!? Where?" Jackson coaxed gently his face screwing up in horror.

She indicated her breasts, top of her arm and shoulder. She took a bite of her sandwich. Jackson was shocked. She had the pictures on her email, Dorraine had sent her copies. She took out her phone and showed him. She emailed him a copy of the file Dorraine had prepared if she ever needed. He scanned through the file pictures quickly intending to read it thoroughly later.

"If I'd have known I would have ripped his head off! Let's hope I never meet him again; I'll be on a murder charge!" Jackson fumed. "I will never expect you to do anything that makes you feel uncomfortable!" He whispered, in her ear then kissed her cheek.

The darkness outside the window was broken by the street lights dotted along the road and was blanked out by the heavy chintz curtains at the window. They lay in bed watching a comedy, which lightened Alva's mood, Jackson was happy seeing Alva chuckle, but he didn't understand some of the British humour. Jackson sat propped up on the headboard, Alva in his arms clinging to him like she was drowning. His mind wandered and he recalled the horror she had just disclosed to him. If he ever came across Drake Trent again, he wouldn't hold back this time.

"Let's pray he never comes to the states again… I won't deliberately miss with my gun!" Jackson thought aloud.

"You threatened him with your gun?" Alva suddenly sat up and looked at him.

"Yes, when I saw him off the day after your birthday, I'm not proud of it, I just wanted to scare him. I never miss where I aim and I aimed at the tree behind him, and caught his earlobe. I frightened him away, though… sorry."

"I'm shocked, but thank you for wanting to protect me… I wondered why when Mont and I went to see him he refused to see us!"

Eventually she fell asleep in his arms.

Would she ever feel safe giving herself completely to him?

The morning dawned and they rose and started to get ready for their day. Jackson had had a shower and was dressing whilst Alva started her regime. Jackson accidently walked in on her with shaving foam and having a shave. He remembered what she had told him yesterday and wasn't going to point it out. He carried on cleaning his teeth. She blushed at her embarrassment but realised he would find out soon enough and quietly carried on. He noticed her shame and planted a kiss on her forehead and told her he was ready as soon as she was.

They spent the day looking around the collection of shops. The area was called 'The Shambles' a rather apt name, they were quaint, old, and funny shapes. The sun was starting to melt the snow, this made the cobbles slippery. He had made quite clear last night he wanted to protect her and keep her safe and only wanted what she wanted. He made her understand she was only to do what she was comfortable with.

They had enjoyed a lovely day and decided to go to a traditional British pub. They found a booth and slipped off their coats. Alva sat admiring her ring. The amethyst sparkled in the light and the two smaller diamonds either side sparkled with a spectrum of colours.

"Jack, I'm sorry about yesterday and freaking out. I hope it's not spoiled our engagement." She told him.

"Don't apologise! I want you to feel able to completely yourself with me. Am I right in thinking he was your only boyfriend?" He asked.

She nodded and blushed. He got close and whispered in her ear.

“I know Ashley didn’t get very far, but still assaulted you?” He asked.

She nodded, biting her lip.

“Then am I right in thinking that Drake beast sexually, mentally, and physically abused you? Was that the only thing he forced you to do? He didn’t rape you, did he? I will kill him if he has!” he demanded.

“It was how I told you… I don’t want to talk about it here.” She squirmed in her seat.

“I’m not asking you to… I’m guessing you are still a virgin though?” he asked casually.

She nodded.

“I’ve not really had any boyfriends… most blokes boys think I’m ugly and fat! I’m wondering about you, what makes you interested?” she asked.

“Alva! You are gorgeous! Most blokes don’t know what they want. I see you all your facets, you’re sweet, beautiful, kind, clever, witty… there’s a long list. Your accent is a real turn on for me!” He smiled at her.

“Aw thank you babe! I have a huge list of the things I like about you too and yes; your accent is very sexy too!” she said kissing him. “I’m guessing from yesterday you’ve had a few lovers. You know my body better than I do… I can’t say I not envious of them.” She bit her bottom lip again.

“Let me get another drink and I’ll tell you and stop biting your bottom lip, I keep wanting to kiss it, you will undo me with that look!”

Jackson, plonked a kiss on her lips then disappeared to the bar.

He returned and settled next to her. Now was the time he would have to bare his soul. He needed to be vulnerable after all she had told him everything and they wanted to be married so needed to know. He leant both elbows on the table his hands clasped together like he was going to pray. That was something he seemed to do was sit in silent momentary prayer.

"I went to work for Lizine one summer in East Virginia. She was a widow who wanted help on her farm, harvesting peas. There were acres and acres, fields as far as the eye could see. She had hardly any machinery so mostly manual work. There were a few guys there working too. The others all knew each other and stayed together at another place nearby. My job came with digs, the house. I'd lived there a few weeks. I worked hard with the guys, but they all would go to a honkytonk of an evening, but I didn't I wanted to save every penny. I had my dream of owning a house and a shop and eventually doing what I'm doing. After a couple of weeks, she seemed different she had put on a little make-up. She had cooked a really nice dinner and we got talking. She was friendly. Her husband had died in a car accident a year before. I was nineteen and she was forty. They had been married twenty years. Well not to go into too much detail she gave me an education. Although it was mostly about satisfying her needs, although, I didn't have intercourse with her."

Alva sat and listened feeling all shades of jade with envy.

"I went home on the agreed date; I planned to go and visit her as often as I could. I got a letter from her after a week saying she had sold the farm and wanted no further contact. I was so heartbroken at that. I really liked her."

He took a chug of his water. Alva sat and listened sipping her wine.

"When I moved to Chicago, a few years later, it was where I learned to be a tattooist and piercer. I met Lainey. I was twenty-one and she was thirty-five. She owned the tattoo parlour. Now I had no piercings or tattoos. They were not something I was into. As you know there are no tattoos. She was separated from her husband, but lied and said she was single. We lasted a couple of weeks and again I thought she was the one, my experience was about her sexual gratification and not mine for a second time. She encouraged me to get a piercing 'downstairs' as she said it would heighten her pleasure, when we would do it, at the time I was thinking about asking her to marry me and was going to surprise her…" He continued and supped on his beverage.

Alva was listening and felt sad that he could have given his heart away before she had met him.

"I was all excited it had healed. I was going to show her. I turned up at her apartment to surprise her, the door happened to be open, I was worried there was an intruder and walked right in to her frolicking on the living room floor with her husband. They had reunited. The she looked up saw me and asked for a threesome. I was shocked, then devastated, and not something I am into I always just wanted one and only one my whole life, I want to say I only gave myself to one woman. I didn't know she was married. I hurriedly left, I went to the shop to collect my stuff and said about it, my colleagues told me about her having a husband, I felt utterly humiliated. Apparently, they would often split up; both would have a romance before they got back together. That really hurt me. It was some kind of game they played."

Alva reached for his hand and squeezed it she saw him raw with emotion. Tears in his eyes.

"I found out she was pregnant!"

"Was it yours?"

"Definitely not! I never actually did doubt it as she wouldn't let me penetrate her without getting a piercing! I never did the deed with either of them! Plus, people from the parlour said she would have been pregnant at least two weeks before she started seeing me! That hurt too! It made me feel really dirty, I guess that was why I had a bit of a 'breakdown' and walked from Chicago home. You know the rest about that and why I slept rough for a while…"

Jackson looked into Alva's eyes. "…I've dated a few times, since then, but not gone further than kissing. I also found I could never get an erection around any woman. I was certain it was divine punishment from God for coveting another man's wife. So, I've been celibate since then because I didn't want to hurt like that! I was broken and my dick stopped working. Then you turned up! I guess that's why I said I was too old for you… I was so used to older women… I thought it was what I wanted. I was scared because you are too right for me! I've never told anyone the complete story…" His eyes brimming with tears, he continued, after a sip of water. "…The moment I opened the door I got the biggest boner ever, that's why I said 'DARN!' and the fact I've never seen anyone so beautiful. It was like 'Hello! She's smouldering hot! Yes please! She's the one.' I've told Mont a few snippets, but not as much as you. I've certainly not told him about my dick. I hope it's not put you off me." He finished.

Alva threw her arms around and loved him like he had never been loved.

"I love you! I'm sorry you've had such disappointment, but glad you are mine. I want to love you my whole life. I'm so glad we are together." She kissed him.

"I love you too Alva! I didn't want to make you jealous, but I want you to understand I'm serious about us. I want us to work. It took me a long time to find someone that could make him work. Now perhaps you will see why I will happily wait. I won't lose you! I don't want you feeling scared of me, or worry about me leaving. I don't want to upset God! I realised recently, there is a difference in having sex with someone and making love, with someone you love. I want to make love with you each time, if you will let me. We have our lives to live together and I want you to want whatever we do and not feel you have to do anything if you don't want to!"

They sat in silence holding hands and staring into each other's soul. It seemed like a lifetime passed between them. They finished their drinks and walked in the freshly fallen snow around several museums eventually time led them to a restaurant hand in hand.

They settled at a table overlooking the moon lit river. The snow sparkled like glitter in the moonlight on the nearby bridge. He truly loved Alva. They ate dinner and laughed and joked. He told her about his musical dreams and how he wanted her and wanted to build a life together. She told him she wanted the same and to find a job she would love and not just tolerate in Nashville and be together.

They walked back to the hotel. The sky began snowing again the pavements were icy and slippery Alva held tight to his arm, laughing all the way.

He leaned down and kissed her slow and tenderly outside the hotel.

"I'm cold!" she told him.

"Let's get to our room and I'll warm you up with a nice hug in bed."

Reaching the door, they went in the dark hotel room.

"I'd like to try again Jack… If you want… but I need you to be patient with me." She told him breaking his thoughts as he switched the lights on. He wrapped his arms around her,

"I can be very patient… I've waited years for it to work, we can stop when you want you… I was going to suggest, if it's the ejaculation that bothers you… I can stop you when I am there and you can move away… would that help?" he proposed.

She liked that idea; she trusted him to keep to his word.

"Oh Alva, that's amazing! I'm going to…" his voice rang into the silence of the room.

He lay there a few minutes before rolling off the bed to clean up. The relief of that first orgasm given to him was immense.

She joined him in the bathroom to empty her bladder and freshen up.

They returned to bed. He felt his cock get bigger and pulsate at the thought of what they had just done and the fact she was still a virgin as well. He was laying between her thighs kissing her, she could feel him.

“I’m so aroused by you!” she murmured. “I consent! Please! Give it to me!”

Without further invitation he plunged into her. He thrust in and out as gently as he could remembering it was also her first time. He felt her hand wiggle between them.

He was delighted at this thought. He paced himself.

“Alva! I think you are a naughty girl, doing that! You are so fricking sexy! Thank you for this…”

“I’ve wanted you for so long and was scared to tell you stuff, I was worried you’d think I asked for it…. I’ll happily surrender myself to you and allow you to do what you want with me; I trust you that much”

“I’m glad you trust me!”

With that he felt her contract around him and he released simultaneously.

He lay still inside her for a few moments. He felt nothing but pure joy. He kissed her.

“J…Jack… w... was I ok?” she asked shaking. Tears welling in her eyes.

“Honey, I think you were amazing! But you being my first I can’t compare you. How was it for you?” He stroked her face.

She burst into tears smiling and nodding. He lay next to her hugging her. He could see she was ok, just overwhelmed by the experience. He held her close until she could talk.

"Sorry! I just got emotional… I really love you, Jack. You asked how it was for me… it was sensual… pleasurable… everything I could ask for. I think I am going to enjoy being your wife. Thank you for making me feel so beautiful and letting me be your first too." She smiled.

"You are beautiful and sexy. Don't be sorry for your emotions… I love everything thing about you and I love your raw honesty and I would never think you would deserve poor treatment."

He had been given two gifts. He was her first and hopefully her only. Although he felt cheated by Lizine and Lainey, he regretted his time with them, his mind wandered to what Alva had disclosed to him, hating her turmoil, and feeling her pain. She had fallen asleep in his arms; he watched her breathing. He drifted off to sleep but ended up in a nightmare and woke in the dead of the hour not wanting to fall back in a slumber.

Alva awoke a few of hours later, it was still dark, but dawn was breaking. Jackson was sitting on the side of the bed hunched over, his head in his hands, she could see his shoulders shaking. He was sobbing!

"Jack? What's wrong?" She knelt up behind him on the bed wrapping her arms around him.

"I'm not sure if I am so joyous that I have you now and we have made such beautiful love or…" he grabbed her hand and kissed the back of it.

"Or what?" she asked.

"I'm so terribly sorry Alva!"

He has changed his mind. Now he has had my virginity Alva thought?

He turned and looked at her and could see the fear and tears brewing, he was so in tune with her he knew what she was thinking.

"Oh Alva! Come and hold me." He took her in his arms, "I know what you are thinking… and stop, I'm not going anywhere! I woke up and couldn't sleep and I know I should have read it another time but I read the doctor's and Dorraine's reports and…"

He swallowed down his emotion, and lifted his legs and rolled back in bed to hold her.

"I read about where he kicked you, leaving you with a fractured pelvis. I had to look up where the 'pubic rami' was and how many ribs, he has broken. I can still see you wincing in pain when you came back. I'm guessing that was why you didn't want to go anywhere those first few days, and then we made you go to the wrestling, and what happened then! No wonder you were like you were all those times we got close!"

They lay facing one another. Jackson took a deep breath.

"I'm sorry that I didn't know when you came for your first holiday… I feel like sometimes I can read your mind. I sensed you were deeply unhappy that first holiday… it all makes sense now… you wanting to be a bird and fly away. You asked me to 'rescue' you and I ignored it. You said to me if I told you I wanted you, you would walk away from him… I could see you were unhappy. Then there was the time you sounded terrified when Mont threatened to call him the night after you were at the shelter. Then there's the blatant disregard you had for you safety that night, you had no idea how you were getting home because you'd stopped caring and you thought that you weren't worth a lick. I recall the last night of the holiday when you told me to stop because you said you would fall in love with me. On your birthday you were physically sick that he turned up, the look in your eyes with him there. That night you kept jumping and flinching and when I came to you and put my hand on your shoulder that broke my heart! Sometimes I dream of that morning he tried to get to you and I threatened him… I'm sure I would be on death row if I had known what he did to you I would have gelded him!"

"Oh Jack! I wasn't sure if I told you, you'd feel obliged to me. He didn't get physically violent until I went home. Before, when I was in Tennessee it was verbal, psychological, and emotional. He only started the other stuff before Christmas. It was my job to 'rescue' myself! When I spoke to Dorraine about not telling anyone she said it can take people a while because of the fear and shame. Please don't blame yourself… it was your letter that gave me courage… you told me I deserved the best. I hid the card and book on my parent's wardrobe so he wouldn't see it. He would have gone nuts!"

"I'm sorry I should have thought!"

"Don't be… it was like a ray of sun during those dark times!"

"I just wish I had known the first holiday I would have done something! I feel like you have suffered so badly and I have lost so much time with you just because I couldn't admit how I felt… I loved you from first sight Alva!"

"Jack, I fell for you when I fell in the restaurant that first night, you held my hand and you grabbed me around my waist when I tripped. You smiled at me. I fell wholeheartedly then and there. I thought later if I had been with Drake, he would have let me fall and laughed at me!"

Jackson pulled her close.

"I don't know if I can ever forgive myself!"

"Jack there is nothing to forgive. If I had asked for help straight out and you had ignored me then yes that might have been cruel. But I didn't tell anyone until last year, when I came back."

They both felt bonded and close to each other. Their intimacy would grow like the Lavender plants in Jackson's Garden. They fell asleep, in each other's arms, until 7am but had all the secrets of their hearts been disclosed?

Chapter 18

From Edinburgh they were lulled into a nap on the train, that glorious bit between sleep and awake was a sweet place to kiss the hours away. London's grey loomed and lunch had been eaten. Jackson was staying with Alva at Alison and Vaughn's. Alva hadn't even thought about sleeping arrangements and just assumed Jackson would sleep in Kenny's old room. They would always refer to that room as Kenny's as he had moved out a couple of years before he became Montgomery Moon. Alva went upstairs and noticed her single bed had been exchanged for a double and Vaughn had put their luggage in there.

Alva confused, went to ask her mum.

"Mum, I've got a new bed."

"No, dad and I have a new bed and put the old one in your room. Why?"

"I was wondering where Jack is going to sleep?"

"That's up to him… he could have Ken's old room… but… we thought you both would like to share."

Alva blushed.

"I thought you wouldn't approve."

"Alva you are twenty and getting married soon hopefully. I know you normally rush things, but I get the impression you've taken your time with Jack so not rushing anything." Her mum smiled reassuringly.

"Thanks, Jack and I wouldn't want to disrespect you and Dad."

Alison chuckled.

"You sound like Jack he is very respectful! And we wouldn't let just anyone stay in our daughter's room!"

Jackson and Alva's birthdays were just under two weeks apart. Whilst Alva would turn twenty-one, he would be maturing to thirty. He wondered what the next thirty years would hold. Montgomery had gone almost silent for the past few days and not even text his pal. Vaughn and Alison had been quiet since they had come back from their few days in York and Edinburgh. Alva couldn't put her finger on what was up. It was Jackson's birthday tomorrow and Alva kept wanting to organise something. Alison kept putting her off and guiding her away. She would just say that they would work it out on the night.

Alison greeted the pair at breakfast.

"Happy Birthday dear Jack! Can you two dress smart tonight Dad and I are taking you both out to dinner."

They spent their day at the Planetarium and Observatory. The building stood high on a hill in the middle of a vast park. The walk from the station wasn't of great length. The trees were bare. As they walked through the park, they noticed a number of runners, who were using the undulations of the park for hill training and dog walkers, little dogs scrabbling along and larger dogs loafing. There was an aroma of food cooking in the air from the pop-up vans and cafes licenced to serve sundries at intervals in the park. They Climbed the winding steep ramp which snaked up to the building, like a serpent protecting a keep, it was hard work and they took their time occasionally stopping to pretend to the other there was something interesting to observe. To Jack this was a wonderful way to spend his birthday, partaking in one of his favourite hobbies, with the woman he loved, the only thing missing was his music and it would be the perfect day.

Arriving home chilly, the night was falling like a blanket across Silkworth, with holes for the stars peeking through, Jackson wished he had a telescope to peer through, he had enjoyed his day in observatory. The house warm and welcoming allowed them to heat up with hot drinks and a chat with her parents. Jackson retired upstairs to take a shower, the hot water would revive him from the day, if he sat any longer in the warm lounge he would drift into a slumber.

"Mum, how posh is this place?" Alva asked, appearing at the lounge door with another round of teas.

Vaughn looked up from his newspaper and gave a wry smile. Alison put the bookmark in her novel, written by Olivia Roswell and checked the time on her watch.

"Smart casual type thing. You could just wear the 'Western shirts' Georgette made you! Pack an overnight bag too. You have about two and a half hours." She told her.

Jackson was now in the bedroom drying himself. Alva always thought he looked hot; he'd just washed his hair and it was tussled from him towel drying it.

"Apparently we need to wear the shirts Georgette made us for Christmas." Alva laughed. "She must have known we were a couple too!"

Their shirts were black with dark purple piping and embroidered white roses and lavender. Alva smiled. She packed a bag for them both and met her dad at the car and put the bags in the boot. They all climbed in with their thick coats and arrived at 'Carolina.'

"Just going to meet Mont and Georgette and we'll go! They want to show us the nursery so we will all just pop in."

They all got out of the car and Vaughn locked the doors.

“He was saying how he was enjoying decorating with Georgette.” Jackson offered.

Montgomery invited them and ushered them to the largest reception room at the rear,

“SURPRISE!” everyone shouted, as they opened the double oak doors.

“It’s a surprise joint birthday and engagement party for you both!” Georgette and Montgomery chorused.

Montgomery had sneaked over some Jackson’s family and put them up in a hotel nearby. He had plotted this since they had got engaged. Vaughn and Alison noticed Enrico Capozzi sitting with his wife Kim and Jackson’s parents, they were shocked, this man had seemed to have an interest in their daughter of late. Jackson was thrilled to see his ‘Uncle Rico’, Aunt Kim, cousins Ricardo, Marco, Isabella and their families he introduced them to his new family. Enrico explained he was trying to keep an eye on her for his nephew, his men realised something was amiss by Alva’s body language and he had ‘borrowed’ the taxi and would follow them and wait in case she ever wanted to make a dash for it. Alva said how grateful she was that day for him being there. Once Vaughn and Alison had spent time with him, they realised his reputation was just that, he was strictly a legitimate business man, but as his father was a mafia don, he had inherited everything and he ran things on fear, reputation and rumours. He had met Kim when she was at university in London, she had a job waitressing in Valentine’s Ristorante, where Capozzi would frequent, at least twice a week, as the food was excellent and he liked the waitress in particular. Jackson had spent many happy summers in England with the Capozzis on their estate filled with lavender bushes.

Carolina heaved with guests, there was a happy din of congratulations and merriment, the clink of glasses met speeches by the happy couple and their parents. Montgomery had set up a stage in the big reception room, with bi-folding doors at the back which overlooked their spacious garden. He had a marquee attached to the house. Along the length to make one large room, but there was still standing room only. The idea of the stage was there to showcase all the music talent ensembled, Common Ancestor and The Fishers had flown in and of course would do a turn each.

Montgomery insisted on a performance of "Darn, the First Time I Saw You!" from them, which they felt obliged to do and was met with rapturous applause. Montgomery had filmed their performance and quickly posted it on his social media pages before the pair could protest. He still had a way to go in his program and learn about respecting other's boundaries.

That night bereavement struck and Vera, Georgette's grandmother was taken ill then died a few hours later, Alva remarked that she had only been sat in the living room cheering and toasting them a few hours earlier. Montgomery was caught up looking after his pregnant wife during her loss. Alva felt sad as she rather liked the lady. The whole family attended the funeral the next week. Jackson went a bought a suit and Alva clung to his hand.

Chapter 19

It was the day after Alva's birthday and three after Vera's funeral, a Friday. Alva sat mesmerised by the news. Her parents sat with her and Jackson watching the morning news intently. Brantley Clayton, her cousin, and Vaughn's nephew was now the city's mayor only a few weeks after the attempted assassination. He was making an acceptance speech. The news was showing footage of him rescuing an old lady and the nurse who happened upon the shooting and saved his life. The newscaster spoke of a deal he and the nurse had made over a coat and she was teaching him about life. It looked like they were now a couple. The family listened with pride, Brantley was much loved, Vaughn and Alison had tried to adopt him, year in year out they were blocked by Conrad Aspinall the solicitor and legal guardian. Then there was a news flash: the 'Drake Brothers' and their father David had been arrested, for the fire and the attempted execution of Clayton, the later with the murder of Brantley's parents. Alva shivered at the sight of them on the screen. Then her heart froze at the sight of Trent's evil eyes, which seemed to be boring into her soul through the telly. Jackson noticed; he would enquire later. Then the reporter padded out the story about the history of the Drake family and how a young girl by the name of Jane Deighton, who worked for the family had been seduced at the age of fifteen by Dennis Drake the grandfather of the Drake brothers. Jane had been forced to keep quiet about the paternity of her two children even though she had been shunned by her family. She had been kept in a house by the Drakes until her parent's had worked out who the father was and twenty-two years her senior, eventually forcing him to acknowledge his offspring.

"That's Grandma!" Alva stared at the screen. "Those children were you and Brant's mum?"

Alva's eyes darted across to her father, who slowly nodded. Realisation and terror welled in her guts pulling them tight, nausea filled her being, she ran from the room to the downstairs shower room and started vomiting in the toilet. Jackson barrelled after her and knelt on the hard tiled floor next to her rubbing her back.

Alison and Vaughn let Jackson see to her. The picture to Alva was now clear, she now knew Trent was her cousin as well as the Drake brothers. She rebuked herself for not realising that had been why his first name was Drake. An accumulation of the realisation that her grandmother probably suffered like she had and history had almost repeated itself. She could have been in danger with her life too if they had realised who she was after listening to the theories as to why Clayton was their intended target.

Alison knocked on the door with a glass of water. Montgomery had arrived with Georgette demanding answers from their parents. Although he knew some of it; not all of the information had been forthcoming. Alison and Vaughn did their best to explain and how they were sure that David Drake, the father, Vaughn's half-brother, had murdered Cheryl (Vaughn's full sister) her husband Tony and the baby that was due. They had not killed Brantley as he was in boarding school. How a false will, to take custody of Brantley had been submitted and the judge had ruled the original stood so they waited to kill Brantley once he had accumulated more wealth. Vaughn, had desperately tried to petition to look after Brantley, but had been refused. Vaughn had said because he wasn't worth the amount the Claytons had he had been disregarded to be 'gone after' and then when 'Moody Moon' had appeared it was an opportunity to 'disappear.'

The news continued with more revelations. They were going to town on the gossip they could dig up. There staring from the screen was Drake Trent and how he was involved with his cousin's prostitution racket, how he'd been arrested on several occasions for sexual assault and rapes, and how he would get off each time. Alva had hidden herself in the bedroom, Georgette and Jackson, who had gone to make tea for everyone in the kitchen, could hear Montgomery and his father raise voices to each other from down the hall. They shot each other a look, neither had heard Montgomery use such a tone, even when drunk, the anger could be felt ricocheting down the Victorian passage and it's high ceiling.

"You knew who he was yet you let Alva see him! You knew what they were like!"

"I never knew for sure it was all rumours!"

"No smoke without fire Dad! You put her in danger! God knows what he's done to her!"

Jackson heard the door slam, he knew Alva had left at the arguing, it was getting near the mark now.

"Alva!" they shouted after.

Jackson ran out to her.

"Look what you've done!" Montgomery shouted.

"If I had thought she was in danger I would have stopped her! He was normally such a nice chap here."

Alison was now in between the fighting stags; they hadn't fought like this since Montgomery was twenty-two and had broken up with Georgette.

"Calm down the pair of you! We're on the same side here! We just have to see if Alva wants to talk and we will support her! She won't tell us anything with you two fighting!" she soothed them.

Montgomery's heart was screaming at him. If you had encouraged Jackson and her together when she first came over instead of stopping them, she might not have suffered and clearly, she has by the state of her his conscience kept telling him!

Jackson stood in the front garden holding Alva.

"What do you want to do?" he asked.

"Run! Run away! Please take me away Jack."

"Shall I tell them we are going for a walk? That gives you breathing space?"

"OK" she nodded.

Jackson went and fetched her bag and their coats.

"Alison!?" Jackson called. "Alva is fine she just needs some space we're going for a walk." He reassured her.

"What the hell has he done to my baby? I'm guessing she has told you!" she demanded. Jackson's face said it all to Alison.

"That's not for me to tell you. Alva will when she is ready and if she wants to."

Had Jackson not been there Alison would have gone after Alva and demanded to know everything in an instant and would try and solve it of her, Jackson had learned during his steps to put in boundaries and he was going to make sure Alva was able to do things in her own time.

They walked down the road in a fast pace, Alva wanted to get as far away from her family as possible, she loved them and knew they meant well, but she hated the control.

"What do you want to do?"

"I don't want to go through it again! I don't want to talk about that stuff. They'll think I'm a dirty whore!"

"No, they won't! They have guessed something is up!"

Jackson's phone rang.

Alva could hear Montgomery ranting about Jackson knowing stuff and he didn't. Jackson listened and took all that was hurled at him.

"Have you finished Mont? Firstly, thank you for your concern about my fiancée. I'm going decide how I will respond later once I have spoken to Alva and let her choose how to proceed. Thanks!" he hung up. "They are guessing what has happened..." Jackson stated to Alva.

Alva's phone was ringing. She declined it.

"This is why I didn't want them knowing they will boss me about and tell me what to think — What do I do?"

"I'm not going to tell you what to do, but there are several suggestions. We can go and make a statement to the police. You have the file that Dorraine took with her affidavit… we can do nothing and deny everything. We can tell them what you told me. You can let them see the file or some of the file and not answer any questions."

"Can we stay in a hotel it will give me time to think?" she asked.

"OK, but I will need to go back and get some clothes and explain."

"Alright! But don't tell them yet. I'm not ready."

After a while Jackson found a bed and breakfast on the other side of town and settled her in. He took a taxi back; the family were all pacing up and down like animals waiting for their pray. They were relieved to see Jackson, who, explained calmly that Alva needed a little space to make her decision. He told them that they were staying in bed and breakfast until she felt able to talk and process things.

They all had calmed down by the time he had packed couple of things. Her parents naturally worried and Montgomery was jealous she had gone to Jackson with whatever it was. Now he was in program himself he had rang his sponsor and, Gareth, who also happened to be his solicitor, they chatted about things and prayed and saw things differently. They had to be grateful that she had confided in Jackson.

He left with overnight things and a promise he would call if they needed anything.

He arrived back, the bed and breakfast smelled of a floral air freshener, he made His way to the room and Alva was waiting. She threw her arms around his neck, as he entered like she hadn't seen him in years.

"Thank you for putting me first every time!"

He held her close and she told him her decision,

"I've decided to make a statement to the police, even if it just helps back up what the other girls are saying." She told him.

"Shall I get the stuff from Dorraine about when he came over and tried to kick the door in?"

"That might be a good idea." Alva agreed.

The night cast a navy-blue back drop to their arrival at the police station. Alva waited patiently to give her statement, including what she had found one day in Trent's flat she emailed the copies she had with the file and oath from Dorraine as well as the other items that might help. She handed everything over to the police, she wasn't certain it would do much good. As they were walking out into the dark cold February evening, they saw Drake Trent leaving, he had just been bailed from the other end of the 'nick.' He caught sight of them both Alva grabbed Jackson's arm tightly, her knuckles turning white. Jackson looked as if he was getting something, Jackson reached into his inside pocket. As soon as he recognised Jackson, who gave a menacing stare to Trent who then turned on his heel and walked straight back in and handed himself back in confessing to numerous crimes and sparing Alva, or so she thought. They would never be 100% why he decided to admit everything at that moment but Jackson was sure he was too scared of him not to, perhaps he thought Jackson was reaching for his pistol or he had found out he was related to the Capozzis.

"I'm going to tell them I have made a statement to the police, but I can't discuss anything because of the legal process. That could buy me time, to decide what to tell them. I think I should telephone, Ella Baker, my old best friend and see if she's OK I don't actually know what happened there. I took his word on it, but I don't know now. There were other films sent to me a couple of weeks ago, by another friend Cassie, of Ella with the Drake Brothers and then at what looked like a doctor's office, it's odd she is extremely religious, I'm worried she was somehow coerced…"

"Whatever you need Honey! You are sweet thinking of others." He kissed her head.

"Jack you've been an absolute rock to me! I feel a bit freer!"

"I'm so proud of you, a lot of women wouldn't speak out for various reasons, but you have! Shall we get some dinner and go back to our room and relax?"

They found a Chinese restaurant and tucked in, Jackson ate his usual healthful meal and always looked as if he was enjoying it. He was always so conscious of his eating, Alva never questioned as to why he ate carefully she guessed it was due to his diabetes.

They lay in bed holding each other waiting for sleep to consume them, but the trauma of the day blocked the slumber.

"Take me Jack!"

"If you are sure Honey…"

"Not only take me, but take me away! I want to RUN!"

A few days had merged into a week from Alva giving her statement, she was welcomed home by the family; they were sitting on Alva's bed the bedroom cosy with purple woodwork and lilac flowers on the wallpaper.

"So, Alva are you going to let me look after you?" Jackson asked. "Give up your job and come and let me look after you? Please?"

"Where am I going to live?"

"My house is your house… I'll even have it signed over to you if you want security!"

"No, you're not signing it over to me! Yes, I will come and live with you though. if you can put up with me, I worry about not earning a wage!"

"Let me take care of you and we can work things out! We can leave it to God." He pleaded gently as he wrapped her securely from behind in his strong arms, offering his lifetime of security.

"I was going to hope Mont still had the fiddle player job going. I don't like the idea of being famous but he said he'd pay me well and therefore I can get a visa until we marry. Plus, that film of us singing together went viral. People are asking for us to release it."

She suddenly grabbed her laptop from the bedside table and opened it. She started trawling through old emails. Jackson started kissing her neck in the hope of seducing her.

"Kiss me, Alva!" he kept repeating.

She remained focused. Then she started typing furiously.

"Watch ya doin'?" he asked pulling away from her.

"Trying to check my contract and write my resignation letter!"

Jackson stopped dead in his tracks and sat back on the bed patiently, he wanted her to get over to Nashville as soon as she could.

She read the letter she had written to him several times, changing odd bits as she went, then sent the email and closed the screen. A smile spread across her lips.

"Right! Where were we?" She leaned back to kiss him.

Her phone rang loudly making her jump, it was her boss. The woman was furious she relied heavily on Alva and continually took advantage of her eagerness to please and bullied her, she made a point of always giving Alva the worst jobs, and shifts, yet others were allowed to do pretty much what they liked. Jackson could see Alva get upset and could hear the woman on the other end ranting.

"I'll talk to her!?" Jackson whispered.

Alva handed him the phone. He let the woman continue with her tirade of abuse.

"I'll sue her for breach of contract!" she screamed at him, "I'll take her to the cleaners!"

"You do that Ma'am."

"Don't you know who I am?"

"No, neither do I care!"

"I'm Victoria Amberleigh! My family run this area now the Drakes are gone!"

"Alva has given you the correct amount of notice. She won't be returning. I will return her keys tomorrow morning at 10am. There is nothing further to say, other than I take your Amberleigh and raise you a Capozzi! Thank you and you have a great day!"

He hung up, letting out his frustration with a huge sigh, Alva sat stunned, no one had stood up to Victoria Amberleigh like that ever! Her family were said to be as bad as the Drakes, although Jackson didn't like to drop Uncle Enrico's name, but knew he would understand, Enrico had made clear his rage at the so-called Amberleigh gang flexing their muscles.

"Alva how on earth have you put up with that rudeness for so long!" he smiled at her.

"Oh, Jack I'm worried now!"

"Why? You are not responsible for her reaction. You have given the correct timings." He managed to reassure her.

She switched her phone to silent so they wouldn't be disturbed.

The evening fell and The Nickelodeon beckoned, The Nickelodeon was said to be the most exclusive restaurant in the area, a waiting list of over a year normally, but somehow Jackson Maddox had a table, which was helped by the fact Montgomery Moon would be dining there and your uncle knew the owner and manager!

Alva and Georgette looked around the dining room and was mesmerised by how art deco the design was, the octagonal opaline glass lights suspended from the ceiling giving it a romantic ambiance, enormous bevel edged mirrors hung on the walls, enhancing the space. They sat at a round table, candlelit pure white starched linen table cloths, the restaurant was fairly calm and peaceful, the bar was clearly where the old organ, would have stood a square clock it's centre piece of the rosewood surround, the music harping back to the roaring twenties and thirties, those glamorous inter-war years of peace. They ordered their meals, it was a specialist seafood restaurant, lobster and caviar were ordered and a job negotiated and planned to start in the fall. Montgomery had his own situation to deal with; to get back with Georgette and hope she would go with him to Nashville eventually. At present Georgette was still pregnant, life was about to change for everyone.

Chapter 20

Alva was happy to be planning a new life with Jackson. He was booked to go back in a couple of weeks, Alva planned to join him a couple of weeks after. Fate had different cards to play that day. The family were in the living room at Vaughn and Alison's drinking hot drinks and chatting. Her mobile rang with its distinctive ring tone of 'DAMN! The First Time I Saw You', which had become a hit thanks to Montgomery.

Alva went pale whist taking that telephone call.

"He lied!" she put the phone down and was shaking.

Jackson stood up and put his arms around her.

"What's happened?" he asked.

"That was the person from the Crown Prosecution. Drake has changed his pleas to not guilty and they are summonsing me as a witness." She burst into tears.

Jackson held her. Her parents, Montgomery and Georgette sat in shock, they all felt bad that she was going to be made to relive it.

"What do you want to do Honey?" Jackson asked gently.

"You'd better take the stand!" Montgomery told her, folding his arms indignantly.

"They need to be punished!" Vaughn interjected.

"I don't think I want to hear about it!" Alison anguished.

“What do YOU want to do Honey?” Jackson asked again gently.

“She has to do it!” Montgomery bossed again.

“I think you will find it’s Alva who needs to decide and she needs our support, not our opinions.” Jackson said mildly.

Alva turned to them all.

“I’m willing to give evidence, but only if Jack will be there with me and ONLY JACK! I don’t want you all listening to what happened, it’s embarrassing enough going through it all again.”

“We want to support you!” Alison said.

“Support me by respecting the best way for me!” Alva was firm.

“I suppose this puts Jack and Mont in a dilemma?” Vaughn reminded Alva the Jack was due to go home after eight weeks.

Jackson was booked on a flight in two weeks.

“So, when does this trial start?” Montgomery asked.

“April and likely to go until May!” she replied.

“So, another ten weeks...” Montgomery sighed. “Jack, I suppose I could get you set up with a laptop top here and sort out you working here for those weeks. Most of the work can be sent over – Do you think that is an option?”

“I’m willing to make it work if you are happy with that… but I don’t expect it though, I would put Alva first in any situation, regardless!” Jackson told him, secretly panicking about his secret, he would need to ring someone later to explain the delay in his return.

“Well, if it will help put that predator away and the others in prison, I’m happy to do whatever it takes too.” Montgomery stated.

Jackson was welcomed to stay a few extra weeks. He liked the thought of the extra weeks but not the circumstances.

He discovered a place nearby called 'Blake House' a short walk from Alison and Vaughn's, which held meetings for his twelve-step fellowship and would attend on the days he could, he wanted desperately to tell Alva which fellowship he was in but couldn't bring himself to just yet, he needed his fellows at a time like this. It was also a night shelter and soup kitchen. He thought that it might be something for him and Alva to do together in their spare time. There were a number of joint projects that went on in Blake House, the charity that ran it could make money by hiring some of the meeting rooms out during the days to other community groups.

***

The family had read in the news that bright morning Brantley had married his bride that weekend. The day of Alva's court appearance was here, it was now April and the crabapple tree in the garden was full of pink blossom, the trial had started a few weeks before. Jackson put on the suit he bought for Vera's funeral and a pale blue shirt and a black and blue tie he'd bought for the occasion. He took proceedings seriously and wanted to show Alva. She wore the simple long sleeved black dress she had worn for the funeral plus the pretty jewellery he had been gifted at Christmas.

They arrived and was greeted by the CPS lady Mrs Stephanie Tate-Howe QC. Jackson had a 'word' with her.

"Ma'am, I think you should be aware that when he came to harass Alva in Nashville, I had to threaten him with my pistol. It is my right as a US citizen to bear arms as the second amendment states. I did and only would act in accordance with the laws of the country I was in."

"Thank you for letting me know if it should come up, I will be prepared with an answer. I was aware an altercation took place; I did see some footage that was submitted by a Sergeant Dorraine Dennis." Mrs Tate-Howe reassured Jackson.

Mrs Tate-Howe talked Alva through proceedings. Alva would need to wait until called to the witness stand. Jackson could go and sit in the public gallery, then after she gave her evidence, she would be able to sit and listen with Jackson.

"The judge is Mr Justice Bull, he is very fair, he doesn't suffer fools gladly. Just keep calm and take your time if you need to stop for a moment, please let me know. The prosecution is likely to make an issue of you and Mr Maddox getting together so soon after you left and will try and make out a lot of it is your fault and provocation. Don't be flustered, remember you are under oath so just be truthful. Alva, I believe you!"

Alva sat alone in the segregated waiting room for what seemed like hours. She was called in; Jackson was sat in the public gallery carrying her handbag. She stood in the witness box and firmly read the oath. She meant every word she spoke. She looked at the people in the court, the jury were made of five women and seven men, all different races and creeds a good and fair mix Alva thought. Mr Halliday the defence lawyer was a man in his late forties with dark menacing eyes, he gave an air of arrogance. Her eyes settled on Mr Bull, an older man in his late fifties with a grey beard and glasses, his black hair obscured by the Georgian powdered wig, he looked regal in his scarlet robes, although he looked formidable, he seemed to give off a safe presence. Mrs Tate-Howe had told her to concentrate on the questions asked, Alva was someone who found lying difficult, unless it was about food and how much she had actually eaten, then she could lie her back teeth off.

She stood composed and answered the first questions firmly and clearly. Drake kept staring at her menacingly, trying to throw her off. The Drake Brothers sneering at her, she was asked about their behaviour towards her, reliving a few incidents, she had been subjected to, she broke down a little before recovering her composure. Jackson watched, wanting to fly across the courtroom and scoop her up in his arms. He knew he couldn't. Alva kept looking over to him occasionally for reassurance. Mostly she would direct herself to the jury or the person asking the question. Jackson was sat behind and a little to the side of Drake Trent, his cousins, the three Drake brothers and their father, David Drake, who was on trial for the murder Cheryl and Tony Clayton and the destruction of their baby as well as conspiracy to murder Brantley Clayton twice. Drake looked behind him and suddenly noticing Jackson, he stood up.

"THAT BASTARD TRIED TO SHOOT ME!" Drake kicked off.

Mr Justice Bull asked him to calm down and any more swearing would have him removed from proceedings.

"THAT BITCH GOT HIM TO TRY AND KILL ME, HE TRIED TO SHOOT ME AND I'M THE ONE ON FUCKING TRIAL!" He was pointing at Alva.

"Officers remove Mr Trent to the cells, he was warned. I will continue the trial without him."

The judge waited until he was removed then he turned to the councils.

"Is there new evidence to be submitted?" Mr Justice Bull asked.

"I was not aware of this serious incident until now, Your Honour do we need to adjourn until this matter is investigated by the police and does Mr Maddox need to be taken into custody?" Mr Halliday QC the defence barrister asked.

"I'm well aware of the fact Mr Maddox drew a pistol and threatened Mr Trent under provocation. The incident occurred at Miss Moon's brother's home in Nashville Tennessee in the USA. Mr Maddox was left in charge of securing the house and Miss Moon's safety, he is a citizen of the United States of America and acted within the state laws of Tennessee and his rights under the second amendment. This matter would be out of the jurisdiction of the British judicial system in any case. Mr Maddox is not on trial. Your Honour, I would ask you to direct the jury to ignore the remarks made about the pistol to Mr Maddox." Mrs Tate-Howe remarked.

"The jury will disregard this matter." Mr Justice Bull directed to the jurors.

One of the questions Alva answered was about a gun. Her mouth was dray and felt hot as she recalled the panic she felt when she accidentally found in Drake's flat. She could identify it by the initials scratched into the barrel, the same gun that had been found in his flat and the same gun used to shoot Brantley Clayton. She was asked where in the home he kept it and she was clear and concise. It was the place where the police had found it. She felt sick knowing Drake was the one who pulled the trigger and that it was Dougie driving the bike. Jackson had heard the remarks made by the ballistics expert that morning how Drake was not a good aim and the injuries had only been the result of the ricochet of the two shots. Jackson smiled inwardly knowing what an excellent aim he had.

Eventually Alva had answered all the questions and was discharged, she made her way to Jackson and sat with him, he took her hand, for the summing up.

"You did good Honey!" he whispered, squeezing her hand. They would save any kissing until outside.

The jury now had to listen to the summing up from the defence and the prosecution. Some of the details were harrowing from the other women. The awful details of her aunt's death were read out. As well as the terrible things the brothers had done to cause fires and everything that had occurred.

The jury retired to make their deliberations on each matter.

Days passed by slowly.

There had been a lot of talk over the situation that Alva had been in. She didn't disclose the full extent but the snippets she did tell, or they read in the public domain floored her family, mixtures of guilt and anger surfaced. There were a couple of falling outs and blames laid. Alva eventually explained this was why she felt she could have never gone to them because of their judgements and criticisms of each other. By now Montgomery was on his fourth step in his program and although he didn't like what had been said, Alva did have a point. Montgomery used it for his inventory and looked at it in a positive light. Their parents used it to look at their own behaviour too. It took a week to find them all guilty on most charges. They had all been sentence to the fullest terms each of them could. Stephanie Tate-Howe was right Mr Justice Bull was a fair judge. Each man was found guilty unanimously on each charge and sentenced to the maximum time they could be, it was said if the death penalty was still an option they would have been flogged and hanged, but it wasn't.

Alva had tried to contact Ella several times, she deeply regretted the horrible text she had sent her when she had been sent the first video. It was a reaction and she hadn't thought about what she had written in anger. After the trial she was worried what may have happened to her and tried to text and call her, the calls were quickly declined and the messages read and then she was blocked, Alva couldn't blame her she had said such vile things to her in a rage she was blinkered by her own abuse to have noticed what could have happened to her friend.

It was now mid-May, the huge rhododendron bush in the front garden a riot of purple. Alva and Jackson decided that the last two weeks he was with her they would volunteer at the night shelter, he missed the one in downtown Nashville, he was keen to get back the clandestine work he was up to, he needed to wrap it up as soon as possible now he had Alva to keep her safe. Alva had been volunteering there until Drake had got involved with her. She cheerfully telephoned the organiser and explained that her fiancé and herself would like to volunteer and gave them the hours they were able to provide for the rest of the holiday.

Saturday came and they arrived a 'Blake House' it was a building that was rundown, it housed twelve small single rooms and two shower rooms and separate toilet block horseshoed around a main hall and large kitchen, finally seven meeting rooms to the front of the building, it smelled of pine disinfectant reminding Jackson of the record company. They were shown around by Shona, the coordinator, and inducted in. Jackson showed Shona his credentials from the shelter in Nashville his food certificate in case he was of use doing that. Shona introduced them to Dean who was in charge of the kitchen. Dean was happy for the help and showed them a few forms they needed to fill out as a regulation and it was not dissimilar from home. They lost count of the sandwiches they made, the aroma of the vegetable and tomato soups made a contrast to other cleaning smells, the pots bubbled and popped. There was an area with clean donated clothing that people could help themselves and facilities to wash their old clothes and have a shower, some people had their own toothbrushes they kept in a pocket. Blake House was in walking distance from Alva's and they continued every day over the weekend. Walking each morning and returning for dinner.

The dawn broke with its chorus of birds, the crows cackling their arguments with magpies. Jackson loved the earliness and the opportunity it bought to learn from Alva the calls of the British birds, when asked what his favourite bird was, he would put on a false Cockney accent and say her name. The couple arrived to pretty much silence other than the four, night volunteers, who were conferring in the office about various plans they had. Jackson and Alva signed in and passed the time of day, heading straight to the kitchen and started prepping breakfast for their guests and setting up for the day.

Each Wednesday the centre hosted a lunch for the elderly day centre. Whilst that was going on Jackson and Alva had volunteered to thoroughly clean some of the bedrooms. They were washing and cleaning up the breakfast things gradually a few more people joined them.

Firstly Elsie Clyde, a sweet little old lady, who volunteered in hope of finding her missing son, he had a mental breakdown and disappeared one day fifty years ago. Jackson empathised with the story; it was close to home for him. The tea was brewing in large stainless-steel pot, when Shona, the co-ordinator, walked in chatting to a beautiful looking lady, across the hall to them. Elsie quietly explained to them that the beautiful woman was the City Mayoress, how lovely and would happily roll up her sleeves and get involved. Maggie approached them sporting a high long dark ponytail, faded blue jeans, black t-shirt, and pink hoodie. She looked relaxed and not how they would expect a mayoress to dress. She was a similar height to Alva. Alva shot Jackson a look, he knew what she was thinking.

Maggie introduced herself.

"Hey I'm Mags!" she shook hands.

"Jack, Ma'am!" he offered his hand and they exchanged pleasantries.

"Alva"

They smiled at each other; the name sounded familiar to Maggie.

"Mrs Clayton, I mean Mags… I hope you don't think it very forward of me, would I be able to arrange to meet your husband please. We go back to Nashville soon…"

An Alva? Nashville? Maggie's curiosity was piqued.

"Now, why do you want to meet my Brantley?"

"Because I think… I might be a cousin?"

"It's not Alva Moon, is it?" Maggie enquired.

Alva nodded. Maggie threw her arms around her then she looked through the serving hatch to see her husband chatting to Shona.

"Brant!" she shouted excitedly.

Brantley was a fairly tall guy. He was the youngest ever mayor of the city at twenty-seven. He was a similar height to Montgomery at six feet, they had a similar shaped face, slightly different noses. Brantley had a buzz cut whereas Montgomery had just short back and sides. They could actually pass as brothers. Today he dressed in jeans and a polo shirt.

"Brant!" she called again impatiently.

He looked up and beamed at his wife and indicated he would come shortly.

He strode across the large hall and waltzed into the kitchen.

"Brant, can I introduce Jack from Nashville in Tennessee…" The men shook hands. "…and Alva Moon!" She let the name sit for a moment.

The realisation dawned on him. Brantley threw his arms around her.

"I'm so pleased to meet you! I've been looking for you guys. Mags wrote to your dad but we got no reply."

"We've been hoping to find you too. We were all so worried when you were ill at Christmas! The hospital wouldn't let us visit or know how you were we had to get everything from the news!" Alva explained.

"Alva, I only found out a few weeks ago that your parents were willing to adopt me. I'm so touched, I didn't remember you guys existed until Mags did some research, and I had a vague recollection, I was only small. We realised there were name changes etc. I managed to get the court papers and the solicitor had kept things from me in order to syphon off my inheritance. Anyway, how are you? I read in the newspaper you were a witness in the trial of our cousins! Thanks for helping put them away, I'm sorry to read what happened to you." Brantley smiled at her.

She blushed knowing people knew about the abuse.

"I'm better thanks… are you recovered now? I heard after you had to give evidence too… and of course your injuries. My there is so much to talk about!"

"There is! Do you think your dad and Mont would want to meet us?" Brantley asked.

"They will love to. I want to ring them now!"

"Don't tell them yet! What about… I take you all to dinner tonight and meet you at King's restaurant? Ring them now and see if we can arrange for tonight? There's a private area they'll let me have." Brantley asked.

After the cousins plotted, Brantley booked the table for dinner at King's which was a traditional English restaurant with a carvery style buffet. Brantley had considered it the best option, that we he could offer people a meal and they could choose what they wanted and there would be no washing up for anyone. He would frequent this particular restaurant with those family he had made with Maggie during their whirlwind of a romance.

Maggie caught Alva in a quiet moment.

"Me too, hashtag me too… Alva, I just wanted to say how very brave I think you are giving evidence. A lot of us who have been subjected to the Drake brothers' violence and abuse, haven't spoken out yet." She pulled down her bottom lip to show Alva the scar Donnie Drake had branded her with at fifteen and her wrist scars "A lot of women won't talk about it, thank you for speaking up for them."

"Thanks… it wasn't easy…I guess initially I just wanted to back up what the other women were saying, then when Brant was shot and I knew there was a gun in his flat, I had to explain to the police… I guessed they were involved. Mont once told me Georgette had rented a flat from them and the brothers had assaulted her."

Maggie told her briefly about what Donnie and his brothers had done to her at fifteen. Maggie and her were kindred spirits who were survivors and proof you could find a good man after what they had been through. The cousins and their partners continued with their volunteer work the rest of the day and enjoyed being able to help people. They parted for the time they would need to go home and change for their evening.

The waitress showed Alva and Jackson to the table of eight, at the back of the restaurant, tucked away and slightly secluded from the general public. It was Brantley's 'special' table. Enough to be on public display, but out of the way enough for some privacy. they couldn't be spotted by the paparazzi. Within a few minutes Montgomery arrived with Georgette who waddled in rubbing her any day due bump.

"So, what's the announcement that can't wait? You up the duff out of wedlock? Mom and Dad will go nuts!" Montgomery joked as he pulled out a chair for his wife with a scrape and plonking himself opposite and next to his buddy.

"You will have to wait!" Alva told him.

Alison and Vaughn arrived and spotted them and walked over and sat with them.

"What's going on? You told me a lovely surprise! I'm so excited." Alison said.

Jackson sent Brantley the pre-arranged signal on his phone.

"It had better be good! I've missed my bowls tonight!" Vaughn stated indignantly.

"I just thought a little FAMILY get together after everything that has happened would be nice." Alva told them.

"Is that it?" Montgomery shook his head and sighed, he tried to show he wasn't disappointed.

A few moments later Brantley and Maggie swept in and went straight and sat down without invitation. Montgomery nearly choked and spat out his drink, when he saw his 'clone' and who was joining them. Vaughn initially thought it was somebody being cheeky and taking advantage of the spare seats, in the very busy, sought-after restaurant. He turned to chastise the cheeky devils.

"Hey Uncle Vaughn!" Brantley flashed a huge smile.

There were tears of joy at the reunion, long chats and lovely food, company was enjoyed, then arrangements made for more meet ups plus a lot of photographs.

Vaughn thanked Alva for finding Brantley and arranging the evening. Time was needed for catching up and more memories needed making.

Georgette gave birth to Kacey-Reba three days later on her birthday.

Chapter 21

Jackson's return home to his house in Nashville felt lonely, he lived for the promise of Alva in two weeks. In his spare time, in between the dances of work and 'other' things, he cleared and sorted items and made room for Alva's clothes in his drawers and closets.

He carried her over the threshold, that summer evening as the sunset on his old life

"Welcome home!" he told her.

He wheeled her suitcases to the bottom of the stairs.

"So where do you want to sleep?" Jackson asked. "I was going to decorate a bedroom, but wasn't sure if you wanted to share… and I thought it would be more fun if we did any decorating together, you can put your own stamp on the place. Eventually we will buy another house together… I hope!"

"Can I stay with you in your room please?" she wrapped her arms around his neck.

He smiled looking into her eyes.

"You don't need to ask! It's your home now. I was hoping you'd want to." he smirked. "I bought brand new bed sets. I've put one on our bed and would make the other up if you had preferred."

"Oh, Jack you are so sweet!"

She slipped her soft arms around his waist and he hugged her shoulders.

Alva went and made hot drinks whilst Jackson hauled her luggage to their room.

When he came to the kitchen, he saw her standing by the sink and crept up behind her and wrapped his arms around her waist he nuzzled her neck.

"You know what I would like to 'christen' every room with you! …" Jackson suggested.

She smirked the thought of that was so very tempting.

"…Honey? Where shall we 'christen' first?" He continued.

He swung Alva around to face him.

"Well…" She pursed her lips and struggled free. "You'll have to catch me first!"

She darted off and he chased her around the rooms many led into the other she ran upstairs and into the master bedroom. Finally, she allowed him to catch her in their bedroom, he threw her on the bed tickling her until she begged for mercy. He stopped then she pushed him onto his back and started tickling him, which didn't last long as he held her close to him.

Jack was perfect! He never demanded anything from her he was always tender to her, she could be as flirtatious and cheeky as she liked and he still respected her. If he spoke 'dirty' to her it was never in an unkind manner. She felt safe with him, so would often try any suggestions he had.

They lay there a few minutes. He caressed her face. He stood up and took her hand.

"Now… remember we can stop at any time." He reassured her.

That was all the bedrooms done, the lounge, the kitchen, and the utility room! She moaned and called out his name each time, now she was certain no one would hear. She had always stifled herself in the past few weeks, especially at her parents'.

Jackson ordered a takeaway. They 'ate' in the dining room, in their robes after he'd cleared the plates away, he came back with some whipped cream and chocolate sauce for Alva. Then after 'desert' he nipped upstairs to run a bath and light some candles and sprinkled some rose petals around.

"It wasn't a home until today and you came, it was just a place I lived, now it's home!" He told her sitting together in the bath.

They had marked each room in the house.

"When you said every room in the house, I didn't think you meant all in one day! I thought you meant over the course of the next days!"

"I did! You didn't tell me you wanted to stop… I thought you were making up for lost time!" he laughed.

"Is it bedtime yet!?" she half joked; she was exhausted.

"Alva Violet Moon! Are you still wanting more?"

"Jackson Wesley Maddox, I could never have enough of you! But I do think we should sleep.

Jackson got out of the bath and told her to wait a few minutes. He came to collect her. then blew out the candles.

He had put a tiny bottle of sparkling wine on the bedside table with a bottle of fruit infused water for himself with champagne flutes. The idea being they celebrate their first night together in their new home.

He had lit all the candles and there was a gift bag on the bed.

"Welcome home Honey! There's a small token for tonight, you've done so well today!"

He had bought her a beautiful dark purple silk negligee. She slipped into it; it hugged every curve.

"Thank you, Jack! It's beautiful! Thank you for today… I never thought I would find someone who could make me feel like you do. A man who wouldn't make me feel sordid or dirty!"

"Good! I never thought I would find a woman half as good as you Honey!"

She climbed in next to him. He offered her a glass of fizz and they toasted the start of their new life together.

Jackson wondered when the next lavender moon would be.

Chapter 22

Life was excellent since June; she had gone and got her social security number the next day and at the end of August Alva had joined Montgomery's band. Vaughn had always been offered to become a musician in the band, but said he was happy to be Montgomery's roadie, and would pick up an instrument if needed. This meant the whole family would immigrate. They started the process of becoming US citizens as soon as they were able to.

A date for an October wedding was written on calendars and in diaries, save the date cards were sent. The whole family had booked to move permanently the third week in September. The one request Jackson had made about the wedding was he would arrange all the music, and her bouquet.

The next thing she knew Alva opened her eyes. The Tennessee sun was flooding through the window at 'California'. She had a nervous excitement this morning it was a beautiful day. Today she would become Mrs Maddox. She was happier than she could ever imagine. She glanced over to the wedding dress hanging up behind the dark oak panelled door. She was in Jacobean room that Montgomery had decorated when Georgette had first stayed. Georgette had offered it to her, there seemed to be something romantic and magical about that room.

The wedding dress and bridesmaids' dresses had caused a worry for her at first. She was torn as who to ask to make and design her dress. Eventually Eduardo had collaborated on the designs with Georgette and then his team made them. Georgette had said although she wanted to it was a mammoth task and didn't think she would be able to get the dresses done in the time with her other orders, she only had three weeks from their move until the wedding, plus Eduardo had a large workforce and a number of highly skilled seamstresses. Eduardo was happy to design with Georgette, he loved her western designs, it would be easier to be able to share ideas online too. The designers were different styles but they had a huge respect for the other.

Montgomery had planned to stay with Jackson at his home, with the Common Ancestor lads; Vaughn had rolled into California during the early hours, merry from trying to 'educate' the guys about different cocktails. Montgomery had driven him home as he no longer drank alcohol. Sneaking his father up to bed before, nipping into his bedroom to make love to his beautiful wife whilst the baby slept in the adjoining nursery, then returning to his best man duties.

Alva rose and went down stairs it was half past five, the waft of coffee reminding her of all the times she stayed. Georgette was up with the baby, Kacey-Reba. Georgette looked up and smiled. Georgette passed the gurgling bundle to her aunt and made coffee for them both, Alva sat and fed niece a bottle of warm milk, she loved her niece and enjoyed doing these little things, it was the baby smell that would set her feeling broody, she would say her 'ovaries are pinging'.

Next Alison joined them. She was joyous, she was excited for her daughter. The girls from Common Ancestor joined them a while later and they all congregated in the dining room, enjoying the breakfast of croissants and pastries Georgette had laid on.

It was a bustle of sore heads over at Jackson's Everyone other than Jackson and Montgomery had been rip roaring drunk last night, Vaughn had also taught the guys several drinking games. Jackson stood, herbal tea in hand looking out into his garden admiring their organisational handy work. The marquee was up, the flooring was laid and the view beyond was a carpet of autumnal leaves covering the lawn, the trees a patchwork of colours. He and his family had arranged all the floral displays. Yesterday he had chosen Alva's flowers, some had to be ordered because of the season and he removed the thorns and they were safely at his parent's florist shop.

"Looks great! I'm glad she is marrying you, Jack! Brother-in-law!"

Montgomery appeared smiling; they had a lot to do that morning. They welcomed the caterers and had organised them to provide a groomsman breakfast. Montgomery decided the next job was to get the guys up and tidying. Jackson was still in his three-bedroom house and the male members of Common Ancestor were littering the living room floor. Beer cans and bottles were strewn around with empty take away boxes. Jack hastily started tidying ready for their guests.

"Sod this for a game of soldiers! They can do that!" Montgomery blurted out in his English accent. "It stinks in here!" Remembering the days that side of sober.

Montgomery started opening windows and curtains allowing the day light to wake them, he made a large pot of coffee, adding several extra scoops for luck and to try to help sober them up. Bodies began stirring, it was like a scene from a zombie movie without the gore.

"Guys! We need to get going! I know you are all hung over…but it's my sister's and my best mate's wedding and we could do with cleaning up!" He suggested.

The guys groaned and agreed. Sleepy eyes were rubbed and coffee drank. Once they had all woken up enough and paracetamol was taken, they packed up their sleeping bags and pillows and stored them away in their cars. The guys ate a full English breakfast, Jackson ate a small version. They then took turns to shower and shave in the two bathrooms, whilst the others took turns cleaning and hoovering and preparing the house. Jackson was thankful for such a large garden; it would easily accommodate the hundred odd people they had invited. Maxwell, his family, Rita, and Dirk arrived ready for the family wedding, with the flowers for themselves and the groomsmen. Some of the guests were part of Jackson's secret work too, although they were invited out of politeness and in a business capacity. Della was languishing in a secure psychiatric ward across the pond.

Jackson was getting more and more anxious as time passed. Montgomery kept reassuring him. Finally, they were ready and all looking good in their black velvet three-piece suits, with blue ties, they were doing alright. They sat chatting about the weather, business and country songs whilst waiting for the cars.

Dorraine arrived at 'California' with Alva's and the bridesmaids' bouquets, corsages, and button holes. The house was a cacophony of joy, bathrooms being occupied, doors shut and opened, the front door left on the latch for deliveries, make-up artists, hairdressers and the photographer. During the rest of the morning the bridesmaids, Georgette, Dorraine, Janey, Joanie, and Felicity were primed and prepped. Perfume wafted through the house. One by one the girls congregated in their lavender blue mismatched dresses in the bar room. Georgette eventually dressed Kacey-Reba as she didn't want the baby to mess up her dress. Georgette and Alva had found a pretty antique pram which they spray painted and could push the five-month-old down the aisle. Alva sat enjoying the attention in her white bathrobe. Once everyone was ready and she saw how lovely they looked she disappeared with Alison and Georgette to dress.

Vaughn enjoyed entertaining the ladies in the bar room, he made them all giggle with tales of Montgomery and Alva as children.

"She's ready!"

Georgette came and got Vaughn to go up and have a private, few moments with his wife and daughter.

Alva's dress was ivory, it had long tuille sleeves, a satin bodice with a sweetheart neckline and a full tuille skirt. There were embroidered swathes of lavender flowers across the bodice and trailing down the skirt. She had her hair in a French twist with a side fringe as she had the day of the CAMOEs. The make-up looked natural. Her veil matched her dress and she had a head dress of flowers that matched her bouquet. She had given Jackson a swatch of fabric for colour match.

Georgette gathered the girls at the bottom of the stairs and disappeared to change the baby's nappy, for some reason she used the office downstairs. There were oohs and aahs as Alva appeared. Just in the moment the photographer arrived. Alva was handed her bouquet of white roses and sprigs of lavender, no thorns. Jackson had made the bouquet himself she welled up a little.

Georgette saw a flash of a figure move silently across the door and toward the wedding party. Georgette heard the cock of a gun followed by Dorraine try and negotiate. Georgette was shaking as she heard Drake's boom echo around the silent hall.

"Did you think I would let you go that easily! You bitch!"

Georgette could see in the glass reflection him aiming the gun at Alva, Georgette silently moved around the office, hiding Kacey-Reba in the adjacent shower room, which doubled as a 'panic room'. Drake continued to rant about how he loved Alva and if he couldn't have her no one could, how he loved her so much he had escaped prison. He went on and on for half an hour shouting at her and screaming in her face.

"The panic alarm at California has been activated!" Montgomery looked at his phone, Jackson went pale, "The police are attending!"

Montgomery had a panic button installed when Della was harassing him, they had not even tested it, he tried to ring Georgette to no avail, the others tried the bridesmaids no one could answer. Montgomery decided to log in and look on the CCTV system and could see everything, his heart was in his mouth, his whole world was being taken hostage by Drake Trent, Jackson was fighting the groomsmen to see what was going on.

Suddenly Drake felt cold steel behind his ear.

"Drop the gun now! I will shoot you; no one comes into my home without my permission and threatens my family!" Georgette said loudly but firmly.

Emmy the dog who had been asleep in her basket sprang to life at the tone of her mistress's distressed voice that only she could hear, barked and launched herself at Trent locking her jaw around the wrist in which hand he held the gun. He swung his gun towards her and with one swift move Dorraine having watched Georgette signalling to her had him on the floor and arrested, within the next minute her colleagues had gained entry and were hauling him off. Emmy was going nuts at the appearance of police dogs in her home, but she soon settled as the other dogs quickly retreated with Drake in tow.

Montgomery had watched in horror and pride as his wife had ended the siege. Jackson was sobbing with relief, eventually he was calmed down and reassured, he was now in the car and on his way to the church.

After some reapplication of make-up after tears, the girls were all in their cars on their way with Alison, Alva and Vaughn were in the bridal car, he was reassuring his daughter everything was alright and Drake would be taken back to the UK and dealt with and how he escaped from prison needed to be investigated.

The church stood opposite a dual carriage way. It had a narrow-pointed spire, it was a pure white building, twelve miles and sixteen minutes away from Jackson's house. He had been allowed to marry there as becausc Rita and Dirk were active members of the church. The bridal cars rolled up. Montgomery greeted them outside. He was dressed this time in a black velvet ensemble with a white shirt and bow tie to match with the others but kept the aviators on and wore his famous Stetson outside the church, he had recently reverted to the beard again. He had toyed going for a complete change when he had married Georgette and had gone as far as shaving his beard off, but after a while he and Georgette thought the look was right for the fans.

Montgomery rushed and spoke to everyone checking his wife and child were safe then checked his parents and sister as well as the other girls.

"Is he here!?" Alva asked her brother that was all she seemed to be worried about.

"Yes, he's here! Are you OK?" Montgomery hugged her tight and reassured her. "I have a message for you from him. He says I have to tell you because he won't be able…"

"Is he still wanting to marry me?"

Montgomery laughed.

"Of course, he is still wanting to marry you… he can't wait! He told me to say 'DARN!' to you, because he knows you will look hot and he doesn't want to lose it in there, and also he can't say DARN! In church." Montgomery reassured her.

Alva laughed.

He smiled hugging his family and kissing his wife passionately being reminded of their wedding day.

"You look stunning Mrs Moon! You did so well in their today, I'm so proud of you, you did everything we rehearsed for an intruder!" he told her as he patted her buttocks through her dress and whispered in his wife's ear, "That dress is going to look nice on the floor later! I'm already anticipating getting you home, you deserve a reward!"

Georgette smirked at her flirtatious husband.

“Brantley and Maggie are here!” Montgomery told his parents who were pleased they had arrived.

Montgomery escorted his mum to her seat, then marched off to stand with Jack and the other groomsmen.

The church interior was a vision of white wooden pews and luscious wine colour carpet. The bridesmaids stood in the foyer. Georgette and Dorraine walked ahead with the pram. Felicity, Janey, and Joanie were handed a microphone each. A piano started a few notes.

Janey started singing, Elvis Presley’s: ‘Can’t Help Falling In Love.’ Then the others joined in harmonising, together with The Fishers, when they got to the part about taking his hand etc. Jackson soloed and Alva had joyous tears.

Promises were made and legalities met.

“I’m worried” Jackson whispered to her during the photos.

“What about?” Alva enquired.

“The saying… ‘To change the name but not the letter, is to marry for worse, and not for better.’ You’ve gone from Moon to Maddox”

“Doesn’t count, my real name was Deighton, or Drake depending on who’s name my grandma went with! It’s only Moon, because of ‘old moody’ there!” She smiled pointing to her brother.

Everyone drove or were driven back to the house for the reception, the event today with Trent pushed out of their minds, they were determined that he shouldn’t spoil it. Jack and Alva followed in their limousine. Jackson asked the driver to pull over and give them thirty minutes. He obliged and went for a walk.

“Right Mrs Maddox! Can we consummate our marriage!?” he pulled her on to his lap. His hand lifting the skirt of her dress.

"We can't! Can we?" she protested, but loving the idea.

"We can! I've told him thirty minutes… but the way you look I'll blow quickly!" He told her.

She giggled.

"What about the guests?" she asked.

"I told Montgomery I wanted to take you for a ride…"

Alva was shocked.

"…a ride around the city and ask you about buying another house… but he doesn't know we've already looked at some!" Jackson was laughing.

"Mr Maddox you are insatiable!"

"Only for you!"

Enjoying their privacy Jackson took the opportunity of consummating their marriage and to tell her how beautiful she looked. She told him how debonair he was and how she loved the song he arranged and his part in it.

"There's more to enjoy Honey!"

Jackson carried over the threshold, proud to have her as his wife. She hadn't lost any weight, but remained steady, Jackson didn't care.

They dined with a hot buffet meal. Montgomery announced the speeches. The younger children were settled with colouring books and crayons.

Vaughn started,

"Alison and I are very proud and pleased to give our daughter away to Jack today. I'll keep this short so those that do drink alcohol can all get celebrating. First of all, I'd like to mention our son Montgomery or Kenny as he was born… without him Alva would not have met Jack. Like all siblings there is rivalry… and competition and I think that had included Jack until our dear daughter-in-law Georgette came into our lives. I still believe Montgomery would, as he said, when he first knew he was to have a sibling 'prefer a puppy'.

Alva was and has always been in a rush. She was born two-weeks early and wasn't going to allow us to get to the hospital. She was born on the floor of my parents-in-law's bathroom as the ambulance crew were running up the stairs. She rushed her way through school, college, and university. She doesn't like queuing; she is the most impatient person I know! The thing she has waited for was Jackson. It took several months after they met to decide he was what she liked. Then eventually she fell for him, even though, there were reasons they shouldn't embark on this journey together. This is the only time my daughter has shown any patience, is when Jack has been involved. Jack, you clearly bring out the best in my daughter. I'd like to welcome you to our family and we wish you a life of happiness. I know you will be true to your word and always protect her, because you have clearly demonstrated you have!

Jack and Alva!"

It was Dirk, Jackson's dad's turn to make a speech.

"I'd just like to thank everyone here today for our son Jackson and our beautiful new daughter Alva. Rita and I feel he's made an excellent choice. It has taken him a long time for him to fall in love and we were worried he might never find happiness, true happiness at that and boy he did, she's lovely! Jack has fought a few battles and won, the most recent being the heart of this young lady.

Mom, Dorraine, Maxwell, their spouses Trey and Dawn and your nieces and nephews wish you a lifetime of happiness."

Dirk finished his short but heartfelt speech to a round of applause.

It was Jackson's turn; he didn't have a speech. He stood up with his microphone and started singing his own composition. It was titled. *'Once in a Lavender Moon'* he had added the legend of the heart shaped window and how rare a lavender moon was, as rare as her and her beauty. Alva couldn't help by shed tears of joy. He then toasted the bridesmaids and best man.

Through my window the moon looks mauve,
The image is like a painting in fauve.
The hue is startling and illuminates the night and,
just like you a beautiful sight.
my heart is full at the lunar event,
astronomy my passion well spent.

Then Once in a lavender moon,
I found the opportune,
under the heart of the North window that was clear,
it was then I asked for you take my name, my dear.
The legend it tells determine,
forever and always, we will be.

The periwinkle tint obscured my vision,
no longer am I at sentence in prison.
Like a dove I was set free,
you and I and constantly be.
For the sign came from the blue
and God then added a little pink hue.

Once on a lavender moon, the greatest event came,
my life will never know the same,
a gentle soul entered my life,
until eternity is over, I found my wife.

The moon was purple and round,
I knew then it was permanent love I had found,

a tinctured moon that shade,
showed me my fate had been laid.
My soul found its other piece
making one jigsaw complete,
I could not ask for more.

The moon looked painted the colour of iris,
a pretty bloom I couldn't miss.
Like a rose without any thorns to hurt,
you are truly a work of art.
I'll happily spend any of my wishes,
to keep all of your kisses.

It was on a Lavender moon that I met you.
moons of lilac occur so sparse,
so, I know our love forever will last.

It was now time for the best man's speech,

"How do I top that? You'd need to be a CAMOE winner to write stuff like that... Oh yeah, we both are!" He laughed; the crowd tittered "I met Jack when I first moved to Nashville. I went and had a look in his shop and got chatting to him, we had a such a long conversation as if we were old friends, that I forgot to buy anything. The next day I went back to buy two new guitars and a keyboard. He looked me up and down and told me to save my money. I thought he was trying to put me off becoming a star as he'd seen numerous spend out and go home, and I didn't have the 'look.' What he actually wanted was for me to buy the second-hand ones he kept out back and spend the rest in the bar with him. He was a fountain of knowledge and knew all the haunts and was well aware of the music industry.

I then managed... somehow... to get a record deal. Once I was making enough, I asked him to become my assistant, then, later my manager and producer. Not only is he the best at what he does, he became my best mate.

I remember meeting Alva, Mom was in bed at my grandparents' home the afternoon of her birth; apparently, I threw a tantrum of epic proportions for an eight-year-old and I had just been collected from school, wrapped in a shawl she was pink and wrinkled and bawled a lot! She still does! I still would prefer a puppy..." He laughed. "*...they do as they are told!*

I could tell you some silly things we did growing up, but mom and dad don't know and we're not too old to be told off, I won't grass on you Alva over mum's vase!... although it was really me who broke it.

I remember Alva coming to Nashville for a holiday and not telling me and causing trouble. A puppy wouldn't do that! She spent a lot of time with Jack and they became friends. She kept talking about him. Puppies don't go on about your best mate either! I had my ear chewed on several occasions as to how wonderful Jack was and he should get a pay rise. I also noticed Jack keep looking at her and I asked him if her was 'checking her out' he lied of course! She was and she is stunning and clearly has great genes. Eventually she went home and time passed by.

A while later she reappeared in Nashville after breaking up with some low life. She wanted to get away from him. Others said she just wanted the protection of her big brother. I think deep down she wanted Jack and the connection between them was so strong, she felt safe with him, like no other, so safe she could confide in him absolutely. Another few weeks of will they won't ensued. I wasn't happy at the idea at first but knew they were so right for each other. Jack finally asked her out on a date. That night I walked past the door to find them snogging on the porch. Over the course of the months, they tried to have a secret relationship... yet it was obvious to most people they were deeply in love. At Christmas they were told we all knew.

The best way I can describe them are blatant liars. Neither could ever lie to me and still can't. He told me he was taking her for a 'ride' around the city on the way home earlier...I doubt it was innocent, I'm guessing they can't keep their hands to themselves and why they were late."

Alva blushed. There were woos and whistles from the guests and Jackson grinned. Alison and Vaughn shot Montgomery a look for being crude, but he would get away with it, for today.

"They were made for each other and I wish them a lifetime of happiness. I'd like you to all be upstanding to toast the bride and groom. Mr and Mrs Maddox."

"Mr and Mrs Maddox!" everyone chorused.

It was time for their first dance. Jackson, had put on a headset microphone and started singing another Elvis classic: 'I Just Can't Help Believing.' Montgomery and Common Ancestor sang back-up.

Chapter 23

After six months marriage Jackson and Alva started trying for a baby. Alva arranged to have her IUS removed. They started that night. They were aware that becoming pregnant may take longer than the average couple because of her PCOS. After those six months faded into a year Alva was frustrated. She had hoped pregnancy would have occurred by now. They arranged to have a few tests for Jackson and everything was with the normal ranges. Alva started trying different things in order to conceive.

Jackson had been working hard with Montgomery writing and producing songs, he had been invited onto a talk show with Montgomery after a documentary about Montgomery had been aired and Jackson had featured heavily. Two weeks later Lizine arrived in Tennessee and tracked him down to his house.

Alva had opened the door to a woman with a young boy about the age of ten,

"Hi, is… er… Jack about?"

Alva called Jack and saw his face drop. Alva made herself scarce but could hear the conversation.

"Go and play in the garden whilst Mommy talks to Daddy…" she heard her telling the boy.

Alva collapsed on the stairs stifling her sobs with her fist.

"I told you when you wrote, he can't possibly be mine… unless you drugged me and I didn't know!" Jackson was firm in his answer. "We'll get a DNA test and I will prove he's not mine!"

Alva didn't like the arguing, Jackson sounded like a different person. If this child was his Alva was worried, he would take to the boy and Alva was jealous. She hated herself for feeling envious, she knew it would be wrong to deny a child his father but she hated the thought of having to share her 'Jack' with 'them' especially if she couldn't give him a baby herself!

"I can't possibly be his father… we never!"

"Well how come I remember you the night before you left?"

"It wasn't me! I'm telling ya, it wasn't me!"

The argument continued for an hour. Then Lizine left and threatened them with court, Jackson was adamant he was not the father.

Alva was silent the rest of the evening Jackson tried to talk to her but she kept bursting into tears, she felt betrayed.

"You told me you were a virgin!" she admonished.

"I was until you! Unless she drugged me…" he remonstrated back.

"So how come you are the father!"

"I don't know!"

Alva slept in a separate room that night.

Over the next few days Jackson contacted the other guys that had worked on Lizine's farm and planned a reunion. Alva hardly spoke those weeks before the boys came on a visit, during the time he got the DNA results and kept them secret.

The day of the reunion arrived and he set up a Barbeque in the garden, the men were instructed to come on their own. Lizine arrived with Ryan.

They all settled at Jacksons eating and drinking. Jackson observed everyone. Montgomery and Georgette arrived, Ryan was a huge fan of his and Jackson had planned that his boss whisk the child out of the way so he could talk to everyone. They all sat in the living room reminiscing, Alva stood up to leave them but Jackson insisted she wanted to hear what he was going to say.

"So… Lizine found me to claim Ryan is our son… presumably because I have come into the spotlight of late… perhaps she wanted Ryan to meet Mont or perhaps she thought I had money…" the other men shifted in their seats.

Lizine turned a flush shade of scarlet and felt as if she was on fire from embarrassment. Jackson continued,

"I'm not here to make accusations, but discover the truth for everyone… the DNA test as you know Lizine, I'm undisputedly NOT the father… but guessing the dates… I'm wondering if it's someone else in the room?"

Seemingly Jackson had not been the only one singled out for Lizine's lusts. A few arguments followed and one of the men confessed to taking her when she could just about consent, and thought he was Jackson after her memory was cleared, she remembered and Jackson left it at that, after which the party fizzled out.

Alva was relieved, but there was hurt and damaged trust between them, he felt Alva hadn't trusted him. It would take a while for Alva and Jackson to get over the hurt, they were both innocent in this.

Was there more he needed to tell her?

***

Alva and Jackson lay in bed hugging. They had now been trying for eighteen months. Jackson was happy with the trying and left the outcome to his higher power. Alva tried hard to control it much to Jackson's dismay. He kept repeating if it was meant to be it would.

"I went to the doctor the other day… all they go on about is my weight… they tell me if I want a baby, I need to lose weight… I try…but I can't stop binging! I tell them I need help but the answer is always I can't want a baby enough If I can't lose the weigh, I just can't stop eating. Mont's answer to everything is a twelve-step fellowship! I ain't 'God squad'! If there is one, is he punishing us for sex outside marriage?" she started to sob.

"It'll happen when it happens… are you thinking about looking? They do work if you work them. You know people who live in the solutions of twelve-steps" he reminded her. "You know twelve steps are non-religious? You can be any religion, atheist, or agnostic? It's about you believing in your own higher power, whatever that is? If you believe in a Christian God then yes sex before marriage is a sin… but that God forgives if you repent."

"I don't think I believe in anything… why doesn't 'It' whatever it is not give us a baby?"

She had a point and a right to feel angry and bereaved. But then why not her?

Every month or there abouts, well somewhere between twenty-three and thirty-five days she would receive from mother nature and dissolve into floods of tears at the thought of her body failing her yet again. The medics kept saying if she was having periods then she could conceive, it meant her body was capable, yet was producing anovulatory cycles. Of course, they were 'doing it right' well-meaning people kept offering advice on how to get pregnant. Alva's PCOS wasn't having any of it. The pair of them had been worn down by the questioning from friends about 'when are you going to have a baby' and 'are you doing it properly?' It wasn't through lack of trying, and there wasn't anything they didn't know. They had done everything under the sun, but it wasn't happening. Each time there was a question or a comment Alva would sit quietly and try not to burst into tears and Jackson would try and steer the conversation elsewhere.

When Montgomery had said about twelve-step fellowships, Alva had looked some up. There were several online which would suit her. Jackson had tried to support her dieting and she had lost small amounts but it was torture. The results wouldn't last more than a few days before the inevitable binge. Each time the periods in between her keeping to a diet got shorter, nothing ever seemed to work. She had heard from Montgomery that most of the fellowships were based on his and she knew Jackson had a copy of the 'big book' in his study. She took it down from the shelf and looked through. What Jackson had said to her about not letting the religious bit sway her played on her mind. She found the chapters in the book which spoke about that part and felt reassured.

It was time. She logged on to a meeting in Jackson's study. The meeting happened to coincide with the same time Jackson attended a meeting, he would always go the bedroom and sit at the dressing table with his laptop. Jackson had mentioned he was in fellowship but never told her which one. Alva had always thought it was an Alcoholics Anonymous meeting as he was t-total.

Alva logged on and was surprised then totally floored to see Jackson in the meeting. She couldn't say anything. All she did was nervously introduce herself, say she was new and sat and listened. Jackson happened to be giving a chair that day. A chair often is a person with significant recovery who carries the message, by sharing, their experience, strength and hope. Alva sat and listened with a face of thunder. She felt he was in this secret club she knew nothing about and yet she realised she desperately needed. HE KNEW she needed yet he said nothing. No wonder he was careful with his food, she had thought it was because he was diabetic.

"I'm Jack, I'm a compulsive overeater, I'm a sugar addict, a food addict, and a caffeine addict. I'd like to welcome our newcomers…

… I have had a weight problem as long as I can remember. When I was twenty-one, I had moved to Chicago and my world came crashing down, I ended up homeless and without means. I needed to come back to home in Tennessee, but had no means and I was too ashamed that life hadn't gone the way I expected it to. I had to walk back, that and lack of food my weight dropped drastically. I was starving. When I eventually got home people remarked on how well I looked, that was their way of commenting on the drastic weight loss. I felt good at first. Then the demons set in. I began to eat extra, not only because I have this vile disease, but because I spent weeks hungry not knowing when my next meal would be. I put back what I had lost and more.

I was off the proverbial 'wagon' again…

Alva listened, shocked.

…After years of unsuccessful weight loss ideas, I was rock bottom, I decide I then consigned that I would remain overweight forever as diets do not work and are harder with each attempt. I was diagnosed with type two diabetes about four years ago. I had a seriously high BMI! My physician kept trying to encourage me to lose weight, whatever I did I just couldn't put the food down. It had a hold over me. I knew I needed help. I knew a lady who had lost a lot of weight and I asked her how she did it. I was attracted. She suggested I try six meetings to see if it was for me and I felt I was home...

…When I first joined a meeting. To say I was nervous was an understatement, I was anxious about the term 'God' not actually understanding at that time it referred to a 'higher power of my understanding. It was reassuring that every meeting I went to people were sharing things I could relate to. I came back for the comradery… I was no longer alone! I was drawn to similar stories and became aware of the solution, that didn't involve any harsh punishing gruelling practices. Now I focus on the program and not my weight. I found I was drawn to particular person at a meeting I asked if they would sponsor me, which they did…"

Alva listened to all the similarities of her husband's story.

"…I read as much literature as I can and when I can. I meditate and pray each morning and night, I ask God as I understand God what their will is for me and what I can do each day to help a fellow sufferer, I also try and state my gratitude to them...

…I'm over three years in program, I was lucky and got abstinent in the first month. I am well my diabetic blood tests are of normality…

…I don't know my weight because that is my higher power's business and not mine. I do one day at a time and I am willing. I have two fellows I sponsor, and give service where I can, these are monumental in my recovery, I give as much as I can when I can, and so eternally grateful to have a life I can live…

…I keep working my steps. Not every day is perfect some days It's perfectly imperfect and some days are hard and some are better. I wouldn't give up my worst day in program for my best day in the food. Thank you for listening and inviting me to chair this meeting."

Jackson talked for ten minutes. Alva sat stunned. She was confused, she felt all emotions: proud he had got help and how far he'd obviously come, she was angry he had not told her, shocked. It explained a lot of things about things he had done or said, why he only drank herbal tea or water, why there were no bathroom scales in the house.

She continued to listen and made a few notes. Jackson could see in her face she felt betrayed, he had to remember he wasn't responsible for her reaction. Perhaps he should run it through his step four but he had been trying to stick to the eleventh tradition of attraction rather than promotion.

Alva found some of the shares, harrowing because she recognised the food behaviours she had.

The meeting ended with the serenity pray and a few people stayed online for fellowship. They were all very chatty. There was a lady called Rhonda who was a newcomer greeter and emailed a grateful Alva a welcome pack. Jack logged out and sat in the bedroom wondering the best way to handle things. He put a call into Paul his sponsor and talked it out with him and then sat quietly and prayed.

Meanwhile Alva was chatting to Rhonda and asking questions. She thanked Rhonda for her time and service then logged out. She sat for a moment before getting up to make herbal tea for him and a coffee for herself. She took them through to their lounge and sat waiting for him.

He eventually came down and stood watching her from the doorway. She saw him and stood up and walked over to him. He wasn't sure what she might do. She wrapped her arms around his neck and dissolved in to tears.

"You! You could have told me! I was suffering and you could have told me!" she raged hitting her fists on his chest.

"I know, but I didn't want to force it on you. You've got to want it. I have to try and keep to the principles… it's attraction rather than promotion. I'm sorry if you think I have let you down."

"Oh Jack! I'm so bloody proud of you though! I could have supported you!"

"You knew I was in a twelve-step fellowship!"

"I thought it was AA as you don't drink alcohol"

"I don't drink alcohol because I'm addicted to sugar! I thought you realised by the way I cook and don't eat certain ingredients." He explained.

"I thought that was because of your diabetes!"

"Are you going to try anymore meetings?" He kissed her head.

"I guess? I am sure it's for me though."

"Don't rush or feel pressure because I am in fellowship you have to want it!"

They stood there holding one another. From that moment Alva became abstinent. She found a sponsor the next day, someone they knew very well, she handed it over to God and started her steps.

Chapter 24

Three painful and frustrating years had passed since Alva and Jackson had started trying for a family. She knew every secret Jackson had or so she thought. They had every test going, scans, blood tests, sperm counts, internal investigations and even exploratory operations and everything came back normal other than Alva's medical problem. She had been slowly working her programme. She found Joanie from Common Ancestor was in the same fellowship was willing to sponsor her. They chatted each day, but no one else from their circle knew. Who you saw and what you heard at meetings stayed there! It was a relief to listen to the stories when she joined a meeting, she focused on the similarities and not the differences.

Time ticked on for Jackson's secret work, this past year he hadn't seemed to get any further than he was, people were relying on him to get things wrapped up, Della was still imprisoned for a couple of lesser charges, she still hadn't been tried for murder, she was due out in a few weeks, but the police could never pin those murders on her, it was all hear-say evidence. Her extradition from the United Kingdom seemed to take forever, she had a very clever solicitor, Lucas Aspinall who somehow managed to stall things several times. Jackson wanted to keep Della where she belonged and knew there were complicit people, he just needed to prove it, Bryan was at the top of his list.

Alva internalised a lot of her thinking.

The pressure and grief had gotten too much and she disappeared, that mid-June day. Jackson had arrived home to a note to say she had gone. He telephoned around, her parents and Montgomery and no one had seen or heard from. He was sick with worry. Since she had left to live in Nashville, she had little contact with people from England and he had to wait until his morning which was their lunchtime to phone her friends and no one had seen her. He asked his sister Dorraine, the police officer and she tried to work out where she could be.

In Montgomery's study, Jackson was sitting with Georgette and his brother-in-law. It had been almost twelve hours, and as time passed the more worried, they became.

"Wasn't Alva here that day? She was using the computer in here." Georgette piped up.

Georgette trawled through the internet history, contorting her lips. Jackson continued with a frantic monolog of worry. She glanced at the key hooks in the office. A set of 'Carolina's' keys were missing. Georgette logged into the cameras at the house. She could see her in the living room crying on the couch. Georgette's heart broke at the image.

"I know where she is!" She took a coin off the desk and flipped it "Heads 'Carolina'? Tails 'California'?"

Montgomery had named his two homes referencing the Jo Dee Messina song and as England was geographically north of Tennessee was how he had chosen each name.

"She's not here so it must be heads!" Montgomery said.

With that she disclosed to Jackson about Alva's fears of him leaving her if she couldn't bare him a child, the situation with Lizine hadn't helped those years ago either.

No matter how she had reassured her sister-in-law she couldn't allay her fears. She also said that morning Alva had seen her specialist and wasn't quite right but Georgette hadn't had the chance to ask her before Alva had called out cheerfully that she was going. The printer was now whirring to life and with that a heavily pregnant Georgette, who was on baby number two hauled herself up. She passed Jackson the set of keys for the English residence and handed him the paperwork from the printer.

"I've booked you the next flight, but you have time to get home and pack. Mont will run you to the airport. I'll send him along shortly. I'm guessing you don't want to split up" she told him.

Jackson shook his head, thanked her bounded to the door. After a minute they heard his car start outside the engine roaring to life like a cheetah was about to speed after its prey. Georgette turned to Montgomery.

"Get him to the airport, make sure he is there, but please don't be too long… I think something might be happening." She pointed to her bump. "I'm feeling uncomfortable like I did with Kacey-Reba and we know how quick she was. I'm going to ring your Mum and Dad, get them over and explain about Alva. That way if you are strapped for time, I can have one with me and one with Kace." She planned with him.

Montgomery kissed her and she promised to keep in touch. He raced to his buddy's house, dodging all the people that seemingly wanted to get in his way, to get him where he needed to be and dash back home. Flashes of his first daughter's traumatising birth played through his mind. Georgette was firm to get him to get Jackson back to Alva but he didn't want her going through that again especially if she was on her own.

Jackson was outside waiting with his holdall at the gate, he packed a few changes of clothes, anticipating he would just get Alva and return. He was pacing up and down the path and rubbing lavender between his fingers thinking about his own lavender moon. Jackson wasted no time in jumping in the truck as it screeched to a halt sending a cloud of dust up. Why was the traffic so busy. Why are all the idiots out today Montgomery kept thinking? This journey was hazardous, too many near misses. Jackson was worried. The sixteen minutes it would take felt like hours as they sped along interstate 65.

"Sorry, Jack, I just want to get you to Alva and Georgette's gone into labour!" Montgomery blurted out.

"Bro! I would have got a taxi! Why didn't you say!?" Jackson chastised him.

"You know what Georgette is like. She wants you two sorted out and wouldn't let me tell you!"

Jackson smiled. Montgomery's phoned pinged.

"Can you check it please Jack?" he asked as he chucked it at him.

"It's from your dad: I'm with Kacey-Reba. Mum taking Georgette to the hospital. Waters have gone. She's ok… Mont you just drop me here and I can do the rest. I'll let you know what happens." Jackson told him.

"No! we are two minutes away and I promised Georgette, I would see you to the terminal. and I always keep my promises!"

A few minutes later they were at the drop off point. Jackson had the door open as the car was moving and grabbed his holdall from the back seat.

"Good luck and let me know!" Jackson called.

"Same to you buddy!" Montgomery smiled and waved.

Now to go and get to my girl, the men thought in unison!

Montgomery rushed and got to the hospital and found the delivery room. Alison was with Georgette supporting her. The contractions were coming thick and fast. He saw the relief on Georgette's face as he entered the room. Alison moved away from the bed and Montgomery enveloped his wife in his big, strong, muscular arms. Alison ducked out of the room to allow some privacy and within a couple of minutes she heard her second granddaughter scream the ward down.

Alison's phone bleeped. Vaughn messaged her.

Double celebration. Brantley has a son. Anthony Kenneth Clayton 7lb 6oz, born 1:30 am BST. said we will tell Mont and Alva.

Alison replied.

"Just heard our grandchild being born. Mont just made it! Will update you soon."

Montgomery appeared in the door and beckoned her into the room

"Meet, Kelsea-Dolly! 7lb 6oz" He smiled passing the baby to his mum.

"I wouldn't have minded you staying Mum." Georgette told her.

She now referred to Alison as 'Mum' and Vaughn as 'Dad' they always had given her unconditional love.

"No worries, I would have if Mont hadn't gotten here on time. But you should have as much privacy as you can. It's a special moment for you both." She sat holding the baby smiling. She suddenly started laughing.

"7lb 6oz?" she queried.

"Why?" asked Montgomery puzzled.

"Look at the message Dad sent to me!" she laughed.

Montgomery laughed and showed it to his wife. He then facetimed his dad and then his cousin.

"Hey congratulations!" he said as Brantley answered. "We have some news of our own!" he switched the camera round and introduced the child. "Guess how much she weighed?"

Georgette spoke to Maggie and they compared notes. She updated her about Alva.

***

Jackson text Montgomery to let him know he was in the country and now waiting for a taxi. Montgomery text him the news of the two latest additions, but said none of them would let Alva know and allow him time to talk to her so he could let her know.

The house could be reached by a drive from a narrow winding road, it was an eight bedroomed mock Tudor mansion with security gates. It was slightly smaller in size to the Nashville home; this home was typically British in style. It had been built in the 1930's and had a solid oak door. It was double fronted the grand stairs faced you as you went in either side of the hall were reception rooms, a WC and a large double aspect kitchen, gym, barroom, and music room to the side. The downstairs was carpeted in plush pure wool carpet, with the kitchen, bar room, gym in wooden parquet and the music room had been built for the acoustics and had a little area for relaxing with a little black two-seater settee

It was dark driving down those lonesome, winding country roads in Essex. He saw the sign for the house and directed the driver to pull up at the gate. Hopping out of the cab, the security lights came on he carried his bag and the flowers he bought at the airport up the drive and quietly opened the door. The house was in pitch darkness, like the surrounding countryside and like the rural area it was quiet and lonely at that time of night. He looked in every room and crept up the stairs not wanting to make a sound. He wasn't absolutely sure she was there; it was so soundless. As he got to the top of the stairs, he could hear loud sobs coming from her room. He opened the door and could see her laying in the bed.

"I'm here now Alva Honey!" He softly called her she looked round and smiled weakly and let out more howls. Jackson slipped his shoes off and climbed in next to her wrapping his arms around her waist. He could feel her anguish.

She showed him her phone, news had already broken about the babies being born. He laid and held her as she sobbed.

"I'm hurting too" he told her.

"I know you want a baby, that's why I walked. I want you to have the joy of being a dad. You should find someone who can bare your children."

"I've handed this baby thing over to God. If it's God's, will it will happen with perfect timing!" He remarked.

He held her tight.

"I'm not going anywhere… it's you I want… babies are a bonus! You are not on your own! As for you finding out about the babies it wasn't supposed to be general knowledge, we were all waiting until I had told you before they announced it so there must be leaks somewhere. I love you no matter what! I always have and I always will. I'm proud of you doing your steps, you've come so far, Honey."

He continued to hold her and she fell asleep in his arms.

The morning dawned and Alva quietly made breakfast after facetiming Montgomery to see her niece. She tried hard not to cry and held it together long enough. She then texted her good wishes to Brantley who then telephoned them immediately. Brantley explained he was really stuck and needed help. Brantley knew they were a couple of miles down the road. Maggie was unwell and he needed to take her to the hospital and they didn't want to take a new-born baby and a toddler with them to the hospital.

"I understand that it might be difficult for you given your issues… but I need your help. There is no one else we can trust to have them… everyone else is sick or out of the country, the Francis family are on holiday in New Zealand, Val and Dave have a stomach bug and Tessa had just had an emergency gall bladder removal… Mags won't just leave them with any random babysitter or nanny from an agency however qualified they are!" he explained to her.

Alva started flitting around putting shoes on.

"Brantley we're on our way!"

"Thanks, the midwife has just called an ambulance. Thanks so much!"

She turned to Jackson and explained. They gathered themselves and jumped into Montgomery's brown two-tone Silverado truck and drove the few miles to the castle like house in the middle of the countryside. She reminded Jackson to drive on the left. As they rode up the drive, they saw the ambulance loading Maggie in the back.

"Don't worry Mags, I'm here. The kids will be ok with me." she waved to her. Maggie weakly waved back she was flushed and looked poorly.

Brantley gave a few instructions regarding the baby and little Martha, the toddler.

"Let me know what's happening… no rush! We can be here as long as you need us." Alva reassured him, giving him a hug.

Brantley climbed in to his red Aston Martin to go to the hospital and sped off, leaving the family car in case it was needed.

That afternoon Alva and Jackson took the greatest care of the two children and played with them. Jackson did a few jobs around the house like unloading the dishwasher and hoovering and did some laundry for them. He didn't put them away he just carefully folded all the bits into the laundry basket. He wanted to help, but not to be intrusive.

Alva appeared in the doorway.

"Brant's just telephoned. She has an infection and are going to give her some IV antibiotics now and then some this afternoon and discharge her home this evening. I would like to offer to stay and help only if you are OK with it and they want to." She told Jackson.

"Fine with me, but no more than three days! Don't use this as an excuse not to talk about our situation!"

"I won't!" she promised him. She text Brantley:

Jack and I would be willing to be available to you and Mags for the next few days if you want us. We can help until Mags is better, cook meals, housework etc and any childcare needed. No pressure just an offer.

A while later Brantley replied:

Thank you so much! We would be very grateful for your offer and would love to spend time with you. If it works better, you are welcome to stay with us, or happy to pay for daily travel and any expenses

Alva replied with:

Happy to stay with you if ok and not invading. No need to pay for anything.

Jackson was happy to see his wife felt valued and useful in the family and suggested he pop out and buy some groceries a card and gifts, then they could make dinner. While out he would pick up their clothes from Carolina.

Maggie returned as the June sun was thinking about setting in a couple of hours to the aroma of a roast dinner. She was touched at

Alva's thoughtfulness; it was something she would have done herself for another person in the past. The children had been well looked after and Martha had a bath and was cuddling between Alva and Jackson on the couch looking at a book and drinking her bedtime milk. Anthony was in his Moses basket swaddled and asleep. Alva went and made tea whilst Brantley settled Maggie. Alva and Jackson had made up a bed on the three-seater settee ready for Maggie's return. Maggie made herself comfortable and was having cuddles with Martha.

Brantley appeared at the kitchen.

"Brantley dinner is done. It just needs serving up. If you are ready? Martha has eaten."

"Thanks Alva… we are both really hungry! I was going to order takeaway! That smells divine! We're ready now if you like. You will join us?"

"Where would you like dinner?"

"We'll slum it and have it on our knees in the lounge, is that alright with you?"

Alva laughed and nodded.

"I will see to any of the children if they need anything until you have eaten and then we will go to bed and give you privacy." Alva brightly smiled.

"I'd like to offer you the room under the observatory. I think Jack might enjoy looking at the full moon tonight!" Brantley knew Jackson was interested in astronomy too.

"We are happy to be called if you want help. I need to talk to Jackson. We're trying to sort stuff out." Alva reassured.

Brantley hugged his cousin and said he understood. He was so glad they were there to help and tomorrow they had to allow him to treat them to a takeaway. Brantley knew the situation about the fertility problems and was sympathetic.

Maggie and Brantley enjoyed their dinner and homemade apple pie and custard. Jackson and Alva made their excuses and went to bed in Brantley's old bedroom with its ensuite, and staircase to the sky.

Alva and Jackson lay there talking

"I spoke to my sponsor earlier. I'm sorry, I could have told you my fears and trusted you… I know for this situation my low self-esteem, critical thinking, resentment, fear, self-pity, impatience, and negative thinking that are on my grosser defects list all play a part. I am praying on them and asking them to be removed. I know I just need to hand it over and pray on it. I can't control the outcome. I feel better knowing you won't walk. Thank you, Jack, for being you. I appreciate you coming over four-thousand miles and one left turn to tell me you are not leaving. I'm sorry for my lack of trust." She explained. "I would like to make a living amends by talking to you about things and not running without telling you!"

"I would travel to the ends of the earth for you! Anyway, I think there is God in this… we ended up being of service to Brant, Mags, Martha, and Anthony. Don't you think we were placed? Brant said there was no one else able to help." He expressed.

Alva finally settled herself to surrender any pregnancy that may be. The Maddox's lay the rest of the night in meditation, the bed was relaxing and comfortable and sleep came quickly.

In the dead of night Alva and Jackson woke to the baby crying, then she heard Martha crying and got out of bed and went into her nursery and put her dummy back in her mouth and pacified her.

"Auntie Alva's here sweetie…there's a good girl!" she soothed as Martha settled back to sleep. East London people would often use Auntie and Uncle as an address for children of close friends and for older cousins.

"Thanks!"

She heard her cousin's voice behind her. It was nice to feel useful but she knew she could come across as trying to take over and her helpfulness as overbearing, it was her 'people pleasing', she returned to her room and tried to keep herself in check. Jackson rolled over and kissed her, before she knew it, she was wrapped around his member and he was inside her making love to her husband. As she found herself unwinding, she felt a hand over her mouth and fell about giggling.

"Alva Violet Maddox! You are too loud when we make love!" he whispered with a smile.

They lay in an embrace for a while, then Jackson got out of bed and pulled on his pyjama bottoms.

"Come!" He pointed upstairs.

Alva sat up and pulled on her nightie, her feet hitting the luxurious carpet in the bedroom, he took her hand, and lead her up the winding stairs with the dark wood barley twist banisters, there were no street lights in the area, so the stars were bright and moon was full illuminating the night. Looking through the telescope, the moon took on a purple tinge.

"See that Mrs Maddox? That's what I mean by a 'lavender moon'! A very rare sight, even rarer tonight, it's a 'super lavender moon' and very special like you! I'm going to go back down and open the curtains so we can see it as we lay in bed. Then I will look at the moon and pray some more, show my gratitude you are here in my arms and you are mine. I will drink your scent in whilst watching the 'lavender moon'."

She enjoyed spending time with her cousin and his family the next day. Jackson had a lot in common with Brantley, both men were interested in astronomy, Jackson was impressed with Brantley's telescope, he had one but was nowhere near Brantley's quality. He had allowed Jackson to spend the past evening in the observatory. The men chatted over a drink, Jackson told him everything about their fertility issues. Brantley listened like Maggie had taught him to and patted his friend on the back. They looked through the telescope and Jackson spoke about the 'lavender moon,' just sometimes it would look mauve, but it wasn't a recognised astrological phenomenon. Brantley agreed.

"There isn't anything I can say to make it seem better. I hope it does work out for you both, any kid would be lucky to have you as parents." Brantley told him.

He was right there was nothing that could be done. They could try and throw more money at the problem; they could buy doctors and treatments. Jackson wasn't short of money, since becoming Montgomery's manager and producer the money kept rolling in and the royalties from the odd song, he had collaborated on would come as a bonus occasionally. Alva too was making money working for her brother, she too had written a couple of his recent massive hits. Love at Last Shot and I Can't Answer Your Song. They had thought about and bought the services of the best people and tried several treatments to no avail. They all had kept on about Alva's weight. Jackson loved her whatever her size, but knew she was ill with it. It wasn't as simple as starting a diet, it was like eating was her default setting. I was hard to describe to someone who didn't have an eating disorder the nature of the beast. She had been concentrating on the program and became abstinent that first week. It was clear that by the grace of her higher power the weight was melting away from her. He had pride in her she was facing her demons; he was as proud of her as she was of him.

They had arrived back at 'Carolina' late morning. Alva had promised she wouldn't stay more than three nights, and felt two was enough. She had changed all the beds before she left washing and drying them all and remaking all the beds. She used her time with the Claytons as a distraction. It was time to get to a meeting for both of them. They decided they would join the same meeting at one o'clock after lunch, British Summer Time, which was 7am in their hometown of Brentwood, Williamson County, Tennessee about twelve miles from the city of Nashville and four from Montgomery's in Oak Hill. They could join their usual early morning meeting, but it was strange seeing everyone this time of day. They sat together on the same computer. It was easier than using their phones. It surprised some usual members, but they wouldn't ever remark other than it was nice to see them both. Rhonda asked how they both were.

"My wife and I are holidaying in England." Jackson answered.

Alva waved.

"It's lovely to be able to help my cousin and his wife who just had a baby and has a toddler!" She chimed in.

A few days passed by, they decided to return to Nashville. Alva was excited to see her nieces but felt embarrassed she bolted. She explained to her family that she had a problem with food and that it wasn't only her PCOS making her hungry. She found some more meetings convenient for her.

Jackson resumed his work with Montgomery. Those months saw a breakthrough in his other work —

Chapter 25

Alva and Jackson's fourth wedding anniversary, rose with the sun that morning highlighting the gold, red and orange tones of the autumn leaf carpet spread across their lawn. She had given him a plectrum box made from fruit wood. He had bought her some more lavender bushes for their garden. The fourth anniversary was traditional to give fruit or flowers. They were careful to never exchange food gifts.

Alva's weight had dwindled, in the two years she had been in recovery she kept to the program and was working her second set of steps with her sponsor. She didn't know how much she weighed or had lost, that was God's business not hers, or that of a medical professional. Clearly a significant amount was clear to see. Although the program was clear that God was a higher power of one's own understanding and that could come in many forms for the individual, Alva had decided she chose a Christian view of God and came to believe that Jesus Christ was her saviour. Jackson had grown up in a very religious household and although had rebelled against this growing up, at the time of his marriage to Alva had found his way back into the fold and prayed Alva would too, she wasn't quite ready to join the congregation of the church in which they married. Jackson went to church alone on a Sunday, and meet with his parents and hoped Alva would get a miracle and join them too. She was on step nine and hoped that Ella would pop into her life so she could make amends for the way she had spoken to her back then, she wasn't in possession of the facts.

Alva's heart felt like a loaded gun that morning. She was due at the medical plaza at 10:30 to have her coil put back in. She had given up hope of getting pregnant and the longer she was without the device the more trouble her periods were or scanty they seemed odd recently. Alva hadn't had a 'proper' period for a while, occasionally this would occur, once a year followed by a massive flood, although the past few were extremely light and sporadic and she had hardly bled. She and Jackson agreed that she would have it back on medical advice and would try again in two years. She had gone alone; Montgomery had dropped her off. Jackson had other priorities that day, he was collecting a special gift, he had commissioned for their anniversary. He wanted to show her he was not going anywhere; his other job would be soon over.

Jackson had arranged to collect her at 11:30am and drive her to a restaurant to meet up with Montgomery, Georgette, Brantley, and Maggie for lunch, before they all made plans for the latter couple's holiday with them. The four children had been left with Alison and Vaughn, who were in their element.

The others were being driven to the meet up by Montgomery.

Jackson paid and slipped the gift in his denim jacket, he was happy that morning, he had also gone to the police station and handed in all the paperwork he had collated over the dealings of Della, her husband Bryan and many of the Pagwell record executives, he was asked to be a key witness should they require. He was going to tell Alva and Montgomery briefly as soon as people were in custody, he was pleased to finally slot the final piece into the jigsaw.

It seemed all the idiots were out driving, reminding him of the day Montgomery had taken him to the airport to seek Alva during that breakdown. It was a dicey journey he was already behind time and Alva always being in a rush wouldn't appreciate being at the restaurant last. He turned on the radio and smiled, reports were starting to come in about raids at Pagwell records and arrests being made, Bryan Pagwell, Della's husband was the first name that emerged with the words murders and embezzlement. It was reported that from prison Della was singing like a caged bird!

Alva stood outside the medical plaza in stunned state of shock, unaware of the drama her husband had caused that morning, they now had their own situation to deal with. She was shaking with what the doctor had just told her. She had just sat nodding, confused, and dazed. She had the pieces of paper proof in her purse. She took them out and looked again at them and burst into tears.

Where was Jack, she wanted him here could she bring herself to tell him? She had another appointment tomorrow for tests and she would need Jackson with her.

Jackson looked at the clock on the dashboard. He was late. He was driving to collect her, he knew she would be annoyed, but hoped his news would soften the blow a little, Della would no longer be trying to sue Montgomery for breach of contract as she had been trying to do so for the past few years and kept coming up with things against him and causing trouble between him and Georgette, at least now Georgette trusted Montgomery implicitly there was no way she believed a word that came from Della's mouth. Della had even made out she was pregnant with Montgomery's child at one point, producing fake scans and doctors' letters, when no child was born, she claimed a miscarriage from the stress.

Jackson's phone rang, he switched on the hands free.

"Jack, are you coming? I NEED you!" her voice was shaky.

"I'm on my way Honey, how are you feeling?"

"I couldn't have it done; they wouldn't let me… there's an issue." she cried.

He could hear the emotion in her voice.

"I'll be there soon… whatever it is we will get through it…"

The line went dead.

During those moments, ahead of them Montgomery saw Jackson's car and mentioned it to the others,

"Alva will be annoyed he's late!" he chuckled. The others agreeing.

BANG!

The four of them watched in horror a Jackson's car flipped over 360 degrees another car had run a red light and sped off. How the other car could drive after that impact surprised all onlookers. Montgomery pulled over and the four of them ran to Jackson's aid. Maggie climbed in through the broken passenger window. Brantley forced open the rear door behind Jackson and got in holding his head and maintaining an airway, like Maggie had always taught him. Maggie sent up a silent prayer. Brantley sent up a silent prayer too. Maggie did what she was excellent at, saving lives. As Montgomery was phoning for an ambulance, a crew happened to be passing and stopped.

Jackson was in a bad way. Maggie was concerned. She spoke to the crew and explained her training and what she thought he would need. She ran through drips and put in cannulaes. One of them radioed ahead and got her to talk to the doctor. She travelled in the ambulance with him. The other's followed in Montgomery's car.

A grave looking Montgomery drove up to her waiting and she jumped in the back and sat next to Brantley.

"Where's Jack? Where's Mags?" Alva asked not wanting to hear the response.

"There's been a terrible accident…" Brantley started.

They arrived and distraught Alva and Montgomery were escorted to resus, while the others were directed to the relative's room. She went in to speak to the staff, Jackson was unconscious and looked awful, blood seeping from his nose, his eyes were closed and puffed with bruising he wore a neck collar too and was attached to monitors and drips. She felt such concern and worry at the sight of seeing her husband in such a state, her heart broke.

One of the monitors flat lined.

"Cardiac arrest! Crash Call please!" The doctor shouted.

She felt it wasn't real. It was like, her heart felt like a loaded gun that morning and something now turned around and shot it.

"JACKSON WESLEY MADDOX! DON'T YOU DARE LEAVE ME! THIS CAN'T BE HAPPENING! YOU PROMISED ME! I'M COUNTING ON YOU, I'M PREGNANT! GOD PLEASE DON'T TAKE HIM FROM ME!" She screamed dissolving on the floor.

With that the monitor sprang back to life. The line flicked back to waves of complexes.

"He's got a pulse!" Doctor shouted.

Montgomery lifted his now tiny sister, she had lost over 60lb, off the floor and whisked her outside.

"How far gone are you?"

"Twelve to fourteen weeks. I only found out an hour ago!" she sighed.

"Does anyone know yet?" He asked.

Alva shook her head.

"I have to go back tomorrow for blood tests and scans to date the baby accurately. I'm not sure, it's so confusing."

"I won't say anything unless you want me to, but you need to keep calm not just for you and Jack but for the baby too. We can help you, with whatever you need" he hugged his little sister.

When Dirk and Rita arrived with Maxwell and Dorraine, Montgomery and the others disappeared home to eat, no one felt like a restaurant anymore.

"Do either of you two know a good therapist?" Brantley asked, in the car on the way back.

Georgette handed him a card she had in her purse. He rang and made an appointment for an hour's time.

"That accident has triggered my PTSD from my assassination attempt." He explained.

"I'll drop you and wait for you if you like." Montgomery offered.

Montgomery had always felt upset and guilty for that. He had felt that he could have been the one his cousins had gone for. They would have had he had not changed his name by deed poll. Even when they had accidently bumped into the Drakes in Georgette's flat, they hadn't realised he'd changed his name or his image.

Maggie patted Brantley's hand; he had done well helping her to save Jackson. She was proud not only for that but recognising he needed to debrief after the incident.

"Are you OK? Georgette?" Montgomery asked.

His wife had lost her parents in a car accident, she nodded, Montgomery squeezed her hand. They drove home in silence.

As they pulled up the drive Georgette spoke breaking everyone's thoughts.

"We all heard Alva screaming and what she said!"

"I've said I won't tell anyone. I hope we can keep it between us for now."

He recounted the mystery that he had witnessed, they all agreed.

Alva and the others waited for news eventually they were told, by some miracle there was no brain injury and nothing more than a broken nose, a couple of ribs, his left arm, and whiplash. They explained they would move him to ICU to monitor the fact he'd arrested, because they didn't know why. He had a lucky escape.

Alva sat by his side all night willing him to get well. She dozed in the chair she was meant to have blood tests to check the baby in the morning. She wasn't sure what to do she was torn she didn't want to leave his side but knew she had to look after herself and the baby. She would have to ask and tell people. The doctor came to talk to her and explained he would try and wake him up the next day. As soon as Rita arrived, she asked Alison to drive her to the medical plaza and get her bloods done and have a check-up. She then drove back to hers so she could grab some clothes, her charger, her 'big book' and wash stuff ready to stay the next couple of nights.

She was searching for things and found a letter in his drawer addressed to her: Alva, to be opened in the event of my death or serious accident. She sat and read the handwritten note that read:

Dearest Alva,

I want to keep you safe and I'm in a precarious position, a few years ago Dorraine approached me and explained there was to be an investigation into Pagwell Records, they needed someone on the inside or close to it. There was a lot of fraud and embezzlement going on. I initially did it to make sure Mont was kept out of it all. Over the time I discovered lots of underhand and dangerous things about Della Fontaine and other executives. I haven't told you because I didn't want you knowing, I am writing this in case I am killed or injured so you know... Dorraine knows about the dossier and she will look after you should the worse happen. My Uncle Enrico will take care of you if you ever return to England. Please though don't ever put yourself in danger, whatever happens to me and if you read this and I'm still alive only talk to Dorraine no one else, you MUST PROMISE.

Just know I love you and always will.

Your Jackson x

"You look peaky dear!" Rita mentioned on Alva's return "Go home and get some sleep! I'll ring if anything changes."

"I'm ok Rita!" she lied to her mother-in-law.

"Did everything go well for you with the doctor yesterday dear?" Rita asked.

"Yes thanks, it went better than expected." She smiled.

"You need to rest in your condition! So, if you need to rest at home, I'll get someone to drop you home." Rita smiled.

Alva looked at her confused.

"Alva, you look different. There's something different about you. I'm guessing you only found out recently? I am guessing you'll be calling me 'Grandma' soon?"

"No one knows yet! Except Mont, that was an accident and Mum, because she took me for a blood test and a scan this morning. I only found out yesterday. I didn't realise I was fourteen weeks! I haven't even told Jack yet." Alva explained, bursting into tears with guilt at him not knowing first.

"Don't worry dear, I won't breathe a word but I will understand if you need more rest. Can I ask how come Mont knows?"

"Yesterday Jack had a cardiac arrest and the monitors went flat and I screamed at Jack not to leave me and why. A moment later the monitor started. It was like he'd died and came back for the baby." She started to weep again.

Rita put her arm around her and sat with her, telling her Jackson wouldn't be disappointed in her for getting support from their families.

That night and day blurred into one. Rita made sure she ate sensibly. Alva made several outreach calls, she sat and read her book, mostly she prayed and gave gratitude for the hospital and the skills of the workers. It kept her from her self-defined 'default' mode of eating and binging, especially on confectionary. It would have been so easy to succumb, the hospital shop contained all her 'alcoholic' foods. Every outcome here was not in her power and she had to relinquish any power she had. Alva took out her note pad at some point during the early hours and wrote songs about the situation called 'The Saddest Song' 'If You Know What I Know (You Wouldn't Dare Say Goodbye)' 'Tears In a Tennessee Tornado' and 'Wake Up, Baby, I Love You!'

Dorraine sat with Georgette that night, she guessed Alva's condition, but didn't say anything, she wanted to speak to her about the crash, but didn't want to worry her.

"So, how's the investigation fairing? You can be honest with me… I want to know… I'm not going to break… he's alive… I'm guessing they tried to kill him?" Alva stated.

"What do you know?" Dorraine asked.

"I'm guessing he's got information on Della, Bryan and that lot and all their shady deals, and you need him as some kind of witness?" Alva stated very matter of fact.

"Yes… how do you know?"

Alva explained she had guessed, but Jack had alluded to things several times and he was trying to keep her and Montgomery safe and the note she had found. Dorraine explained they had found a hit man had been hired who was accomplished and causing accidents and killing people, he had been following Jackson all day and couldn't get his car on its own to murder him and set the car alight like they often did and so out of frustration he worked out the route he was taking and bypassed a little ramming him, he was a stunt driver from Hollywood and the car he used must have been reinforced to have driven after that impact. Dorraine then told her Della had ordered it from prison and there had been arrests but now they had the dossier from Jackson's secret work they wouldn't be able to wrangle out of any charges. Jackson had been working on gathering evidence as long as he had worked for Montgomery and had been recruited by Dorraine as part of a long investigation, which he had been willing to give up when he was stuck in England all those weeks, but then explained it was good because he then looked less obvious. Alva was proud he was so brave.

Over the next hours the medication was titrated back so that he could breathe on his own. Eventually everything that was needed for him to wake up was done. Alva sat patiently praying for him to wake up. He was groggy and opened his swollen bloodshot eyes. Alva jumped up and kissed his forehead and smiled through her tears. She stroked his head. He nodded back off to sleep again and this happened a few times. He eventually rolled on his side independently and opened his eyes and looked at her. She smiled and reached for his hand.

"Hi! I'm sorry I was late!" he croaked.

His throat was dry and hoarse from not drinking and having a tube down it. She put the cup and the straw near his mouth and he drank.

"Don't worry about that! I was here as soon as I could. You had me worried!"

"Alva, you look different… you look more like my 'Lavender Moon' Where's my jacket?" He asked.

She scouted round and found a bag everything he'd wore was dumped in, things were bloodstained and had been cut off of him.

"Can you get the box out of my jacket… I hope it's still there."

Alva fiddled with his jacket and pulled out a red velvet box and handed it to him. He handed it back.

“I bought you an eternity ring to celebrate our four years wedding anniversary and to show you I’m never going to leave you, whatever happens!”

She opened the box. It was an exquisite platinum band with different coloured gems around it. She sat looking at the ring tears rolling down her cheeks.

“I had the strangest dream… I dreamt I was out of my body and you were screaming at me not to leave you because you were pregnant.” Jackson closed his eyes. “God said, it wasn’t in his plan and I had to go back!”

Did he really dream it or did he have an out of body experience she wondered? Reaching for her bag taking out paperwork.

“I couldn’t have the procedure…” She started.

“You were telling me there was an issue when I crashed…”

“I wasn’t able to have it done… you see, they asked questions and did a couple of tests…”

She placed the scan pictures in his hands. He looked down at them and looked at Alva in such a joyful way.

“I’m going to be a daddy!?” he clarified. “Get over here and kiss me Mommy!”

She kissed him a little before continuing,

“I was so shocked when the doctor told me… I still am. I couldn’t recall when my last period was. Then she said about unprotected sex and I had said we hadn’t seen the point as I didn’t get pregnant. She did a test to be sure and it came back positive. Mont found out because you died for a second. I had to ask mum to come with me yesterday and your mum guessed. Sorry I didn’t tell you first!”

“Honey, you needed all the support you could get! How far are we?” he squeezed her hand.

“Fourteen weeks… and I worked it out when it happened. Perhaps I only get pregnant on ‘The Lavender Moon’.” she told him.

Psalm 136:9

Epilogue.

"She looks just like you! Have you thought of any names yet?" Jackson asked looking down at the week-old bundle of pale purple in her arms.

"I thought Lavender? I also wondered if we had 'Moon' as a middle name as it's our 'family name' I'm glad, we picked purple stuff and neutrals… but I was convinced she'd be a boy! You're not upset, are you?"

"Of course not! She's perfect, I'm just so grateful! I like Lavender, she is our little Lavender Moon Maddox!"

They sat on the bed together; it had been a long night with a colicky baby. Jackson sat and reflected, just over a week ago he was woken up by Alva convinced something was happening. They had carried on their day, every moment was slow for Alva, her impatience was infuriated by such matters. She had been like this until twenty hours passed and a massive contraction had hit her. The midwife had examined her and she was 7cm, Alva tried to have her at home, next time she was examined she was 9cm. Then it stopped and was now back to 7cm. Alva was rushed to hospital in excruciating pain. She had been hooked up to wires, drips, monitors and epidurals. Another few hours passed resulting in an emergency ventouse delivery, which almost ripped her apart. Jackson had been there every step of the way; he had held her tightly and felt completely helpless at times. Her pregnancy had been quite smooth, now the proverbial had 'hit the fan.'

Alva was still feeling sore and she felt really down but relying on their programs they knew they could get through it. Jackson had been wanting to ask her something for the past few days,

"You know we've been having trouble trying to find a house to live in? Well, the people that were renting my grandpa's, Maxwell Barnes' home have moved out and it is empty. It was left to us three

American grandkids; the English cousins got the money from the estate and I have spoken to Max and Dorraine and they would be happy if we bought their shares off them. We can look this afternoon? That's if you feel up to it.

"I'd like that, Jack! I really feel like I need some normalcy in my life at the moment, it's been so hectic."

The house, happed to be fairly close to Montgomery's and her parents' new home, Alva loved the house. The brick-built observatory in garden was the star, the indoor swimming pool and a vast expanse of garden helped too. The main house was large and there was a smaller house on the property too. It was a derelict cottage, hidden by a copse of trees. The smaller house was the original home, but Barnes had the bigger one built in the 1970's and moved in and the four-bedroom late 1800's home fell into disrepair.

The main house itself was similar to her brother's and had lots of rooms that could be used.

"Do you think it's too big for the three of us? twelve bedrooms is a lot?" Alva remarked.

"I have an idea, so come with me!"

They explored the house; Jackson had the idea to convert half into their home of five bedrooms.

"Then we can make the other part into a meeting house and recovery centre for other twelve step groups or run weekend retreats for those with addiction. Like Blake House! Also, the cottage will need renovating… I was thinking of the cottage being a shared house. Making a few flats with a communal kitchen for people that are homeless or someone escaping domestic violence. Just to give them a step up. Maggie and Brantley have a fund and are willing to give a donation for the homeless flats even though it's not in the UK. And Montgomery suggested the centre would need a manager and thought Georgette's aunt Monica would be well placed to help, I believe she has experience with such matters too. Georgette would love her to live here too, she's alone in the UK otherwise."

Alva threw her arms around his neck.

"Jack it's a wonderful idea! I love Monica like an aunt too!"

"I'll arrange for Monica to come back with us in September when we return from Cousin Ricardo's wedding and when in England you can do your ninth step over Ella."

So, with that, their twelfth tradition would be continued forever more, with the retreats and meeting house. Lavender Moon Hall.

Psalms 104:19

AMEN.

Printed in Great Britain
by Amazon

38157544R00145